LÉONIDAS NIGHTSHADE

AND THE AMETHYST SCHOOL FOR SPELLCASTERS

Dion Marc

LÉONIDAS NIGHTSHADE AND THE AMETHYST SCHOOL FOR SPELLCASTERS (LÉONIDAS NIGHTSHADE BOOK 1)

Cover art illustrated by Dion Marc

Interior book illustrations by Dion Marc

Edited by Sue Laybourn, No Stone Unturned Editing Services

Proofing by Anita Ford

Formatting by Leslie Copeland

LÉONIDAS NIGHTSHADE

AND THE AMETHYST SCHOOL
FOR
SPELLCASTERS

Dion Marc

CONTENTS

DEDICATION

I have three separate dedications for this novel.

First to my grandma who taught me right from wrong and to never give up even when all else seems lost.

Second to the LGBTQI+ community who came before me and paved the way so that I may live an open and honest life.

And finally this novel is dedicated to the real life Coco, Tamara, Min and fellow Harry Potter cast and crew who made me feel welcome and safe during a very intense time in my life. I love you all and thank you from the bottom of my ice-cold heart for making me feel that I belonged backstage with you all. Through sickness and health it was and is a true marriage of the heart. By the time this novel hits the shelves we have probably done over four hundred shows together, something I'll take with me to the day I die.

    Love

    Dion

AUTHOR NOTE

Dear reader,

Before you dive into the world of Léonidas Nightshade and the Amethyst School for Spellcasters, I want to provide some background information that will enhance your understanding of the story. The majority of the novel takes place in 1952, a time when being gay was illegal in most countries and the consequences for this "crime" were severe, ranging from death to chemical castration. Keep in mind that the term "gay" was not used to describe same-sex attraction during this time, so I have chosen not to use the word. If you see the word used it means "happy." Also, the word "fag" was commonly used as slang for cigarettes, so if you come across that word in this novel (which you will) it refers to cigarettes and not a derogatory term for gay men.

This book also deals with long-term depression and some of the factors associated with it. I have written this novel based on my own experiences living with depression and Bipolar disorder as well as some of my real-life struggles. It is my hope that this story and these characters will help someone, anyone feel heard and know that they are not alone. I want to emphasize that even with long-term depression and mental health struggles, it is possible to live a fulfilling and successful life, as I have learned and experienced myself.

It's important to note that this is just the first book in a planned series, and each character will grow a year older in each instalment. The characters are not perfect people at the start and will continue to grow and develop as the story progresses. Just like in real life.

Finally, I stand in solidarity with all of my LGBTQI+ friends and colleagues, and I do not condone hate speech from any TERF authors, no matter how much I may have loved their books growing up. It is my hope that this book fills the gap and can be enjoyed by everyone.

You are perfect and you are loved.

I hope you enjoy this story,

Love

Dionysos Marc

Life can be cruel, and it may seem like the world is constantly against you, drowning you in a never-ending downpour of hardships. But don't give up hope, for after the darkest storms, the sun will eventually peek through the clouds. And when it does, the warmth of its rays will dry your tears and remind you that you're a survivor. You have fought bravely, and every challenge you've faced has made you that little bit stronger.

    - Dion Marc

A problem shared is always a problem halved.

    - My Grandma (and probably someone else originally)

For a friend with an understanding heart is worth no less than a brother.

    - Homer (Book 8, The Odyssey)

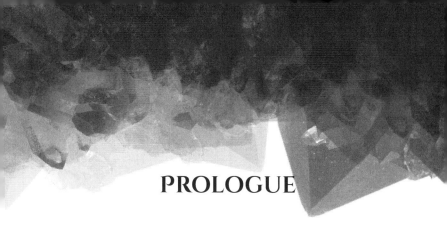

PROLOGUE

Rubble fell like cascading stars as the old walls of the forgotten city of Dusios were bombarded by cursed spell after cursed spell. A city from the times of ancient Gaul that was once a home to fae kings and queens when visiting the earthly realm. A site that contained much in the way of history, particularly that of the magical variety.

With their wands drawn, Amelia and Edmonton Nightshade hurried through the ancient site with their enemy hot on their tails. They would not have been forced into this altercation if not for the betrayal of those they once called friend. Valor? More like dishonour.

BANG!

"We haven't much time," called silver-haired Edmonton as he dodged a cursed blast.

BANG BANG BOOM!

Another wall with a tapestry rich in tradition was brought to its bitter end by a blast of vermillion light.

1

"I know, darling, but we must try," replied Amelia as she grabbed her husband and forced him down. BANG!

"How much further?" she queried, face full of panic.

Pulling back out the parchment, Edmonton quickly studied the map.

"We are in the palace proper now, so the library of prophecy should be...just around that bend there," he said, gesturing to the small arched doorway to their right. Unfortunately, making it across would put them both in complete exposure.

"Is there any other way?" Amalia begged.

"Love, I'm afraid not."

"Okay then, for our son," she said resolutely.

"For our son," he chorused.

With wands fully extended, they jumped into the fray.

Amelia swished her wand up and out as she manifested an opalescent arch by calling magic from her soul and using her crystalline wand to focus it into her intent.

BANG BANG BANG! The protective barrier was assaulted by dozens of cursed blasts, filling the air with the acrid stench of burning magic.

Edmonton, under his breath, began working on a unique summoning, muttering words a mile a minute. "Tha mi a' galar oirrean na buailteachd, tighinn gu bhith an cruth-chruaidh fhìor." Each word was said in a way that almost sounded sung, for his aim was to summon a creature from the fae realm, a realm that existed just beyond the moon's reflection. Only a true-born Nightshade could hope to achieve this type of summoning, for all fae summoning required the caster to have fae blood for it to work, and Edmonton Nightshade was no ordinary spellcaster. He was a true high-born fae prince of the Nightshade court. One of the hundred and eleven royal families that ruled over the other realm.

Slowly the air rippled as the veil shifted, and the slimy creature was summoned. Neither Nightshade stayed long enough to see the creature's true form, instead turning and sprinting off towards the bend leading to the library of prophecy.

A few hurried moments later and Amelia and Edmonton had reached their destination. Once through the library's golden filigree doors, Amelia quickly performed a sealing charm and oh, how the air sang with her magic. She was a very skilled spellcaster, the best in her year at Amethyst.

Wasting not a second longer, they began hurriedly searching the bound written accounts of the great seers looking for the ancient prophecy concerning their young son Léonidas.

Volume after volume was pulled off shelves and scanned for any mention of their fae prince son before being discarded.

"This is taking too long." Edmonton grimaced. Pulling his wand back out, he placed it flat on his hand and chanted, "exerevnán manteftós!" The wand began to spin in a circle as it searched for the prophecy.

Feet hurried behind the door.

"They're in here," called an excited male voice.

"Oh, sugar!" Amelia cursed before she too pulled her wand back out.

"There isn't any time—"

BOOOOOM!

A violent explosion rocked the room. The enemy had begun its assault on the door. The locking spell would not last much longer. They needed to hurry.

Edmonton tried to feed his searching spell more magic from his soul but it was no use. They just didn't have the time. They both met each other's gaze. Their hearts sank.

"It's the only way."

"I know." His voice broke.

Turning, they both began to mutter words of fire, a "flogmós" and a "kavma." Flames spat from the tips of their wands, quickly filling the room with its disastrous kiss.

"They're setting the room ablaze!" cried another voice, this one thick with a distinctly Scottish brogue.

"Out of my way, you bloody fools," growled yet another, though this voice was unmistakable. *It* sounded like evil personified, the rustiest of nails on the powderiest of classroom chalkboards.

"Exólis!" he commanded a moment before what little of the door and protective charms fell in defeat.

Jacquard Morioatus and his Preneurs De Magi stormed the room.

With a silent wave of his treacherous wand, Amelia and Edmonton were bound in chains of magical iron twisting around their bodies like ravenous pythons.

"You think you could escape from me?"

Laughter echoed around the room.

"Hide from me?"

More sinister laughter.

"Svésai!" he commanded sharply, doing a reverse flick with his wand. The flames that kissed the library were instantly extinguished, leaving behind walls, floors, tables, and empty shelves covered in a thick, pungent, black goo. The Nightshades had done their job, for not one book appeared to be left in the library of prophecy.

Jacquard Morioatus yelled in anger, a horrid sound as

he upended the burnt reading table. His eyes flickered with burning fury. He would take his vengeance.

In a flash, he flew at Edmonton, digging his wand tip into the fae's pale skin. It was enough to draw a few steady drops of blood. Edmonton grimaced but said not a word.

"What was on that prophecy, Mr Nightshade?"

When he didn't respond, Jacquard dug his wand in deeper, the tip so sharp that the drops of blood turned to a steady flow.

Gritting his teeth, Edmonton bit back, "What prophecy."

"Ohhhh, we're not going to play that game," cooed Jacquard.

Swiftly, he turned his blood-covered wand on Amelia and cried, "polyódynos!" Lightning cracked like a whip from his wand cursing Amelia with unimaginable pain. Her screams filled the room.

"Stop it!" yelled Edmonton, his resolve shattering.

"Then tell me what was in the prophecy, Mr Nightshade."

"*NO DON'T!*" cried Amelia, between her ragged sobs.

"Polyódynos!" he repeated.

Thunder cracked once more. The combination of magic sent Amelia into the air. Her screams magnified tenfold.

"*AMELIA!*" cried Edmonton, struggling with all he had in him against the magical bonds.

"What will it be, Mr Nightshade? The prophecy or your wife?"

Edmonton struggled. Though in a moment of crippling grief, he made eye contact with his soulmate, her grey eyes rimmed red. But it was in that moment where grey eyes met mauve the desperate decision was made.

Edmonton stopped. It was done.

"You can do your worst to us, but we will *NEVER* tell you."

"Is that so?" Jacquard laughed. His laughter chorused around the room.

With a reverse flick, he commanded, "pávein!" The curse on Amelia halted and she slumped down into her bonds.

"You see, I know a way of torture that even the gods hide from," he gloated as he sauntered over to Amelia. His blood-red eyes promised pain as they locked on her floating body. "Perhaps a little demonstration is in order to...loosen your tongue, Mr Nightshade. After all, we only need one of you alive, and I for one have grown rather hungry chasing you."

Jacquard tapped his wand three times on Amelia's unconscious skull. On the fourth tap he drew out a thin cord of ghostly stardust.

"What are you doing? You sick bastard!"

He stopped and turned back to Edmonton, flashing him a smile.

"Why I'm stealing her magical essence of course. All you have to do to stop me is tell me what was in the prophecy."

"I'll never tell you."

"Well then. Bye-bye wife."

He drew out the last of her magical essence. It swirled around him as he pointed his wand at a thick blue vein just above his wrist. The thread poured into his vein, filling him with not just Amelia's magic but her life force as well. Jacquard only thought it was a pity she was unconscious, for he knew that the pain was maddening.

Later when both Nightshades lay frozen in a torturous death, he searched the room with his band of magic abusers. Wand in hand, he began to explore. Whilst every page on every book and every letter written on parchment had indeed been burnt, not everything was dust, at least not entirely. There must be something that had survived. After all, this was a fae palace.

One particular spell occurred to Jacquard, one that would make the search just that little bit easier. He snapped his fingers at one of his followers. "Bring him to me," gesturing at the fae prince. A few seconds later, they brought him the fae prince. He cut a deep line on Edmonton's flesh, allowing a flow of freshly coagulating blood to pour over his wand. Using his wand like a quill, he began to scratch runic symbols on the burnt wooden desk. One symbol was a locating charm, the other a blood-searching charm, and the last was a charm of repair.

After a moment, the symbols began to glow as the room filled with smoke, creating a phantom of its once magnificent self. It was there that he found the missing prophecy in the corner of the table just inches away from Edmonton's ghostly hand as Amelia started setting the room ablaze. His greedy eyes searched the prophecy, though to his utter burning rage, most of the script had been scorched away. He only knew this was the correct prophecy for it glowed, unlike the others, which meant the magic he'd cast had worked.

Jacquard tipped his wand on the form which solidified the page. Of the twenty-four prophetic lines only five remained. Three from the start of the prophecy and two lines from the very end.

The first three lines read, *Lost, Ancient, forgotten and old,*

A great power will rise that was long foretold,
When fae born prince becomes god blessed—

And the last two lines read as *Glory, fame, and fortune beyond measure,*

Is what awaits this powerful successor.

Jacquard tried every trick in the book to restore the missing lines, but unfortunately for him, there wasn't a spell or charm that would repair the ruined prophecy. It was in that moment that he made a new plan. Find the god-touched fae prince and use his blood as an offering to the dark gods, or if that failed, take him to one of the last seers to have survived the great seer culling of 1576. Jacquard didn't just dream of glory, fame, and fortune beyond measure but also craved it like the drug fix of all fixes. He vowed that one day soon, all he dreamed of would come to pass. "Fae-born prince I'm coming for you", he sang as he left the ruined city.

Lost. Ancient. Forgotten and old
A great power will rise that was long foretold.
When fae born prince becomes god blessed

Glory, fame and fortune beyond measure
Is what awaits this powerful successor

CHAPTER I

THE SAD BOY WHO GREW HORNS

LÉONIDAS I

"Please...No...NO..NOOO! NOT MY PARENTS! PLEASE! NOT MY—" I screamed a second before I bolted upright. *Please let him leave my parents alone, I needed them.* But the burnt room faded to solace and black eclipsed all. *Thump thump thump* went my broken, bleeding heart.

Come back, I still need you...

Wiping the sweat from my shaking body I sighed deeply, trying to calm my frantic heart. It was just a dream...a nightmare. The same bloody nightmare I'd had every year on the days leading up to the winter solstice. Without a single doubt when the equinox turned cold a cursed dream plagued every sleep. It was one of the death of my parents in vivid detail. Their screams still rang in my ears like police sirens but infinitely worse, a permanent tinnitus. I rubbed my eyes trying to stem the flow of tears I already knew would never stop because pain lasted forever. I missed them both so very much. Without them I felt like a little boy on a broken raft left out in a stormy ocean without a single trace of land.

This pain of loss I knew would never leave me, for the greatest lie I had ever been told was that it would get easier as the days passed; well it hadn't, and I knew deep down in my bones that it never would. It seemed the shadows that followed me would continue to disrupt the waters of tomorrow.

If I had been given the option I would have followed both my parents into the dark and welcomed it. But reality was never that simple. The death of my parents sent my family into crippling debt. I had no birth certificate and thus had no way to prove I was my parents' son. So any money my parents may have had or put aside for me I would never receive. Not that I would want to spend their money but as a result my maternal grandparents had to foot the bill for my care and for that fact and many others I felt a torrent of shame and self-loathing.

I was nothing but a burden and I would never be anything else.

In the dark I fumbled on the nightstand for the side lamp switch. I clicked on the light and read the clock that sat next to the lamp. It read 6:58 a.m. It was time to get up and start the day.

I stuck to the bedsheet like taffy does to teeth. taking me several moments to excavate myself from the mummification that was happening. The sheets were so drenched in my perspiration I knew I had to remake the bed and wash them before nightfall otherwise the smell of sadness would never leave. It could have been worse, at least I hadn't wet the bed...again. How...embarrassing.

My tummy may have grumbled but I continued until a

fresh set of linens covered my bed and those that were sweat-covered lay in the laundry hamper.

Grabbing my jacket and a pair of overalls, I quickly got dressed for the day, putting my ruined pyjamas in with the sheets.

I'd have had a shower if we still had hot water in the evening. And these days we couldn't always afford to keep the water hot so I always waited until my hardworking grandparents had had theirs first, just in case.

Grabbing the pen I kept in the first drawer, I made my way over to my calendar, it was that time again, another cross, another day closer to my inevitable death. It was December 17th, 1951, just four more days until my fifteenth birthday and just four more days until the anniversary of the death of my parents. Birthdays...I hadn't celebrated a birthday since the day I'd woken up and found my grandparents sitting in the living, both with faces filled with barely repressed pain. No, birthdays weren't for celebrating, they were just for mourning...at least they were for me.

I tied the old musty curtains open using the stitched ribbon that was attached to the center of the curtains, filling the room with the faint whispers of early morning light. Looking out the window, I was disappointed, yet another day with snowfall.

I hated the snow. I mean it, I *really* hated the snow. It got into my socks and froze my toes, it dripped into my hair and plastered it to my face, and it flushed my skin pink and turned my nose raspberry-red but worst of all, snow meant that our food crops would fail, destroying one of our only sources of income. The last few years had been pretty bad. Bad enough that Grandma had to take a second job in the village cleaning houses, and this was on top of maintaining our home, which due to its size and age was a full-time job in itself. I tried to help out whenever possible and I had been, honest. Every morning I would go downstairs and Grandma would have a list of chores which I did gladly and without complaint. I had to do my bit.

We lived in a small private forest near a town called Beddgelert in Wales. Everyone here had a *very* thick accent although my grandparents and I did not, thankfully. I could never tell if I was being patronised or being asked a serious question by the townsfolk, not that I often went into town —I wasn't a social person but sometimes—when we could afford it Grandma would take us into the city to watch one of those technicoloured masterpieces. So far my favourite had been *Alice in Wonderland* by the same people that made *Snow White*. It actually also happened to be the last time we could really afford to go...that had been in August and it was now December.

Downstairs, I took a left and headed for the kitchen. Stopping only briefly at the shrouded portrait hanging in the front room. Though like always I never looked at it, it was just too painful, one day maybe I'd be able to.

We had an average sized kitchen. Along the three walls were cabinets, bench spaces, and appliances and in the centre of the room sat a small four-person wooden table with a patchwork tablecloth. Everything we owned was old and well-worn but everything was always clean and tidy.

Left on the table was small plate of Grandma's famous current slice cut into cubes and stacked neatly into a pyramid. Grabbing one from the top I eyed my prize with hunger. Quickly I devoured it. licking my fingers after, getting every crumb. I didn't care that the filling tasted more watered down than usual or that the pastry wasn't its usual crispness. I enjoyed it because Grandma made it regardless of what ingredients she may or may not have had to miss and substitute.

I really wanted to grab another slice because my stomach still grumbled but I knew better. Another one now meant none later.

Stuck to one of the cabinets with scotch tape was my to-do list. After a quick glance I noticed it was rather short, just two items:

Darling, please spend a few hours this morning foraging for mushrooms, I think in meadow west of Henry's oak should still have a few white snow oyster mushrooms still surviving in this frost, a dozen should do.

And 2. Grandpa has hurt his shoulder—nothing to worry about but we will need you to splinter a few of the larger logs into kindling for the fire tonight, the paper has reported that tomorrow is going to be the coldest it's been this winter. Love Grandma see you around 5pm.

With my to-do list memorised I headed for the back door and with one look outside I knew I'd need the wool-lined boots my grandparents had gifted me the previous winter solstice. They were very warm but they were just a fraction too small now so I resented wearing them for any long period of time but I'd just have to make do. We couldn't afford new ones.

Boots on, I grabbed the wicker basket we used for mushroom foraging and headed out into the snow. That first burst of fresh air was chilling to the bone. The sun had risen just beyond the horizon but not quite past the tall snow-covered silver birches lining our property, giving our humble home a soft halo from the refraction of the sun on the snow.

After unlatching the gate I headed in the direction of old Henry's oak.

Old Henry was an eagle owl that made the oldest oak tree in the forests of Beddgelert his home. Every night without fail I could hear his comforting hoot as he flew by, and sometimes he would even sit on the roof singing his song, hunting for any mice in the fruit and vegetable crops. With him around we need not own any rat traps. Hearing his call meant all was well in the woods, but the last few nights there hadn't been a sound. I had been rather worried. Grandpa told me that it was probably because we were having an unprecedented cold spell but I still worried. Henry was a constant. The idea of him leaving made me sad. He was an old owl after all and he had been on this earth far longer than I.

Another ten or so minutes and I was more than halfway to Old Henry's oak, I had passed the stepping stone bridge and the wisteria grotto. I just had to make it through the prickly bushes and take a turn when I passed the tree that had been struck by lightning twenty or so years prior and I'd be at old Henry's oak.

My grandparents grew vegetables year-round, it was just small-scale as we didn't have much land for anything large scale but in spring and summer we could afford things like going to the cinema and the local milk bar. Some nights Grandma and Grandpa would go into the town hall for dances. Sometimes I'd get real jealous as it was adults only.

We grew potatoes, carrots, turnips, red onions, and garlic as well as tomatoes. But winter's kiss came and killed almost all our crops this year. So far only a few of Grandpa's potatoes and onions had survived.

I wished I could do more to help.

Something was wrong. The air smelt of death. There were five sets of foot prints heading right for old Henry's oak. I took off in a run. Even though our property ended a while back, these forests were protected by the council due to the unique wildlife.

The fact that the five sets of foot prints led right up to his tree caused my pulse to quicken and my panic to spike.

"Henry? Hennnnrrry!?" I called again and again but there was no response. Not that Henry was known for responding to my call. I examined the footprints. It looked as if they had come to the tree but then turned around. How odd. I called out for Henry again but there was still no response. Should I climb the tree? My heart beat rapidly. There was no harm in checking, right? At least I would know he was safe.

As I looked around the meadow I saw nothing but pure white snow and the trees it suffocated. There was no one here, it would be safe...right? On impulse I made a decision.

I swung my left leg around the trunk and scooped both my arms around the lowest hanging branch, pulling myself up and onto it. From there I continued until I had scaled most of the tree. Snow dampened my clothes, allowing the chill to bite my bones. I'd most likely gain a cough for this.

The ground now looked so far away that I almost fell from fear. But I just needed to concentrate, Henry's nesting hole was just above the next branch. Swinging both arms tight around the above branch, I held on and pushed myself up and over, my arms burned and sweat moistened my back to an irritating itch. But I had made it. Hollowed into the tree was Henry's home. This high up I could actually hear something, slowly I crawled my way over to the hollow. Inside there were three little balls of fluff chirping away. That was why Henry hasn't been flying past the house, he'd been raising a family. I sighed in relief as I backed up. Best I leave them be. I'd overreacted. The animals of these forests had become my friends at least that was how I thought of them.

Once I was far enough away I turned around and nearly screamed in fright. The tall majestic owl I knew as Old Henry had returned home with a rodent clearly visible in his beak. He had been out hunting for food. Kind of like what I was meant to be doing—a kindred spirit.

Henry didn't seem angry to see me and thankfully he hadn't immediately pecked my eyes out, maybe if I slowly climbed down all would be well. As I began to move Henry cocked his head as if to say "what are you doing?" I struggled not to laugh but a smile did escape my lips. A fragment of innocent happiness.

WHOOOOOSH GRAHHH!

Blood splattered my face as an arrow pierced old Henry right in the head, his face still cocked to side. I let out a scream as I tried to wipe the blood off me but instead it mixed with the snow that saturated my clothes. I looked off in the distance where the arrow had surely come from. There, a few fields away, was a group of five or six boys. My shock and fear switched to anger as Henry toppled over the side. I could hear Henry's babies crying out for their dad, their now-dead dad. My vision turned red as I hurriedly climbed my way down, bark and splitters cutting into my fingers but I did not care.

The last three or so yards I slid down the trunk not caring when I heard the tell-tale sound of my overalls ripping. They'd killed Henry and they were going to pay. I sprinted off in their direction.

. . .

Hours passed and yet I couldn't find the boys...the murderers. The sun had moved from east to west and the sky now had the barest hints of red fading in from edge.

Defeated, I headed back to the oak tree. I was so tired and sad, and after all it was my fault Henry had been still enough to be shot. People around me always died. I was nothing but a burden. This was all my fault.

If Henry was dead his babies would need someone to look after them and that was the absolute least I could do. No one deserved to be left behind. So once more I climbed the old oak, though this trip was made even harder by the fact that I was carrying the wicker basket meant for mushroom foraging, which I still had to do. Grandma would be disappointed in me if I returned with nothing for dinner.

Even though my muscles ached and my bones screamed I didn't stop until I had arrived once more at the hollow. My chest heaved as I struggled to catch my breath. It was a great distance up and climbing a snow-covered tree was not easy. I didn't know when my heaving for breath turned into painful sobs but sure enough giant beads of tears streamed down my face. It wasn't just the death of Henry that made my broken heart ache. I also cried for my parents, for my nightmares, and for my grandparents who had to go without so that I might live.

I was nothing but a burden.

Something soft pushed into my side. Startled I turned around and came face to face with another majestic eagle owl. Younger than Henry but older than the babies in the hollow. This must be Missus Henry, the babies' mother. Instead of attacking me she instead put her head on my knee. Was this majestic owl trying to comfort me? Was that even possible. She looked back up and into my eyes, tears of grief moistened her feathers.

"I'm so s-sorry," I whispered. Her stare was as if she was peeling back the layers of my soul. Leaving me raw and open.

We stayed like that for fleeting stolen moments, it wasn't until my back ached and my legs grew numb that I finally moved. I didn't know what else to do so I asked, "Will you be okay?" It was probably stupid of me to have been trying to speak to an owl, but for some reason deep in marrow of my bones I thought this one could, what did I have to lose if I was wrong.

The owl gave the smallest of nods before moving past me and back into her nest with her babies, now a single mother.

Down the tree I headed, off to pick mushrooms. Would I be okay? Unlikely but what choice did I have. I would just add this trauma to my ever growing list.

Just as Grandma had predicted I did indeed find a cluster of snow-white oyster mushrooms in the meadow west of Hen…The Old Oak tree.

They grew in a shelf-like formation with overlapping clusters. On the underside of the white mushroom was rows and rows of what looked like fish gills or a good book being fanned open. Unfortunately the amount Grandma had asked for was not available, the frost must have dropped to unforgiving temperatures and that was saying something because fungi were pretty tough to kill. Six was all I had, we would just have to make do. The broth would just be that little bit thinner than normal. I was just grateful I wouldn't go to bed hungry.

Grandma had given me another task to complete but the sun had started its descent and I deeply feared cutting wood in the dark. That was where monsters hid and evil spread like wild fire.

Daylight dwindling, I decided to cut through the restricted meadow, who would know?

Crossing the fence line, I quickly disappeared amongst the snow-covered brush. My tracks were soon covered by the fresh fall of snow that had started to swirl in the winter wind.

A snap of a branch had me looking up, breaking me from my thoughts. Across the way stood a majestic stag with fur the colour of the moon's luminous light and a set of mighty antlers that instantly reminded me of the branches of tree. A white stag was very rare. Maybe the reason why this meadow was restricted was because it was this mighty creature's home. The world seemingly slowed as he turned to face me unafraid and content. It was an unbelievable sight.

My blood turned to ice. Just beyond the tree line were the boys who killed Henry, and to my horror they were armed, ready to kill once more.

Not again, never again.

"NO!!!!!" I screamed, running towards the stag to scare it off but to my horror and dismay he remained unmoving.

This couldn't happen again, this *wouldn't* happen again. I felt something stir in my chest like a cold shiver or goose-bumps but yet different. Why was the stag so calm? Why didn't it move?

I screamed at the boys to stop but it was too late, an arrow was let lose.

Too far away, I was too far away, I was never going to make it. I continued to run as tears fell down my face.

"RUN! Why aren't you running?" I couldn't bear to watch another animal die. Deep in my soul where the pieces of my broken heart lived, I wished for the stag and I to switch places. Why should another thing die and I live? I let out a breath and it was as if time stood still.

Then

Air rushed at me unlike any kind of gale force wind I had ever experienced before. So strong it was that I was lifted up off my feet and into the air. Before I knew it I soon stood where the stag once was. I didn't know how I had done it but somehow I had. A mix of confusion and joy caused a loud sigh to escape. The sigh turned to a scream as white hot pain lanced through me. The arrow had hit its target but now thanks to some strange magic, that was me. I took a step back as burning suffocation begun to claim my body.

"Holy Hell! What are we going to do?" I heard one boy cry.

"Let's just grab the arrow and go, no one will ever know," said another. His voice sounded older, he must have been the leader of these murderers.

I fell to the ground, it was no longer cold. Fear left me as the realisation I would soon join my parents. A tear akin to happiness welled in my eye before making its maiden voyage down my skin. The sensation was lost as a strange numbing ice slowly welled within me.

As my vision started to fade to black a blurred figure peered down at me. At first I thought it must have been one of the boys until I realised it was far taller, broader, and with a full beard...with flowers woven into it? And...and something was wrong with his head there were... horns protruding from it, no they were antlers! This couldn't be real...this was an illusion, a dream, a figment of my imagination. People like this only existed in story books.

"It is not your time, son of the Fae. You have many things to live through yet."

What did he mean? And who cared? It was finally my time to be with my parents once more. No more longing, no more waiting. My grandparents were finally free of the burden of my care. Maybe now they could live their lives free from the financial responsibility.

I let out my final breath as my eyes closed.

"No you don't," was the last thing I heard before blistering pain burst through my head.

I screamed.

Wasn't death supposed to be a welcome numbness? An end to the agony of living? The pain of the arrow had long since faded from me, my body had already turned cold... than why did my skull ache as though it was being hit by a sledge hammer over and over?

This wasn't what I thought death would be. I didn't think there would be eternal pain at the end. Another cruel realisation about this existence.

And then as suddenly as it came on the pain instantly subsided.

Relief filled me as my eyes flew open and I found myself lying on my bed, with the curtains drawn and the room bathed in night's shadow.

I wasn't dead?

I wasn't dead...

I wasn't dead, relief faded as I was filled with remorse. I once more was robbed of the opportunity to be with my parents. I took little comfort knowing the blistering pain I had felt was at least gone. Feeling around my chest I found no wound, no wet blood, nothing.

How very odd, how very odd indeed.

Slowly I sat up; slightly dizzy my vision blurred.

Was it all a dream? Surely not, but then how did I get back here?

Getting to my feet, I decided I'd talk to Grandma, she would understand my dreams if that was indeed what they were. As I passed the solitarily bonze mirror I saw a flash of something, was there something behind me? Turning quickly I checked, but the room was dark and appeared to be the same as always. Frowning I looked back to the mirror.

"Ahhhh what in the…"

My eyes must have been playing tricks for this cannot be so. I raised my hands slowly to my silvery strands of hair and began to slide them through. Shaking with fear I prayed to all the gods of this world and the next that this was some illusion, mirage, trick of the light or in this case lack of light but as my hands made their way through my scalp they came to a sudden stop as they met two ivory horns…no, they were antlers, my hands were touching antlers that had grown out of my scalp. how was this even possible? My mind flashed back to the head-splitting pain I had felt in the field. This could not be real…could it?

Hurriedly I switched on the lamp before racing right back to the mirror. And sure enough the antlers that came to three points still remained.

"GRAN…GRANDMA!" I yelled, my voice breaking in utter dismay. Having purple eyes, snow-coloured hair, and pale pink skin had already made me a freak but now two abnormal antlers growing out of my head—that was too much. Too much indeed.

PRENEURS DE MAGI I

Down in the dark depths of the icy sea cave known as Fingal on the island of Staffa in the inner Hebrides of Scotland sat a very cruel and callous man—he had no heart to speak of. This evil man was none other than Jacquard Morioatus, the leader of the infamous Preneurs De Magi. A group of spellcasting terrorists dedicated to stealing the magical essences of all the most powerful in magic kind. This type of illegal magic had long since turned their eyes red and their pupils white. For taking one's magical essence was to steal one's life and this type of act was forbidden by all the laws of all the gods in this realm and the next.

Lounging on a grimy throne made of cursed skulls of victims long since lost sat Jacquard, bored out of his mind. There had been little action in the last year and his fevered search for the god-touched fae prince had long since ran dry. It was no wonder that the search had come to a halt for those parents of his had destroyed almost all of that blasted prophecy. Only five lines had survived. Three from the start of the prophecy and just the very last two lines.

This cruel man had these lines memorised, of course and so the first three lines went *Lost, Ancient, forgotten and old,*

A great power will rise that was long foretold,
When fae born prince becomes god blessed—

The rest was unsalvageable apart from those last two lines: *Glory, fame, and fortune beyond measure,*

Is what awaits this powerful successor…

And he so dreamed of having this ancient great power for draining the average spellcaster these days just didn't give him his fix, didn't satisfy his cravings, his ravenous constant need for power. The withdrawals were slowly becoming worse and worse as the years of dark magic abuse took their toll. If he did not feed daily on someone's magical essence it was like fire ants crawling under his rotting flesh.

Living a life of such horrendous deeds had slowly warped his once charming face into something akin to a wrinkly mole rat. With long greasy strands of hair that reached far below the middle of his back and only grew in a small patch on the top of his bald head.

"Langdon, find out how far away Criedy is with today's batch of flesh-sacks, I'm getting twitchy," grumbled Jacquard.

A short, portly man appeared from the darkness. His suit covered in all kinds of grim and body fluids.

"Right away, Jacquard," he responded before turning and pulling out a long crystalline rod, just a fraction thicker than that of a fountain pen. This tool was called a spellcaster's wand.

"Anangéllo!" chanted Langdon while waving his wand effortlessly in the air spelling the name of whom he wished to reach. Purple light was summoned forth, spilling from the tip of his wand. Once the message and his intent was certain the magic crackled into the ether, leaving behind a smell of burnt wood.

A few moments later a response was received. Clouds of purple light burst through the ether and formed ghostly whisper thin letters which read "There has been an unexpected hold up, expect us late with possibly great news."

This message piqued Jacquard's interest. *Great news? Could it be about the boy?* he wondered for that was the only news he desired. The last flesh-sack that had truly filled his cravings was Edmonton Nightshade, this prophesied boy's father.

He scratched his forearm absently. Withdrawal was starting to hit. If Criedy was to arrive late he would need to find another fix beforehand. The only downside of living in a sea cave on an uninhabited island was that there was no one to snatch away easily. For this act he would need to leave and head north east into one of the few populated ports nearby. Unfortunately for Jacquard his face was well-known. He would need a disguise if he were to travel incognito.

Pulling out a wand not dissimilar to Langdon's, Jacquard withdrew a little of his stolen magic and preformed a spell of illusion to transfigure his face into that of a much younger man. One with long blond locks and chiselled features, a visage that would make any lonely lass swoon. The only things he could not hide with any form of magic were his malevolent red eyes and cold, white pupils. For this he pulled out a set of black antique spectacles from his jacket pocket.

"Langdon, we are heading into town to feed."

CHAPTER 2

THE LADY WITH THE PURPLE FEATHER COAT

LÉONIDAS I

"GRANDMA!" I shouted, running down the stairs two at a time, she must be home. The sun had clearly set and all the lamps in the upper hallways had been lit. "GRANDMA!!" I called again. And still there was no response. It was not until I had passed the last step of the wooden staircase that my heart was set at ease. Though Grandma's voice sounded dull and muted, very much unlike her.

"Léonidas darling, we are in the kitchen and we...we er... we have a...we have a guest."

A guest? Why would we have a guest? We never had guests...and wasn't it considered ill-mannered to have a caller after five?

I was so curious as to why we would have a guest this late that as I entered the kitchen I completely forgot about my sudden growth of antlers, and instead fixated on the unknown sitting figure dressed in purple feathers that seemed to glitter in a way that seemed abnormal, as if they had their own luminous light causing them to flicker like the stars in the night sky. How very, very strange.

Looking to my grandma who sat at the head of the kitchen table like she always did, with her dark brunette hair neatly curled and pinned in place with a black snood, I silently asked her what in the Gatsby was going on. She gave me a short smile that did not reach her blue eyes before she quickly introduced the unknown guest. "Léonidas, this is Fenella Guaire, she is...hmm." It was clear that whomever she was my grandmother disapproved.

"She is—" began my grandma once more.

She was cut off as the lady in the purple feather coat rose to her feet and turned around. She had skin the colour of midnight and eyes as green as the freshest summer apples. Her feather coat fell almost to her ankles and with it she wore pristine white gloves.

"I am the headmistress of The Amethyst School for Spellcasters, Mr Nightshade. And you may call me either Headmistress Guaire or Professor Guaire if you are in attendance of one of my classes." She spoke with such poise that her slight Scottish accent was almost proper posh.

In one of her classes...what? And what is a spellcaster?

Again I turned and looked at my grandma looking for answers but none were given, she did not meet my eyes. Turning, I desperately sought my grandpa's gaze but he too would not meet my eyes. What in the *Wizard of Oz* was going on here.

"Mr Nightshade, as of 6.52 p.m. on the night of the 17th of December, approximately three days ago, you summoned and used magic—"

What? Used magic...wait three days ago? What?...WHAT?

"It is a decree of all governing bodies that all spell-casters must attend the Amethyst School for Spellcasters."

"I'm not magic," I blurted out.

"Did you not complete a location switch spell on the night of the 17th of December?" she responded.

"Errr..."

I...must have...but...no...Magic?

"I won't go," I burst out.

"Mr Nightshade, I think you have the wrong idea."

"I have?" I asked confused.

"Yes, it seems you are under the impression you have a choice here. In this matter you do not, the laws are clear."

"I do not?"

"You do not," she repeated.

I stared back blankly, I had nothing else to say, my brain had shut up shop and vacated the building. This was all too much, too much to hear, too much to comprehend.

Grandpa chose that moment to chime in. "Laddie, you've grown horns, it's not like we can hide that from the townspeople."

Oh darn it, the antlers. I had almost completely forgotten about that nightmarish infliction. Instinctually my hands went skywards, sure enough they were still there in all their solidness.

"I...I...I can wear a hat—" I tried, stammering.

"Come now, you'd look pretty daft in whatever hat would be big enough to cover the horns, laddie."

"But—"

"I'm quite surprised you aren't more concerned about the antlers, Mr Nightshade, you will now be a target."

"A target? You mean more than I already was with the white hair, stupid purple eyes, and anaemic skin?" My temper rose.

"Leonidas! Manners!" my grandma scolded, her disapproval apparent.

"But—" Desperately I looked around the room for an ally but none were to be found. I felt betrayed, deserted and by the expressions on my grandparents' faces they knew it.

"Yes, more of a target than ever. For your true nature has been revealed and what is worse is that it was witnessed by a group of norms.

"My true nature? What? Norms? What? You're not making any sense."

She smiled. "Yes, Mr Nightshade, your true nature—"

"I'm not Mr Nightshade. That was my father's name."

"Léonidas Agápe Nightshade, watch your manners!" Grandma yelled, scolding me once more. Using my full name like that meant I was about to be in a world of real trouble but I couldn't help but not care. This was just so absurd. Growing antlers, using magic, next she was probably going to tell me I wasn't human. This was pure legend.

"As I was saying, Mr Nightshade, before you interrupted. Your true nature has now been made apparent. You are in fact not just a spellcaster but also Fae-born, for normal spellcasters would not be able to meet a god such as Cernunnos and live to tell the tale."

"This is absurd, I didn't meet..." I began, but the blurred image of the bearded man with giant antlers flashed into my mind's eye. Wait...had I met a god? Had I met Cernunnos? I knew of the god of course—Grandma had read me tales of the horned one, the god of wild things. Yet even knowing it was still somewhat hard to believe. Me? No friends, pale freak, met a god?

"I'll shall take your silence as confirmation that you know of which I speak to be true," said Headmistress Guaire.

Whether it was the shock of it all or just my subconscious, I pulled out a chair and sat at the table. There were just too many things I could not deny. There were antlers sprouting from my skull. The distance between the stag and I was too great to have been able to make it by just running alone and the bearded stag man who'd said… what was it? Oh it was *It was not my time* or something like that. But there was one thing that still hadn't been addressed.

"What do you mean Fae-born?"

This question of course was aimed at Headmistress Guaire but from the corner of my eye I saw the sharp stare my grandma gave the lady before sharing a reproachful look with Grandpa. My stomach sank as dread continued to fill me. There was something my grandparents had been hiding from me, wasn't there…

"I'd think it was rather obvious, Mr Nightshade, you are fae-born."

"But—"

"Meaning you are not a normal fourteen nearly fifteen-year-old boy."

"Okay, but—"

"Only fae-born and those who carry god DNA can lay eyes upon a god."

"Sure, but—"

"Others would have their eyes erupting in fire and their brains turned to smoke if they so much as saw a glimpse of a god let alone one as powerful and revered as the horned one."

"Yes, but—"

"I think that's enough information for now, he's only a child," cut in Grandma, trying to put a stop to the conversation.

Getting interrupted constantly was fast filling me with anger.

"You mean to tell me that Léonidas doesn't know?"

"Know what?" I tried but again was ignored by all.

"We were keeping the laddie safe," Grandpa defended.

"What do you meaning keeping me safe!"

"Manners," chorused Grandma and Grandpa.

What was going on?

"Don't you think he should have been told? Maybe this whole thing could have been avoided if he knew," stated the headmistress, her tone quickly becoming as frosty as the peaks of the mountains north of here.

"What should I have been tol—"

"He's too young," said Grandma, getting to her feet, her face stony, ever the matriarch.

"Clearly he is not," replied the headmistress, gesturing at my horns.

"They only have to attend the school when they are sixteen, Léonidas is not yet fifteen! You have no jurisdiction till then! I know the laws! And you have no business telling me how to raise my grandson."

Grandma was angrier than I had ever seen her, she looked ready to go to fisticuffs with the headmistress. Grandpa's face had turned a poisonous shade of pale ash— he was not the type to like such conflict. This must be about my parents for that was the only thing my grandparents ever got this angry about, not even when paying taxes had I seen them this mad.

"Excuse me," I said, but of course I went ignored.

"He is Fae royalty, heir to the kingdom of Belladonna," declared the headmistress.

"Excuse me," I repeated, why was no one listening to me? After all, they were talking about me, should I not have had a voice in this conversation? And what did she mean by royalty? What a laugh. We didn't have two pennies to our name, let alone a title.

"Excuse me!" My tone rose and still the argument between the three of them continued.

"EXCUSE ME!" I shouted.

A force unlike anything I had ever felt surged through me, the sensation was almost like static under the skin yet something in my soul was pulled and released. Suddenly a violent wind seemed to gust from behind me. No, there was no window behind me, it must have come from...me. It poured through me like a cold shiver that electrified my nerves. Completely by accident I sent the table and chairs flying backward. The clattering and banging making a horrid sound.

Was I a danger to people?

I looked to Grandma, she looked...disappointed...in me? Turning, I looked at Grandpa but he could not or would not meet my gaze. Instead, he turned and picked up the table and fallen chairs. Lastly, I looked at Headmistress Guaire. She was the only one to have kind eyes on me in this moment. I was a burden and would never be anything more. Desperately I craved comfort. I was really confused, I was really angry, and above all I was really scared. I never wanted my grandparents to be disappointed in me.

Magic was not the reason I found this all so hard to believe, because my grandma had taught me about magic, how we are all energy that feeds into the universe and how some people had a higher calling and gift for the craft. The real reason I was feeling this type of way was because who am I? I'm just a sad somewhat orphaned teenager whose grandparents were forced to take him in. That only had the creatures in the forest for friends for the towns people found him freakish with pale skin, purple eyes, and snow-white hair. Why would I be special? Why would I deserve this when the universe saw fit to take away...my parents? No, magic wasn't what I felt inside, truly. For what I felt was like a cold, scared, starved little boy trapped on a small leaking row boat set out in the eye of a vicious storm in a sea that was vast and never ending. Trying to paddle to safety with no oars and no compass for direction. That is what I felt inside and that...was not magic, that was reality.

"I think now we can all find agreement, yes? That Léonidas Nightshade must attend the Amethyst School for Spellcasters. He has now displayed use of magic twice within the span of just a few short days."

Silence fell on the room as the undeniable was made apparent. Was I really going to attended a magic school? It was...absurd to say the least. The idea alone of attending a school was a pretty daunting one for my grandma and grandpa had home-schooled me since I was six. What if people found me weird there like they did here? But if I were being honest what I feared above all was my grand-parents deserting me.

Just over an hour later Headmistress Guaire had finally left but not without ensuring I would be in attendance at that school the following night. She'd originally wanted me to leave this night but Grandma absolutely forbade it. So I'd get one more night at home before being sent away. I still had so many unanswered questions. My mind was a chaos of uncertainty and doubt. The only thing I knew for certain was that my life would never ever be the same.

PRENEURS DE MAGI I

Dropping yet other innocent corpse to the floor, Jacquard Morioatus turned his head skyward as a rush of euphoria and potent power pickled his soul as he finally had found his much-craved fix. A magical essence was far better and hit harder than any man-made drug ever could. Nothing could ever be so potent, so pure, so undiluted. So all encompassing. A large smile stretched across his face as he extended his arms into the air with glee and twirled around the small cabin he had acquired by force as stolen magic filled him.

The cabin had housed a family of three though now their corpses lay frozen in time, with expressions of the deepest terror, on the cold hard stone of the grimy floor of which they were now left to rot.

One essence or soul was never enough to satisfy Jacquard, not any more. He had taken the wife and child for their essences were the most potent, with their auras being the most vivid in colour. Jacquard had given Langdon the assumed father whose soul had been clearly tainted by the drink. It still had power, just not as pure and satisfying to consume, like a dirty well-used needle, it could still give you the fix you craved but the needle had become a little blunt, a little bent, and finding the vein had become that little bit harder. And in the end it was never enough.

A knock at the door had both men freezing mid euphoria. Who dared to disturb Jacquard Morioatus? The knocking continued as neither man moved, it went unanswered. A second later a force of bitter wind swung it off its hinges and in walked Callum Criedy, a bald, middle-aged white man with bad teeth and even worse breath. After Criedy in walked, Adolf Romanino, also a bald, middle-aged white man though he had excellent teeth and a muscular thug-like physique, entered.

"Aww did you start the fun without us?" joked Criedy in his Brummy slur.

"About time that you two both showed up," Jacquard retorted curtly, he was not amused by their tardiness.

"No, boss, you'll be happy when we show you what we brought you," promised Criedy

"Oh? Now do tell, Criedy, what gifts have you brought me?"

Smiling he turned to face out the door as he pulled out his spellcaster's wand and uttered, "Eiságein!"

Three young teenage boys bound in magical bonds floated against their will into the room. All three of them had been gagged and blindfolded. These were no ordinary boys. no, these boys had seen something, something that Jacquard very much wanted and craved. For these boys had seen the fae-born prince who became god-touched and knew roughly where to find him.

"Oh, please do explain," crooned Jacquard as dark malevolent things flickered across his cold, blood-red gaze.

The door to the small cabin closed as their muted screams faded into the icy night air.

LÉONIDAS II

Sitting atop my freshly made linens, I stared into the universe. I tried but failed to contemplate everything. So many strange events had transpired. The hollowness in my chest felt more like a great chasm than ever before. Confused, empty, and just so very tired. if I had indeed slept for three days as everyone had said, shouldn't I feel more well-rested and not...and not this crushing exhaustion?

No, for the truth was I always felt this crushing exhaustion, I was always tired and empty inside. Even though I didn't understand I had come to accept it. I knew my parents were the missing piece of my soul, lost forever more.

Fenella Guaire was an intense person, she had that sharp ever-watchful, ever-analysing stare that owls like Henry did...another piece of my broken heart fractured as I replayed the memory in vivid detail. The arrow flew and ended his life. Why were people so cruel? What did Henry ever do to anybody? Nothing.

Hunting was a sport I did not understand, why kill something that cannot defend itself against you? What kind of cowardice was that? No, no I did not eat meat and it wasn't just because animals were friends not food. But more so that when I was very young I learnt it the hard way. My tummy could not and would not handle breaking down meat. I could recall a memory of Grandma cooking a roast dinner, I must have been six or maybe even seven. This was the only time I had been served a plate with meat on it. After taking one bite of roasted lamb I'd vomited blood. I was taken to see a doctor and it was decided that I had a rare "digestive intolerance to meat." Although dairy and eggs were fine to consume. I think that might have been the real reason why Grandpa set up the farm to be just fruit and vegetable.

Why had the headmistress called me a fae? It was just... so...so absurd...wasn't it? but if I thought about it maybe there was so truth to the fiction? I didn't exactly look like my grandparents... My ears were longer and more pointed. My skin far paler and my eyes more doe like... I needed to stop that train of thought.

My grandma had told me of the Scottish folk tales

regarding the fae but I had always thought of them as kind of bad. I mean there are just so many tales of the fae stealing children and replacing them with changelings. Was I bad? Was I a...a changling? No, I couldn't have been for I had clear memories of my father and there was no denying that we shared the same snow-white hair and bright lavender eyes even if I had only been five when I'd last seen him.

Breathing out I tried to let go of this creeping doubt that started to pollute my mind, They were my real parents. A voice in the back my mind reminded me of the simple fact that I knew no other family, not even my paternal grand-parents. Though there once was this dream I had that I thought might have been a memory but there was this unnatural vivid brightness too it that just couldn't have been real. Most memories turned dull after a while and this one had not. It was just as bright, just as vivid as it ever was.

"Darling," said Grandma, breaking me out of my thoughts.

"Yes, Grandma?" I said turning to face her as she stood in the open doorway. Her working clothes had been replaced by her favourite patched-up house robe and her hair was now set in rollers with her ruby head scarf tied to keep the set in place.

"It is well past your bedtime, what are you still doing up?"

"Didn't I just sleep for three days?" I retorted bitterly.

Grandma stared at me for long moments, pursing her lips before sighing and entering the room. Pulling my legs up to my chest, I hugged them tight as Grandma sat at the foot of my bed.

"Darling, penny for your thoughts?"

"Not much..." I mumbled into my knees.

"Not much you say? Well one would think you are doing a lot of pouting for not much," she said casually.

A soft snort escaped me.

"Well as I always say a problem shared is always a problem halved."

Grandma was right, she *did* say that *all* the time.

"Nothing..."

"Darling, come on out with it, what's wrong?"

"What's wrong? More like what's wrong with me."

"Oh, Léonidas, come now, let's not have talk of this. There is nothing wrong with you."

There *was* something wrong with me, I knew it to be true. She need not lie but I didn't want too upset Grandma so I changed topic.

"Do I really have to leave and attend this school, Grandma? That lady in the purple feather coat said so many things. Things you never told me...why?"

My grandma went quiet as a dark expression crossed her normally kind visage. Long moments passed before she closed her eyes and let loose one silver tear that fell down her cheek. It seemed she had decided on something as she quickly got her feet.

"Come, darling, time for bed."

"But—"

"Time for bed, I think tonight I'm going to tell you another story, maybe it will give you some comfort."

"What kind of story?"

"One I had hoped to not have to tell you till you were much older."

What was she saying? Was this a true story? Or was this another ancient history or folk tale? Either way I quickly jumped under the covers eager to hear what Grandma was about to tell me.

She once more took a spot at the foot of the bed as she cleared her throat and began the story.

"Many years ago, long before the war that killed many and displaced many more, there was a young mother who knew only the ways of the earth, who had a child that defied explanation. When her daughter turned sixteen, a lady with a purple coat made of feathers appeared, telling the young mother and the young father that their daughter was special and was destined for great things, but the young mother already knew that for she had seen the magic first hand.

"The lady in the coat told her that a long past ancestor was a spellcaster who was burned at the stake for being called a witch. This lady told her that the magical bloodline had been suppressed and only with the birth of her daughter had become known once more. What was the young mother to do, she had not the skills to look after such a child, for when she turned her back the child had turned trees to ice and grass to gold. So when the lady told her that there was a place that could look after her child and teach her right, she had very little option but to agree. The sixteen-year-old daughter went off to the school that was far away and came back only each summer break."

I moved a little closer to Grandma as she continued.

"The mother missed her daughter desperately but took comfort in knowing her daughter was destined to be great. One summer, before her final year, she came home with a boy. A boy unlike any other. One with hair of snow, eyes of belladonna-bright, and ears that tapered into points. The daughter told her mother that she had fallen in love with a prince and not just any prince but one of the fae realm.

Well, the mother did not know what to do so she welcomed him with open arms but she feared of the stories of the fae that took humans that were to be seen never again. In the beginning everything was fine so the mother began to believe that her fears were just ill-informed prejudice like those that hated people of a different hue. In the post-magic school years the daughter did indeed become great like the mother always knew she would. She even had been given permission to cross the realm to that of the fae. An honour that almost unheard of in this age. The mother begged her daughter to not go for she feared that her fears of never seeing her again may come true but the daughter did not listen and so she went across the veil to the ancient realm of the fae."

Grandma's normally steady hand shook with weight of the words she told.

"The mother waited for many months for her daughter to return. The seasons changed and so did the earth. Three years the daughter was gone but on the eve of winter solstice she returned once more, but she and the prince were not alone for with them they brought a baby boy who had the prince's snow-white hair and eyes of belladonna bright but the baby boy also had her daughter's high cheekbones. Cheekbones that her daughter had been given from the mother's own mother. She knew this baby to be her grandson. And so the mother became a grandma and her heart was full with joy once more. Even though the grandma wondered why her daughter never once told her of what went on in the realm of fae. The grandma saw more of her grandson in the year that followed then she had seen of her daughter since she went off at sixteen to the school for spellcasters.

"Then the war happened and the daughter and the

prince were sent off by the secret governments to accomplish secret missions of things that were not to be said. So the grandson had to move in with the grandma and grandpa full time. The grandma of course welcomed her grandson with open arms and with a smile on her face but she secretly worried her fears would finally become true for people were dying left, right, and centre. In the few years that passed the grandma saw less and less of her daughter but she tried to fill that void with the care of her grandson and for a time that worked. But as the roses died in garden the grandma knew bad things were on the horizon.

"One night the daughter and the prince returned whilst the grandson slept. They were in a panic for they had learnt of something that had worried them deeply. They spoke of little to the grandma and only told her to keep their son safe and that if they should not return but solstice night, they were to move into a safe house they had bought secretly in Wales. Once more the grandma begged her daughter to not leave but just like before she could not stop her. Solstice night came and went and the grandma knew she had finally lost her daughter like she had feared all along. Even though their hearts were broken, the grandparents took their grandson to the safe house like they had promised. The grandson hated it and even in the beginning rebelled for he was sad and missed his parents greatly.

"One day while the grandson was out in the forest with his grandpa, the lady in the purple feathered coat returned once more. The grandma hated the women for if she had never sent her daughter away maybe all that had come to pass may have only been a bad nightmare. The lady told her of the death of her daughter and the fae prince and with that all the grandma had feared had come to pass. Before the lady had left she had told her like she had for her daughter that her grandson was destined for great things and so as the years went by the grandma feared of the day the lady would return once more."

Rendered Speechless, I didn't know what to say, it seemed like my grandma had just told me the story, one piece of the puzzle of the death of my parents.

"Grandma—" I began but she rose from the bed.

"Now it is well and truly time for bed," she declared.

"But—"

"No, Léonidas, that is enough for tonight, after all we have an early rise in the morning."

Sleep? I wouldn't be sleeping, not after all that had come to pass. Everything Grandma had said was just so unfathomable. That I was left with so many more questions. Who ran this secret government? Did my nightmare actually show the truth of their deaths or was it just my mind drawing conclusions to questions that went unanswered? If my father was a prince did that make me a prince? Where was this school? Did they have telephones to call home? Would I be the only fae there?

"Night, darling," said Grandma as she gave my forehead a kiss and turned out the lights.

"Just because the lights are off doesn't mean I have any less questions," I called back to her.

Chuckling, she said, "Yes, darling, I'm well aware."

I tried to turn on my side but my antlers got in the way. Looked like sleeping on my back it was…well, more like staring into the abyss and contemplating life anyway.

CHAPTER 3

GOODBYES AND NEW ADVENTURES

LÉONIDAS I

Before the sun had started its ascent into the dark, cold morning sky to light the day, Grandma had awoken me to start packing for the journey ahead. I still hadn't a clue of the school's location, only that it was far, far away. Luckily, I didn't own much so packing went rather quickly. Just one lot of summer pyjamas, one lot of winter pyjamas, three button-up shirts, two pairs of trousers, four pairs of underwear, one pair of shoes, and six hankies Grandma had made from old blankets. One toothbrush, one tube of toothpaste, and two well used, well read books: *The Wonderful Wizard of Oz* by L. Frank Baum and *The Odyssey* by Homer. One old suitcase was enough for it all and I was still left with a lot of room.

Not owning my own suitcase, I had to borrow Grandpa's. It was a rusty brown colour with two silver latches, a handle, and was just a tad bigger than that of a pillow. I knew it to be old for Grandpa had told me it was a wedding gift from his parents. Grandma apparently had a matching one though I had never seen it.

A manic Grandma rushed into the room, rollers only half taken out.

"Darling, are you packed yet?"

"Yes, Grandma," I replied, gesturing to the closed suitcase.

"Good," she said before sighing. "I had wanted us to be on the road before now. Anyway, not to worry, we'll still get there in time."

"Where is there?" I inquired.

"Oh, darling, it would take too long to explain for now. Just far enough away that...well let just get a move on." And with that she left my room in a hurry taking out more rollers as she went.

From the staircase she called, "Darling, Grandpa has left you some oats, best eat now before they go lumpy!"

I didn't much care for oats, I mean, no one would if you had it almost all the time.

Downstairs, Grandpa sat stoically reading the newspaper.

"Morning, Grandpa," I said trying to fake being cheerful.

"Morning," he replied as he turned the page. Grandpa was a man of very few words, and I kind of liked it that way. There was no middle words, just whatever was straight to the point.

At the stove I spooned myself a bowl of oats before checking the cupboard for honey. Darn, we were out. Instead I grabbed the golden treacle and a spoon and sweetened the oats to my liking...which was as sweet as possible to hide the bland glue-like taste of oats.

It was another full hour before Grandma had finished

fussing around and was ready for the journey ahead. Grandpa had even filled the family motor vehicle up with fuel in the time it took Grandma to get ready. The Morris Minor was quite an ancient auto machine. It was old enough that most people around town had something at least five or six years newer. Grandma always said it was held together by cello tape and a prayer whereas Grandpa always said it had good bones...whatever that meant.

Grandma had on a green dress she had made from old drapes she'd been gifted from one of the houses she cleaned on a regular basis. It was in a popular style we had seen Lana Turner wear in *You belong to My Heart*—it was the one with the collar and wrap-style front and long sleeves. Her hair was neatly brushed into soft waves with a matching green snood hair net to hold the style in place. Grandma had completed the outfit with spectacles, although this was more for driving then for any form of vain fashion accessory.

"Right, darling, we best be off," she declared, slightly short of breath from her rush down the stairs. Grandpa stood, folding the newspaper up neatly into thirds and extended his hand out towards me. "I'm gonna miss you around here, Léo, this place won't—" The ghost of long shut-away emotion crossed his eyes before he coughed looking uncomfortable, and ended with, "Yeah, it just won't be." I rose and shook his hand. Physical touch wasn't something my grandpa was ever into or at least not while I had known him. Maybe he was different before he went off to serve in the first war but at least now, a shake of the hand was to him as good a hug or at least it was the closest I was going to get to one from him.

Grandma handed me a scarf and instructed me to tie it in a turban style around my antlers. After several moment of failing to hide them, Grandma said, "Goodness gracious, here let me do it." Within a few seconds my horns were covered by the pale blue scarf. I had never worn a turban before. I wondered if I looked odd but alas there was no time to check as I was being ushered out of the house quick-smart.

The morning was rather frosty outside, even the birds that sung at first light had taken shelter from the snowy weather.

Suitcase packed into the back of the old motor vehicle, I turned to face my home one final time. It would be a while before I returned. I did not what to say goodbye so instead I said I'll be back soon. I would be returning here in the summer and in summer I'd be able to help Grandpa with the new crops. I would maybe even have a few tricks up my sleeve to help guarantee a more prosperous yield.

Having that idea somehow gave me the strength to leave, I was just going away to gain more skills to help my family...my remaining family. Maybe then I'd feel less hollow inside and less like a burden.

"First stop London," announced Grandma.

London? We did indeed have a long drive ahead.

PRENEURS DE MAGI I

Laughter and glee filled Jacquard's cold, pale chest in the place where his blackened heart once was. The first substantial lead on the god-touched fae prince he'd ever had. He was firmly on cloud nine. Now all he had to do was snatch the boy with his greedy fingers.

Jacquard considered himself a practical man of sorts, so of the five teens who had been brought before him he had only kept two alive. Yes, two was the magic number because with a spare you had leverage, you had an example to showcase what would happen if you didn't obey him and you have the pure desperation in seeing someone getting tortured to create that fear.

"Where was the spot it happened, boy?" Jacquard Commanded, gesturing to the field out in front of him.

"It was...I think—" began the scared brown-haired sixteen-year-old named Mathew.

"You 'think'?" snarled Jacquard, The boy instantly took a step back in fear, his heart beating a mile a minute. "Do I need to remind you of what will happen if you are wrong?"

"N-n-n-no...s-s-sir," stammered Mathew.

"Good, now where was it, *exactly.*"

Mathew stepped forward toward the place he thought he'd seen the strange freak die. His father had taught him how to be a great tracker.

"Come on, boy, we haven't got all day," called Jacquard from a few steps behind him. Mathew looked to the sky where the wind brought the smell of wet earth to his nostrils. It was cold out with the ground still covered in winter's worst. Returning his attention back to the ground he prayed to his god for any sign of the strange boy's death and his sudden growth of horns. But nothing came. Gulping, he turned back to face the scary man with wrinkled skin and greasy, long, black hair.

"I-I-I can't be sure...sir."

"Really?" warned Jacquard.

"The-the-the snow, has covered everything but-but-but I-I think it-it-it-it's here," he said, gesturing to a spot on the snow.

"You think?"

Quick as a flash, Jacquard pulled out his wand and spoke the word of death, "Apothnískein!" as he swiped an *X* through the cold air. A flash of red pounded through the air toward the boy Mathew. He began to try to shield his face but it was too late. The spell hit its target. Skeletal hands cracked through the earth's surface as Mathew was struck immobile. Bony figures infested with worms and spiders began to pull him deep under the snow. All Mathew was able to do was scream as his body was taken away. A few fleeting moments later and Mathew was buried alive. His screams could still be felt in the hallowed ground.

Jacquard turned to the remaining boy Tristan who had just seen his friend die a very gruesome death. "Now, tell me exactly where it happened."

"Right away, Mr."

"Ah see, *now* they're learning."

LÉONIDAS II

London was odd—too many men in top hats with very serious faces. The kind one could get when experiencing bad indigestion.

Getting to London had been a long, long, loooong quiet drive. The sun when we started was on one side of the horizon and now it was firmly in the other. Grandma hadn't been in the mood for talking and the motor vehicle's radio receiver had long since given up the ghost. So instead I had been rereading *The Odyssey*. Thankfully when we stopped for gas a while back Grandma had suggested rereading it may make the time pass just that little bit quicker. Although Grandma was probably just over me trying to start conversations she was unwilling to have. Her common response to anything I had asked thus far was "later, darling," so when exactly was later?

So far I had gotten up to the part where Odysseus visits

Hades (the underworld) and to his shock sees his mother there who had died whilst he was away. The passage in particular was, "O my Mother," cried Odysseus in deep distress, "why dost thou mock me thus? Come to my heart, dear mother: let me hold thee in mine arms once more, and mingle my tears with thin." I hope there to be an afterlife for, like Odysseus, I too wished desperately for my mother to hold me in her arms once more although Homer's depiction of Hades was rather a grim one, I must say.

"Darling, we have arrived," spoke Grandma, her voice unusually thick.

"Right," I said closing the book. This was getting all too real. Was I really going to go to a magic school? What were the chances? It was rather an odd birthday present.

Outside the family vehicle I saw ships and docks and people in flocks, some men in coats and ladies in frocks. Having never been to city like this before I was momentarily shocked at the sheer number and volume of people walking about even this late in the afternoon. After a moment it became somewhat apparent that a ship must be needed to get us to our next destination, a destination I was still yet to be told... I hadn't ever been on a boat before, I wondered if it was scary.

Sighing, I knew I was not perfect, but all this secrecy was about to break my last nerve, like a fragile house of matches, it threatened to collapse. No answers—just more and more secrecy.

We walked past the beautiful large ivory-coloured ships with crowds of cheerful people, we went right up to the edge of the dock where only one ship was tethered. The more I looked at it the more unsure I became, could one call this particular vessel a ship? It was rather small and old, and on approaching, a smell of rotting fish and damp mould assaulted my nostrils. It was almost enough to have me bending over, vomiting up the oats I had eaten those many hours earlier.

Please gods, goddesses, Divine energies let this not be the mode of transportation we must depart in. I crossed my fingers...but to my utter dismay Grandma walked me right up to the rickety, rusted old thing. Even the thick ropes that held it to the dock seemed weathered and about to break. This ship vessel thing was absolutely pure nightmare fodder.

"This is where I leave you, Léonidas. I am not allowed to take a step further with you."

"Whaaaaat?" I squawked, mouth agape. "Surely, Grandma, you jest...right? Please tell me I'm not going on this...boat *alone*."

"Calm down, darling, trust me, it will get you to the island safe and sound."

"What island? Grandma, there is much you still haven't told me. What island? Why can't you come with me? I do not understand!"

Sighing, Grandma stepped closer.

"For people like me it is forbidden to step even a single foot on the boat let alone the island. For all I know, if I was onboard the boat may never be able to find the island."

"What do you mean, Grandma? What island?"

"Darling, Kírke's island, Aeaea."

Oh yeah that makes sense...wait what did she say?

"Huh? Pardon?"

Is that why Grandma had suggested I read *The Odyssey* on the drive here?

"Darling, unfortunately I'm not allowed to say more. I myself have not a clue where the island is. I just know that your mother loved it there and would tell me very little about the island itself."

"But—"

"If I had it my way you'd never be going, darling."

"But—"

"But it's not up to me, This is not my choice. And your grandpa is...right. We can't hide the antlers."

I gestured to the turban.

"Long-term, I mean a turban doesn't suit you, darling, even if blue is your colour."

"So you're going to leave me?" I choked out. Tears filled my eyes. She didn't want me. No one wanted me, it would seem.

"Léonidas Agápe Nightshade, we will have none of that nonsense. Today you are fifteen, you are no longer a child. This self-wallowing behaviour is unbecoming and you will stop it right this instance," Grandma chided.

"But—"

"No buts, we are not leaving you. We will see you next summer and you best be ready to work for summer means plenty of farming and harvesting."

"Yes."

"Yes what?" she said sternly.

"Yes, Grandma."

"Good, now do your grandpa and I proud, also..." She pulled a very long box from an interior coat pocket. I wasn't sure what I was more shocked at, the fact I didn't see it bulging in her coat or that the coat had a pocket long enough for it.

"Now this is for you, darling. Happy birthday," said Grandma with a smile.

What was it? The box was long, about the same size as the distance between my wrist and elbow, and was covered in a fine inky green velvet flock. The box alone looked expensive.

"Can we afford this?" I found myself asking, mesmerised by the box

"Darling, this is a family heirloom so yes we can afford it."

"A 'family heirloom'?"

"Yes, darling, it was your mother's."

My mother's...my hands shook as I began to open the box lid.

Inside, on what looked like a checkered silk cushion was a long rod, almost the full length of the box. It was a soft white hue with swirls and symbol like letters engraved all along the crystal-like surface. It must have been expensive.

"What is it?" I asked Grandma.

"This is...was your mother's spellcaster's wand. It is now yours."

Spellcaster's wand? My mother's? I went to pull out the wand but Grandma hurriedly closed the lid.

"Darling, use your brain, will you please? Not out here where people can see. Wait till you're aboard the ship at least."

Oh right, secrecy and all that.

"How?" I said simply.

"It was retrieved after...after her passing."

"Oh."

There was a heavy silence where I knew both of our hearts stung with loss. It only ended when Grandma spoke. "Now there will be no tears, understand?"

"Okay, Grandma."

I bent in, giving her a big hug. "Thank you, I love it even if I don't really understand it."

"That will come in time, Now..." looking at her wrist watch, "the boat is about to leave."

"There isn't someone to come collect me? Or a person to take tickets?"

"Darling, what ticket? At any point have you seen me with a ticket?"

"Oh right, True."

Suitcase and wand box in hand, I turned to face the boat proper. It really looked like something from one of those horror film posters I had seen at the picture theatre, the one's my grandparents had absolutely forbidden me to ever watch; maybe now that I saw this nightmare that was a good idea.

Steam started to billow from the top of the ship as the sounds of a rickety engine ignited or...misfired as it didn't sound promising.

"Darling, it's time to hope onboard, quick now."

Grandma gave me the biggest hug before she stepped back. When I turned around the ropes tying the ship to the dock had somehow been untied.

OH GOODNESS! I needed to run for it, the ship looked like it was starting to depart from the dock.

"Bye, Grandma, I'll miss you!" I yelled as I ran up the ramp before it was too late.

"Darling, now remember a problem shared is always a problem halved, and if A and B don't equal C then there is an issue with A and B, and if something seems too good to be true then it usually is! And ALWAYS TRUST YOUR GUT!"

I already missed her, as the burning behind my eyes seemed suspiciously like tears.

One step...

Two steps...

Three steps...

What in the world?!

Colour and smoke illuminated around me as I officially stepped foot on the ship. Only the instant my foot made contact with the unknown smooth flooring everything ripped around me as I seemingly changed location in time and space. Accompanying the ripping of lights was a gust of wind swirling like that of a tornado. Sound too seemed to dial in and out before the smell of putrid fish was replaced by oranges, citrus, and sea salt.

The last thing to change before my vision cleared was the sensation of touch. One second my shoes were on firm ground and the next they sank into sand.

A vast island lay before me, with trees and plants of technicolour splendour. Turning, I looked back behind me. There was no dock or ship, no people or smoke. Only vibrant blue waters that almost sung to me with their beautiful serenity.

"Toto, we are certainly not in Kansas anymore."

PRENEURS DE MAGI II

Two unmarked graves now lay within the earth as Jacquard had inevitably lost his patience with the second boy.

"If you want something done right you must always do it yourself," exclaimed Jacquard as he raised his wand once more. The snow hid the answers he sought. It was simple really, he must remove the snow if he was to uncover the truth.

"Diarreín," he chanted as he tipped his wand to his index finger before flicking it downward.

Heat began to leach the earth of all its moisture like a boiling hot summer day. Bit by bit snow turned to water that became moisture that puffed into vapour before finally being consumed by the air. Within a matter of minutes the earth was soon visible. Grass lay killed by winter's kiss and the land appeared barren like some war-torn land. For only mushrooms and soil remained.

Next Jacquard raised his wand once more before pointing it at the ground. "Ziteín Aíma!" This spell cost him greatly because the earth was a force of grounding and neutrality that desired to control but not to be controlled in return.

With his vast array of stolen magics Jacquard searched the dirt for any sign of blood. It rumbled in annoyance but in the end gave in to his will. Several yards away a patch of earth lit up in a vibrant green flash. *So the first boy was indeed correct with his placement, pity. Oh well*, he thought uncaringly. Life meant nothing to this man, everyone and everything was expendable.

Getting back to his feet, he wandered over to the glowing earth. Had he finally found a way of tracking the fae prince? If this was indeed his blood it would allow Jacquard to find him, and depending on the specific protections that may have been placed on him he may even be able to be summoned. But first he needed to make sure this was indeed fae blood, and for that it was time he visited the vampires.

"Langdon!" he called.

"Yes, Jacquard?"

"It's time we went vampire hunting."

Jacquard smiled as he scooped the glowing earth into a secure glass container before clipping it to his belt. He would trust no one with his prize, none would touch it and live to tell the tale.

"Also, I'm hungry. Let's steal some magic along the way shall we."

The eyes of his followers glowed, they would all greatly like to give their insatiable cravings a fix and Jacquard was included to give it to them all as his cravings were always the most ravenous, the most demanding, and the most desperate for all consuming magics.

"Fae prince I'm coming for you." He laughed.

'

CHAPTER 4
THE AMETHYST SCHOOL FOR SPELLCASTERS

LÉONIDAS I

N o, I wasn't in Kansas anymore. The sheer beauty and vibrancy was like a slap to the face—it was so intensely shocking. The sand that now covered my shoes was the hue of the summer sun and if spring was considered a colour that would be the shade of the trees growing in the distance.

Were my eyes telling me lies? Could this all be real?

"Grandm—" I began before realising she wasn't here. No, Grandma was back beyond the sea...somewhere. Even the time of day seemed off. It looked to be at least a few hours earlier then the place I had just been.

Turning, I took a few steps forward into the cool cerulean water, only I did not cross back. All I achieved in doing this was to fill my shoes with salt water. With a gulp I realised there was no going back for me, there was only forward. My heart ached, I missed my grandma already and it hadn't even been more than a minute or two, but I would do as she said with the knowledge I would return home come summer.

"Hello?" I called.

There was no response as my words died on the wind.

With no other clue what to do I headed for the trees the colour of spring. Maybe with some higher ground I'd be able to see where it was I needed to go. It seemed to me a map or a tour guide should have been provided considering I hadn't a clue where to go. Also why wasn't there any snow? Seemed rather strange considering today was the wintriest of days—the solstice. It truly seemed like a pleasant midsummer's afternoon.

Approaching the small tufts of grass growing on the sandy edge, suitcase and wand box in hand, I noticed a narrow path made from polished purple stones that seemed to lead up into the magnificent trees. Each stone was maybe the size of tea saucer and had a translucent quality like tinted glass.

"To follow the path or to not follow the path, that is the question," I muttered.

As I saw it I really only had two options in front of me. Stay on the beach and twiddle my thumbs hoping someone would eventually find me, or see where this path led. One option boring, the other possibly a lot more fun. So follow the path it was.

Sun rays spidered the ground, creating light shows of splendour and awe. The trees smelt of citrus and honeyed pine with trunks that seemed to almost travel into the sky they were so tall and old-looking, actually old was the wrong word. Ancient was a better description for what I saw.

After a while I heard the birdsong in the trees. Some sounded familiar whilst others sung a song anew. The path led me into a short meadow with the tiniest little stream. The grass here sprouted little flowers with yellow cotton wool-type buds that smelt of some type of fruit nectar, the precise type I was unsure.

Walking to the small stream I watched my reflection flicker with the sun's gaze. Was it safe to undo the turban? Or should I just keep it on? I really didn't like the look but more importantly my scalp was becoming rather itchy. Dare I risk it? After all this was a magic school, surely there were plenty of students with horns...antlers...right?

So in the end I decided I would just risk it, I could always put it back on. Setting my suitcase and wand box down, I quickly unwrapped the turban until it returned once more into its original function as a scarf. The fresh breeze in my hair was pure ecstasy. Closing my eyes, I breathed in the citrus scent of the field. It calmed me in way that felt revitalising. Mixed in the with the smell of citrus was something herbaceous and sweet that I couldn't quite put my finger on, bright and clean. Making a mental note to asks someone what trees grew in this field, I was ready to continue.

Snap!

Whirling back around I froze, as a gasp escaped my lips. Standing before me was a familiar-looking moonstone stag. Its majestic presence seemed almost otherworldly, and I for one could not help but feel a sense of awe in its presence. Its piercing eyes seemed to hold a wisdom beyond my years, and I couldn't shake the feeling that he was calling me forth. My heart pounded in my chest, *thud thud thud*, matching the rhythm of the leaves rustling in the gentle breeze.

Had I truly seen it before, or was my mind playing tricks on me? What were the chances that this was the same stag from the field near home? The questions swirled in my head as I gazed upon the creature, feeling a mix of fear and excitement.

I took a step forward, drawn to the stag as if by an unseen force. My heart raced with anticipation, and I couldn't resist the urge to discover what lay ahead. I didn't know what I would find, but I was determined to uncover the secrets that this strange and magnificent creature held. The sound of my footsteps echoed softly in the quiet of the day as I approached the stag, ready to uncover its mysteries.

"Hello?" I called to it.

Though it did not respond it did take a step closer to me. I could've sworn it was the same stag though it would have to be impossible...right? I mean I was clearly some great distance away from home. For one, there wasn't a drop of snow around. And two, we were surrounded by water. Yet everything about this majestic creature told me it was.

Taking another step and then another, the stag with its tree of antlers began to approach me. I was so mesmerised I hadn't realised that I was also taking small steps towards the stag. It wasn't until we met in the middle that it dawned on me. A small wriggling in the back of my mind. Weren't stags dangerous? Though the voice was muted whilst the stag licked my hand. Did he want me to pat him? Slowly I raised my right hand to his snout. The moment my skin brushed his fur something flashed into my mind. A long piece of parchment with writing in verse scrolled across it in an elegant script. It was only a flash but it was accompanied by a short, whispered voice that seemed to call from the text itself.

"Lost, Ancient, Forgotten and Old,
A great power will rise that was long foretold"

As quick as it appeared it was gone. How very odd. Sighing, I opened my eyes having shut them as the... apparition? Appeared.

Where was the stag? My hand was extended, touching... nothing. Squinting my eyes, I wondered if this was all just in my head? That thought freaked me out. Hurriedly I grabbed my belongings from the stream's narrow edge and hopped back on to the purple stone trail with a fire little under my backside. I wanted to get as far away from what... whatever that was as I possibly could.

Somebody soon better start answering my questions for I was about to explode.

Trees of evergreen passed into shades of magenta and flowing vines of red and marigold hung down like technicolour lightbulbs on corded ropes. This place was a paradise of this I was certain, it was pretty much the only thing I knew for certain but at least I knew something...I guessed.

The trail soon came to an abrupt stop. Large squared-off platforms formed a kind of gateway. Each block was maybe the height of a door, only squared off like a cube. Each looked to be made from the same purple glass as the stones in path. Only these blocks appeared to be more opaque, as if they were shielding something beyond so that whatever lay behind it was a complete mystery.

"Now what?" I sighed. Did I have to climb up them? Surely that was too great of a task. Must I find some other way? Had I taken the wrong path? Only, it was the only path I saw so that seemed rather unlikely.

"You're a little late to the party," called a distinctly sassy feminine voice. She sounded like Mae West, so much so in fact that I half expected her to actually be said star.

"Listen, sugar, I've been twiddling my thumbs for two hours, waiting for you to show up." she called again. Yeah she was quite cross.

"Sorry," I called up, "I didn't know the...way?"

She laughed before somehow jumping down from what appeared to be a great distance without breaking a leg.

"Well I hope you are better skilled at spell casting than you are at punctuality."

Was that an insult? I couldn't tell. Her voice showed no malice just sounded matter-of-fact like the same way one would say "The rain is wet" or that "fire burns." She was maybe a few inches taller than me with setting sun skin. Her hair was long and coloured like freshly crushed cherry juice. It was waved in the style of Hollywood starlets like Rita Hayworth and Lucille Bremer. Really classy yet with a hint of pizazz. She was very beautiful. In the same way her hair reflected the silver screen actresses, so did her makeup. She had lips the colour of crushed rubies and cheeks flushed in that film star way. Was she a film star? Maybe... she could be from a newer film that we couldn't have afforded to see yet because of money being so tight.

"Well?" she asked.

"Huh?" I said dumbly, I was still kind of shocked at her beauty. Though I must admit I wasn't particularly adept at dealing with people either.

"Well, sugar, *are* you better skilled at spell casting than you are at punctuality?"

"Well, you see...I...I don't really know," I admitted somewhat shyly.

"Really? I'd assumed you would know if you were invited here. Didn't your parents have you tested?" she asked.

"Tested?" There was a test? I didn't know about a test.

"Listen up, of course there's a test, darlin'. How else would they keep out the norms? Ohhhhh...you ain't too sharp, are ya?"

Okay, that kind of stung. I could've reacted offended but this person had said the same word the headmistress had used last night, one I hadn't understood. So instead I thought I'd ask her.

"'Norms'?"

"Norms is short for normals, non-magic mortals."

"Oh, makes sense." One piece of the jumbled puzzle clicked into place.

"Other names for non-magic people are Normies, Nomagi, Morties and the others."

"So many names," I commented.

"Oh, that's just the English variations. There's at least another thirty-two names but I'd rather us move on. Tonight's the winter solstice feast and I have prefect responsibilities I must get on with."

"You're a prefect? What's a prefect? Sorry for all the questions, you must be irritated by me already."

"Questions are just dandy, sweetheart. That's why I'm here to give you the lowdown. Now a prefect is kind of like a school captain. There are twenty-two of us per house. A spellcaster with masculine energy and a spellcaster with feminine energy for each major language."

"Oh, so a boy and girl—" I began but was cut off swiftly.

"Darlin', if that's what I meant, I woulda said it plain as day. What I said is exactly what I meant. Energy, it's a spectrum, see. Some spellcasters with the male parts got all feminine energy, and some with the female parts got all masculine energy. And some, they're right in the middle, neutral as can be. Your energy, that's who you are. Your anatomy, it don't mean a thing."

I could feel a headache coming on. This was a lot of new information.

"Don't worry, there's no pop quiz on your first day," she said kindly. She must have read my expression or something.

"Anyway come on, we must move on. Pull out your spellcaster's wand."

"My? Oh, my wand...right!" This I knew.

After quickly putting down my suitcase I opened the wand box. This was the first time I'd got to hold it. Gingerly, I pulled it out of the velvet box. It was icy to the touch, though it rapidly grew warm from my body heat. Wordlessly I placed the wand box atop the suitcase and then turned back to face the prefect. I was in awe.

"You look as if you've never held a wand before," she commented.

"I haven't."

"Well now, honey, let me ask you this. Are you sure you're supposed to be here? You act like you don't know a thing about this world. Did your folks not give you the rundown before you arrived?"

She didn't mean for her words to sting like they did but that didn't stop the rise of loneliness and isolation that grew within me at her words.

"They're...d...dead," I choked out.

"Sorry," she said putting her hand on my shoulder. "Normally we get a file about the new students but Headmistress Guaire said it was classified."

A solitary tear rolled down my icy cheek before falling down onto my mother's wand. Bright blue light began to emit from the crystalline rod, an all-over glow. I looked up into the prefect's eyes to find a small smile there.

"Well now look at ya, you are most certainly meant to be here."

"I am?"

"Of course, you just did magic."

"I did?" I hated how hopeful my voice sounded.

"Yes, you made your wand glow! No norms could ever do that!" In the space of only a few moments there had been a shift in the prefect. She had almost become tender.

"How rude of me, I just realised I hadn't asked you your name," I said sheepishly.

"Yes indeed, I won't deny it. I was waitin' for you to ask. I am Prefect Coco La Roux of the winter solstice house."

"Nice to meet you, Coco, I'm Léonidas Nightshade," I said, extending my hand. After a brief moment of hesitation, she reciprocated the gesture and we exchanged a handshake.

"Nice to meet you, Léonidas Nightshade."

Letting go of my hand, Coco turned to face the giant purple glass blocks.

"Now it's best we get going. These woods change at nightfall."

"They change? What do you mean?" I queried.

"No time to explain, you'll find out at some point. But for now let's just say daylight equals safe and nightfall equals unsafe."

"That sounds ominous."

"Yes, now turn and face the Amethyst gateway."

Turning, I looked directly at the spot she pointed but all I saw was a series of stacked blocks.

"Point your wand directly at the centre cube and say 'lýo' and turn the wand like you would a key."

My palms instantly become sweaty. What if I couldn't do it? I thought as doubt reared its ugly head. But before I let it over take me another voice spoke up, this voice told me that this was my destiny. I needed to at least try so I gave it a go.

Pointing my wand at the centre block as instructed I chanted "lýo" whist I turned the wand like a key.

And...nothing happened. Disheartened, I looked at Coco.

"What did I do wrong?"

"I don't know, sugar. Did you feel it in your chest?"

"Feel it in my chest?" I questioned.

"Yes, darling, you gotta *feel* it for it to work. Give this a go. Close your eyes and imagine, deep down in your chest where your heart lives, there's a well like the one you'd dip a pail into for a drink of water."

"Like *Snow White* and the wishing well?"

"Exactly like the well in *Snow White* only instead of water it is filled with your magical essence. Can you do that?"

"I think so."

"Now whilst you're picturing your magic well you must also feel your connection to the universe. Imagine energy being pulled up from the ground and filling your magic well."

Concentrating, I gave it ago. I pictured a well filled with magical essence deep within my chest. It was small but mighty. Next, I focused on my feet and how they touched the earth through my shoes. I tried to imagine I was a tree taking root.

"Now, Léonidas, give it a go," Coco encouraged."

Opening my eyes, I said the word while using the wand like a key. "lýo!" I chanted.

A rush of magic surged through me, leaving me momentarily breathless.

"See, you did it!" said a pleased Coco.

I did?...I *did*! A rush of euphoria filled me. I actually did magic. I watched as the amethyst cubes began to change. The opacity seemed to leech away like milk or water being poured into tea. It slowly became clearer and clearer as it diluted. *I just did that!*

The magic made no sound just continued to disappear until it was like a wall of crystal-clear glass.

"Now what?" I asked.

"What do you mean? We walk straight through it," Coco informed me.

"We do?" I was a bit worried I'd make a fool of myself.

"I promise, Léonid—you know what, I'm just going to call you Léon. The full name...too much."

"Oh okay." I didn't really care what people called me, a name was a name, just as long as when they did say my full name that they'd say Nightshade. I always wanted to be tied to my parents even if it was just in name only. It was all I had and at least that was something.

Coco led me through the clear crystal. As we passed though it a cool sensation not unlike running water kissed my skin though I was left completely dry. Magic was *incredible*.

I could not believe my eyes. There beyond me was a purple castle. Though I was unsure if that was the correct term for it was as big and vast as any city. With towers so great that they reached up into the clouds. Magical blue smoke seemed to wrap around one of the towers like a python's hug. We stood on a cliff edge, probably a couple of hours' walk away and it was still all I could see. Part of the castle on the east side appeared to merge into a cliff face or actually, maybe it was made from it. It was hard to tell.

"Welcome to the Amethyst School for Spellcasters, Léon. Your world is about to change."

All I could manage to say was, "*I'm definitely not in Beddgelert anymore!*"

Coco led me to a series of stone carved steps leading down the rocky cliff face. There was no hand rail and by the looks of those steps one slip would send me to my certain death.

"Coco…um…is there any other way down?"

"Don't tell me your scared of a little height?"

"Well it's not *that* little—" I began.

"Léon, don't you go gettin' all tangled up in your thoughts, just don't think about it," she cut in.

But how could I not think about it? It was a looooong way down. Left with little option, I followed her command and eventually after one close call we made it down to the ground. I feared the day I would ever have to walk back up them.

The setting sun filled the sky with pinks, purples, and burnt golds as the onyx of the night was being welcomed. Down here the castle looked even more massive. There was probably not a building on this earth that was as extraordinarily large as some of those towers appeared to be and to think someone had to build them…no thank you. I'd hate to see the ladder needed to wash those windows.

On closer inspection it appeared that the castle wasn't made of a purple brick like I first thought, but instead made of the same crystal as the cubed blocks and the small stone path I had followed here had been. I hadn't realised that when they said it was the Amethyst School for Spellcasters that they actually meant it was made from amethyst crystals. Wrongly I had just assumed it was named after a person's name. It must have cost a fortune to build! I doubted the crown could afford to build such a structure.

"How many people go to school here?" I enquired.

"I'm not actually certain. But I'd estimate in the vicinity of four hundred thousand, give or take fifty big ones."

Gulp. That's a lot of people.

"Is there really that many witches out there?"

"Listen here, sugar, don't you go throwin' around the word 'witches.' That's just a term those patriarchal Christians came up with to belittle, dehumanize, and control those who didn't fall in line. It's a word meant to make folks feel good about beatin', violatin', and killin' us. We're spellcasters, a title that recognizes our bond with the universe. It's a sexless term that don't discriminate and don't carry a near two thousand year history of abuse with it."

"Oh I'm sorry, I didn't know," I responded, feeling rather dumb.

"Well now you do. And besides, I'm not a part of the administration office. The school houses every Spellcaster's child from sixteen to twenty-two. There is a university on the other end of the island called Emerald College for Spellcasters to study tertiary education in magical studies. But let me tell you, getting in ain't easy. You gotta pass some of the toughest tests and exams you ever did see. Only ten lucky ones make it in each year. So, honey, when ya ask if there's really that many Spellcasters out there, the answer is a big, fat *yes*! Only point-five percent of the world is born with magical essence, and that's millions and millions of people."

Pondering this, we walked in silence for a good thirty or so minutes. By now the sky's purples had begun to turn blue and the god of the sky kissed the sunset.

I really had no clue this all existed. I mean Grandma had

taught me about the energies and I guess what you'd call magical histories but I don't think I ever truly believed it to be complete fact until this moment. The world was far odder and larger than this simple boy from a small vegetable farm could have ever imagined.

We approached the castle city's mighty gates. They were taller than any oak tree growing in any kind of forest. The crystal seemed to have formed from the ground rather than being man-made. Its purple was royal in colour and just as opaque as the cubes before I had cast my first spell with a wand. Would I need to do that same spell to enter? Turning, I readied myself to ask Coco the question but she beat me to it.

"Right, so this is a little different. The gates are imbued with a far superior magic."

"Then how do we enter?" I asked.

"To enter you must draw the secret symbol on the gate, only this drawn with your spellcaster's wand will open the gate. The symbol is thus."

Pulling a pen out of her pocket, she quickly drew the symbol on the back of my hand. The symbol in question was an infinity/sideways *8* where each loop sprouting a line that ended in a circle that finally at the end became self-contained by joining each circle via a connecting line.

"I have to remember that every time I leave the building?" I said in utter despair.

"Well of course you do. But as a first year you probably won't be leaving the safety of the castle for a while and by then it will be ingrained in your memory."

"What happens if I forget it?"

"You would be stuck out here 'til someone notices you're gone."

"And how long would that be?"

"Oh, sugar, probably a few days. If you know what's good for you, you won't forget that symbol. If you're worried about leaving, just make sure you always have a partner with you and never, I repeat, *never* leave the castle at night. These lands are filled with all sorts of dangerous creatures that come out under the stars."

"Well I'm screwed," I muttered.

"Why is that?"

"Well, I've never had friends before nor have I ever attended a school. What if people think I'm odd. I mean, I have antlers growing out of my head..."

Why was I telling Coco my personal insecurities? I didn't even know her from a bar of soap but still there was something about her that I couldn't help but trust.

"Oh do you now, I hadn't noticed," she said with irony, raising one manicured brow.

My cheeks reddened and suddenly I couldn't meet her gaze.

"No, let's not have you moping around like a wet rag. Sure, there ain't nobody else here with horns like yours but there are students who are wolf shifter spellcasters, and vampire spellcasters, siren spellcasters, nymph spellcasters, and we even have one vaewolf that goes here. So this place is filled with unordinary people, so buck up, sunshine."

She was so straight to the point, no nonsense. How could she be so sure of herself to be like that? Like she didn't care what anyone else thought of her. The small amount of anxiety I was starting to feel was extinguished like the bucket thrown on the wicked witch of the west. I really hoped I would get to see more of Coco, Maybe we could be friends at some point. I wondered if it was too early to ask her to be my friend...did people ask others to be their friends or did people just find each other and that was that?

While I pondered this, something else she had said ran through my mind.

"What's a vaewolf?" I asked, confused by the word. "I don't think I've heard of such a word before."

"Here's the skinny, a vaewolf is a vampire wolf shifter hybrid. Only one family in the world are both vaewolves and spellcasters and they are *royal. Their* male heir, future king goes here and let me tell ya, he's quite the looker, but a real twat if you know what I mean."

"This is all a lot to take in," I remarked.

"I suppose it is, sugar," she agreed.

Turning her attention back to the gates, Coco instructed me once more in the correct method of opening the gates but instead of doing it she made me put my suitcase down and draw my wand once more. It seemed as though Coco would help me but she wouldn't do the work for me. Taking a shaky breath, I began the opening symbol. I'd be lying if I didn't say my hand shook with the amount of pressure I was suddenly feeling. I didn't what to mess up again in front of Coco.

"That's right, now just join the circles and encase the symbol," she instructed.

Beads of sweat fell down my face and took refuge in my frosty brows, but as the wand tip created the last line it was done.

"Well done, Léon!" Coco congratulated me.

A rush of euphoric happiness blessed me, I had done something right, finally.

Fissures began to spiral up from the point the exact spot the wand touched the amethyst crystal. Soft sounds of locks could be heard though no key or key hole was visible.

I looked at Coco to make sure this was indeed the correct result and by the expression on her face it was. As the cracks spiralled, little carvings became visible by a biolumi- nescent blue light that glowed from within.

"What do the carvings mean?" I asked.

"The tale of the first spellcasters," Coco responded matter-of-factly.

Sure enough as the fissures grew and the light emitted more, little figures became visible within the carvings. Although a story in the carving was too hard to read or understand, so I asked Coco to which she responded.

"Léon, I'm not one the ancient history teachers, ask a professor like Professor Henare if you're put in his class. Great teacher, Loves a word game."

"Oh, okay," I said, a little disheartened.

One final crack and the doorway was made clear. Handle and all.

"Well go on, open it," Coco said, exasperated.

Slowly I reached out and turned the handle. The door by itself swung in as if it had been hit with a strong gust of wind. Sound was instantly released. It was as if we took out ear plugs or the needle hitting the record after being held up.

I went to grab my suitcase and wand box but unbe- knownst to me they had vanished.

"Where are my things?" I asked in alarm.

"The school has taken them up into your room."

"How?"

"By magic of course."

"They will go to the right room?"

"Obviously."

I was still so unsure of this new world but it would

seem I'd just have to trust that Coco spoke the truth. With wand in hand I entered the castle.

Students walked in all directions, some leisurely with smiles and laughter in their eyes and others in a panic as if late for class or an important date. Some students were dressed with of blue and others in shirts of red, green, and yellow. Female students wore purple pinafore style dresses over their different-coloured shirts and boys wore slacks in the same royal purple. This must be the school uniform… which I didn't have. I started to speak but Coco cut me off whispering, "Don't worry, your uniform will be laid out on your bed when you enter your room." I was about to ask how but as if reading my mind once more Coco added, "Magic."

"You know, is magic used as an explanation for every-thing here?"

"Why yes, most likely."

"You know that doesn't make sense, right?"

"Once you start your studies tomorrow you will start to understand how magic works and things will begin to make sense to you."

Hmmm I was unsure of this but like everything else I'd just have to trust her.

CHAPTER 5

A CONTRACT FOR SECRECY

LÉONIDAS I

The layout of the castle was labyrinthine, with seemingly endless corridors connecting to staircase after staircase. It would be easy to get lost looking at the intricate gold filigree designs carved into the walls of amethyst crystal. I'd need a map just to find my way to the lavatory, let alone to a classroom. Coco, being my guide, took me on a tour of the castle, starting with a communal quarter where students were either immersed in their books or engaged in lively group discussions.

The quarter was filled with lush green plant life and even a small water feature in the centre of space depicting a woman wearing a sheet of white that barely covered her form. Gripped in her hand was a spherical ball sprouting a steady stream of water that sparked in the dying daylight, creating a rainbow of oranges and browns.

From there we entered another building, turned left and ascended six flights of stairs before arriving at yet another corridor. It was truly a maze of halls and staircases, eventually we even crossed an exposed bridge—gee, it was a long way down. Whoever decided that the amethyst used for the bridges needed to be semi translucent should be locked up. I nearly peed myself I was so afraid. But it was there, finally that I got my first proper good look at the magical world of Amethyst. It was even more grand seeing it from the inside as it was when I first saw it on the cliff face. Hundreds if not thousands of buildings and towers were scattered across an evergreen cityscape. Some appeared to be rather ancient whiles others looked distinctly modern with squared-off roof tops and open-air situations. I had no frame of reference for what it was I exactly saw. It was all so...so...grand. And just so beyond anything I could have imagined.

"Amethyst is more of castle city then just a school for spellcasters. The city is broken up into nine regions. Which are: North-Side, South-Side, East-District, West-District, North East-Province, North West-Province, South East-Province, South West-Province, and Central Isle."

"So where are we now?" I queried, that was a lot of information to take in. "Also why does every region have a different name like a Province or District?"

"Keep up, sugar, see how the city merges into a cliff face there?" she asked, pointing.

"Yeah, I can see it, looks like the crystal is growing from the rocky edge."

"Precisely. Now if you ever get lost know that the castle city only merges into the cliff in the North West-Province."

"Right, I think I can remember that but why is some places called Province and others not?"

"You see, everything comes together in the middle, which is why we call it the Centre Isle. That's where things start to branch out, you know. The North and South sides, well they're the big guns, so we call them the 'sides' to show just how mighty they are. And the Provinces, bless their hearts, they're the second largest regions, so they come next. And if we're talkin' about a district, well, honey, that's the tiniest little piece of the city pie. Makes sense?"

"I guess so..."

"You 'guess so'? It either makes sense or it doesn't."

I thought about that for a second. I guessed it made sense that the largest were called sides and the explanation was sufficient.

I nodded. "Yes, it makes sense."

"Good."

We continued on.

Soon, I became rather disoriented by the numerous twists and turns, and the thought of having to remember it all by myself was quite daunting. The rest of the mixed emotions caused my heart to feel a pang of homesickness.

After about ten or so minutes of walking in silence I asked Coco dumbly, "So I take it there isn't any lifts here, huh?"

She laughed. "Yeah, no, sugar, there ain't any here unfortunately. Just think, your legs will get muscular."

"Do the stairs ever get any easier?" I said, beginning to puff with exhaustion.

"Nope," she cackled, "never."

"Great." I sighed dejectedly.

The castle smelt quite clean, like a more muted citrus smell. Maybe like lemon verbena or watered-down lemon juice. I liked it.

"So I know I haven't asked this yet but ugh, where are we going?"

"Headmistress Guaire's office, of course."

"Oh…" I mouthed mutely. I didn't know if I liked the headmistress, after all she had been very direct and challenging with my grandma, and also Grandma clearly didn't like her but then again, they had history. Could I ignore that? Would I be expected to carry the grudge? I was left pondering this while we took a series of lefts and rights. Eventually we stopped at the end of a hallway in front of an archway housing a spiral staircase.

"This is where I must leave you, Léon."

"Whhhhaaattt?" I squeaked.

"This spiral staircase will lead you right up to Headmistress Guaire's office."

"Okay, so why do you have to leave me?"

"No need to get those feathers ruffled, sugar. I'll be back to see you once you're done with your induction shindig. I just gotta have a little heart-to-heart with Professor Arundell about a paper that's due tomorrow, bright and early. So don't you go worryin' those cute little cotton socks, I'll be back before you can say Coco La Roux, where are you."

"Oh okay, just don't leave me alone in this maze you call a school."

"More castle city," she corrected.

"Castle city," I amended.

"Don't worry, I'll be back. See you in a bit." With that Coco and her cherry juice hair bounced away.

Turning I breathed out. "Guess the only way is up…" I started climbing the spiral staircase. At least it had a banister.

My legs burned, my chest heaved, and my face was slick with sweat but I had finally made it up those darn stairs. The sheer amount of them in this castle was clearly a design flaw. At the top of the stairs read an engraved sign above a polished oak door *Headmistress Fenella Guaire*.

Before I had mustered up the courage to knock the door swung inwards as if pulled by a magical thread. Gulping, I took a step inside.

Fenella Guaire's office was so unlike any other part of the castle city school I'd seen so far. This space had been built of another type of stone, one that refracted different hues like pink and gold, blue and purple, green and black. It kind of reminded me of an oil slick like the ones I would sometimes see on a wet road.

Book after book lined the walls of the room, every kind of colour and hue. If there was a type of book that was not in this library I'd eat my shoes.

Sage, mint, and the musk of books filled my nostrils as I tried to catch my breath and still my beating heart.

"Welcome to Amethyst, Mr Nightshade," Headmistress Guaire called in a crisp no-nonsense voice from the corner of the room.

I turned to face her as she had unbeknownst to me walked up beside me. She towered over me wearing that same purple feather coat that shone like stars as when I had met her only a day or so prior. But this time she wasn't in a large-brimmed hat; instead she wore her hair short, short enough that she possibly could be considered bald as there was just the faintest hint of denim-blue fuzz on her scalp.

"Hello," I said, thrusting out my hand to shake hers.

She just looked at my palm with reproach. "No, let's not."

I let my hand fall back beside me.

"Come with me," she said as she started to walk over to her desk before taking a set behind it. Mutely I followed her before at her clear suggestion taking the seat opposite to sit.

Her desk was devoid of almost anything. What

remained was only a folded bit of parchment, a fountain pen, and another bit of parchment.

"I had expected your grandmother to have been more punctual. Mr Nightshade, you are late."

"I'm so—"

Raising a hand, she continued, "Amethyst isn't like other schools, we will punish students who show no regard to the rules and break them. Do you understand?"

"Y...yes," I stammered.

"Good, now, I understand you were home-schooled, so we will be giving you a grace period of one week to adjust. Do you understand?"

"Yes."

"Yes what?

"Yes, Headmistress."

"Good, you are learning. Now here in front of me is your class schedule and map of the castle city. If the map leaves the city gates it will burst into flames, so I suggest you don't do that. Now, as a first year you normally would get your choice of three electives. Unfortunately you are starting mid-year so your classes have been chosen for you."

Headmistress Guaire handed me one of the folded pieces of parchment. After a "go on" look from her I began to unfold it. Inside was a small blue book that had my name inscribed across it in a white script and a small map that was folded down to the size of a bar of soap. I looked at the blue book first. Opening it I soon realised this was a yearly schedule.

"A school week here is six days with double classes on Saturdays and Sundays, your one day free is Monday, although you will be spending your first few trying to catch up, I'm sure. It works on a revolving two-week calendar. So once a fortnight you must check what the schedule will be for the following weeks. Your classes are as follows and yes, they are written down in your schedule.

- Cultural Studies with Professor Bani

- Math and Numerology with Professor Sars

- Tinctures, Tonics, and Spelled Brews with Professor Evans

- English and Language Studies with Professor Nkrumah

- Defensive and Offensive Spellcasting with Professor Sokolova

- Divination And Runic Studies with Professor Mary-Weather

- History with Professor Hirayama

- Alchemy Basics with Professor Ceylon

- Magic and Non Magic Animal Studies with Professor Sutpo

- Cooking and Home Studies with Professor Albrecht

- Transformative Charm Studies with Professor Connaway."

That was a lot of classes. How on earth would I ever be able to remember them all?

"Today is Saturday so tomorrow you will start with Sunday of week two. If you look at your schedule you will find that first up you have a double Divination and Runic Studies class with Professor Mary-Weather followed by a double Magic and Non Magic Animal Studies with Professor Sutpo. Mr Nightshade, all our teachers demand respect and complete focus if you are to succeed. Do you understand?"

"Yes, Headmistress" I replied.

"Good, now it is required to sign a contract forbidding you from ever disclosing this location to anyone alive or dead."

It was?

Headmistress Guaire handed me the last piece of parchment. Opening it, I saw a single phrase writing in what looked to be...dried blood...*surely not...I must be mistaken... right?* The phrase read

By the blessing of the ancient gods and the weight of my immortal soul, I, Léonidas Agápe Nightshade, do swear upon this sacred oath that the location and very essence of this hallowed institution shall never be revealed to any living being or spirit, lest I suffer the wrath of the winds and the fires, the seas and the earth, cursing me for all eternity...

What a weird phrase. A contract for secrecy seemed very extreme but maybe that was the reason Mother had never spoken about it to Grandma? Keeping secrets though...I couldn't say that it didn't deeply bother me. Secrets were like lies of the heart.

"Now of course this is no ordinary contract, this is spelled," said Headmistress Guaire.

"Spelled?"

"Yes, Mr Nightshade, spelled."

"What does that mean?" I asked before hurriedly adding, "Headmistress."

"What it means is that if you were to break the contract you would be cursed forevermore by wind and fire, sea and earth. A death well long and drawn out."

"Oh," I said simply, if that wasn't more than a little daunting.

Slowly I signed my full name. The ink seeped into the parchment like blood dispersing in water. A weighted sensation fell across my body for the briefest second. The sensation made it apparent that the contract was in place.

"Now, there are a few more things to discuss such as which house you are in."

"There are houses?" I added, confused.

"Yes, Mr Nightshade, there are. They are the following: the Summer Solstice house named Théros, the Autumn

Equinox house named Metóporon, the Winter Solstice house named Kheîma and the Spring Equinox house Éar. You are sorted into the house based on what season you were birthed during."

With rising dread in my stomach I knew which house I'd be sorted into.

"As you are born not just during the winter season but on solstice day you, Mr Nightshade, are sorted into Kheîma, the Winter Solstice house."

"Do I have to be?" I couldn't stop Myself. I *hated* winter.

"Why yes, Mr Nightshade. You do. If you look at the map you will find that Kheîma house is located in the southern towers of Amethyst located in the heart of the south-side. You will also find that a set of uniforms have been selected for you and are folded neatly in a dresser with your name on it."

"I get new clothes?" I said in awe. I didn't get new clothes very often.

"Why yes, Mr Nightshade, you do. All school supplies are provided for all students regardless of personal or family wealth."

"Oh," I replied simply. Still, new clothing! I found that so exciting that I couldn't wait to go try them on.

"We have just two more things to discuss," declared Headmistress Guaire. "The first is the school laws. They are as such:

One. Always arrive on time to classes and assessment. You have three strikes before you are placed on tardiness watch. Break the three tardiness watches and you will be placed in detention on your day off for the whole day.

Two. School uniforms are to be worn correctly during school hours. No rolled sleeves unless required for class practical.

Three. Smoking is not permitted in school grounds. If you are so inclined you must leave the castle walls.

Four. Never leave the castle walls at night unless accompanied by a professor.

Five. There is to be no public displays of profane or unbecoming behaviour.

Six. If you witness anyone breaking the school rules or behaving dangerously you MUST inform either a prefect or a professor at once.

And Seven. This goes without saying I'm sure but, no killing students or teachers. Doing so will not just land you in prison but also a complete magic blocker and memory wipe. It would be as if you never came here."

I was glad to be sitting down for a wave of nausea hit me, this was all so complex. I would never willingly break any of the rules but what if something went wrong? People and animals had been known to die when they were involved with me. My parents, the owl, and almost the stag. Was it even safe for others if I was here?

"Mr Nightshade, you are exactly where you are supposed to be," said Headmistress Guaire. Her tone, if I wasn't mistaken, almost sounded soft and caring. A side to her I had yet to see...wait wait wait...could she read my mind?

"Don't worry, Mr Nightshade, I cannot read your mind...well, not without casting a charm to do so."

If she wasn't reading my mind then how did she know that I was worried she could read my mind?

"Because, Mr Nightshade, you have a very expressive face."

Oh...okay...wait! I said that in my head...

"Mr Nightshade, we must move on, we are yet to talk about the fact you are Fae."

Later, I would be rerunning the conversation a hundred times over.

As I descended the stairs following the meeting, my thoughts were in a whirlwind. The headmistress' final words were so shocking they had left me in a state of disbelief. Could it be true that I was the descendant of royalty? The grandson of the current king and queen of the Belladonna court that lay beyond the veil in the Fae realm. How could someone be both royal and impoverished at the same time? And why didn't I know about my other grandparents? Didn't they want me? They probably saw me as a proper burden...I knew I did.

I was so far in my head I hadn't realised that Coco was nowhere to be seen. Where was she? Had she been waiting on me and given up?

"Coco?" I called down the corridor. There was no answer. Darn, what was I going to do? What was I supposed to do? Should I wait?

I tried calling her name out once more but still there was nothing. Walking over to the window, I looked out at the lands beyond. It was very nearly nightfall, maybe fifteen or so minutes before the sun disappeared completely.

Fear spiked my chest at the idea of walking this city alone at night... That was not an option, not for me.

Pulling out the map the headmistress had given me, I searched for Kheîma Tower. If luck was on my side maybe I'd see Coco there or even meet her along the way. That line of thought settled my nerves. I'd meet Coco there.

For a map of a castle I thought it was incredibly well drawn and to be honest somewhat easy to read. I'd never read a map like that before but it looked to be well laid out.

At the very end of the meeting the headmistress had shown me how to use the map. All I had to do was tap it with my wand and utter my destination and the quickest route would be made apparent. Easy enough...right?

Tapping my wand on the parchment I uttered, "Kheîma Tower."

A spark of light flickered on the parchment. Not long after, small lines of iridescent blue started to seep out of the ink and into the parchment, illuminating my path ahead. Accompanying the route was a series of small notes written around the map border. They appeared to give hints and tricks to make sure the journey was a speedy one. One such note was, *avoid the main corridors after 5pm due to student traffic*. Unfortunately for me, I hadn't a clue what the time happened to be.

The path to Kheîma Tower took me outside, down two sets of stairs, and across a courtyard. And from there it was a somewhat straight path to the tower. Magic was incredible, the fact it could do this and tell me where to go felt almost futuristic rather than something out of a fantasy tale.

Looking around, there was still no Coco. Breathing out a sigh, I took off, following my new map. She'd forgive me...right?

Students walked in all directions. Some smiled at me as I passed whilst other just seemed to stare at me and after a while it started to make me feel quite self-conscious. What were they staring at? It couldn't be my pale, anaemic skin tone because I could see many with skin as bleached of life as mine. It couldn't be my purple eyes for I'd passed students with the colours like that of a Spanish onion. I was confused until I passed a large ornate mirror that covered an entire wall. The students behind me, not thinking I could see, were making crude gestures about my antlers. The antlers I kept forgetting I now owned…permanently. I wished I'd never removed the scarf that Grandma had covered them with.

Why was it that when I was being led around by Coco no one seemed to pay us any attention but now that I was isolated and alone they couldn't stop their staring and passing judgment?

After a boy dressed with a red shirt and with equally red hair pointed at me and laughed I started to really wish I knew the magic to disappear entirely. Why did my antlers draw so much undesired attention? Coco said people wouldn't even care…had she lied? If only I still had Grandma's scarf. Head down, I picked up my pace. My nose practically glued to the pavement.

According to the map I was about halfway there. Turning down a corridor, I found myself back outside. This place was such a labyrinth all it needed was a Minotaur maybe that was me…

The air smelled of citrus fruits and freshly cut grass. I breathed in a few times. I was being stupid…so what if a few people stared? I was the new kid. Maybe I was just reading too much into it…and maybe those kids just had really itchy scalps…

BAM!

"Watch where you're going, freak" said an icy boy's voice,

Looking up I saw the face of the person I had just accidentally stumbled into.

"I'm so so sorry," I apologised profusely. The boy was wearing a mustard-yellow shirt, which if I was right meant he was in the summer house Théros.

"Listen here, smart guy. You better watch your step or

those freaky horns of yours are gonna poke someone's peepers clean out, got it?!"

"I didn't mean to, honest, I didn't," I continued my apology but soon, like a swarm of bees a group of students began to form around us to see what all the commotion was about. All it took was a few seconds and all I could see was an ocean of students dressed in coloured uniforms looking down at me. Not one face showed me any kindness. I had no support.

"What's your name anyway, Horny Boy?" He jeered in a way that was pure menace. He wasn't really asking for my name, it was all a show but I answered him anyway.

"My name is Léonidas."

"Léonidas? Ha. I think I'll stick with Horny Boy, it has a...ring to it."

Dread filled me like a sickening poison. "If you don't mind I'd prefer it if you didn't."

"Well I *do* mind, Horny Boy." he responded, sharp-tongued.

The pudgy-faced boy turned to the crowd of onlookers and chanted, "Horny Boy! Horny Boy! Horny Boy!"

"No...no...no!" I began, but it was too late.

"HORNY BOY...HORNY BOY...HORNY BOY," the crowd chorused.

I whirled around. I hadn't a clue what to do, I felt wild like a horse that some cruel person was trying to break. The sea of faces all jeered at me calling me this inappropriately crude name.

The boy with pudgy face and yellow shirt turned back to me, his expression was one of victory. I wanted to hit him. Yet I knew that wasn't like me to do such a thing... though he kept up his name-calling.

Did one expect a snake not to bite when pushed into a corner with no way to escape?

Quick as a flash, I had withdrawn my wand. It was an empty threat and by the pudgy boy's face I could tell he knew it. But the growing crowd all broke into a cheer, they could smell blood.

"Get him, Braxton!" yelled one student, dressed in the same yellow uniform.

"Teach him a lesson!" called another.

What was I going to do with the wand? Stab him with it? I was so stupid, so very stupid.

Braxton withdrew his own wand, it looked similar to mine—maybe an inch or two shorter.

"Come on, Horny Boy, I'll let you get in the first shot," he said, smirking.

I went to put the wand away.

"Uh uh uhah, it's too late now."

"Look, I'm sorry for running into you, I don't want to fight yo—"

"EXAPOTHÍN!" A burst of wind was expelled from his wand, the force hit me and was not unlike being hit by a large falling tree branch. The spell sent me flying into the side of a building. My head hit back and with a sickening snap made contact with the wall. While stars flickered in my eyes I felt a drip of warmth running down my neck. I reached back to check the damage, to only come away with traces of blood on my fingertips. That arsehole just drew blood from me. Rage unlike anything I had felt before ignited in my veins. I raised my wand once more and before I knew it I had sent out a spell. One without even muttering a single word. It was a subconscious wish that came from deep in my bones to cause this bully pain. Purple lightning erupted from my wand.

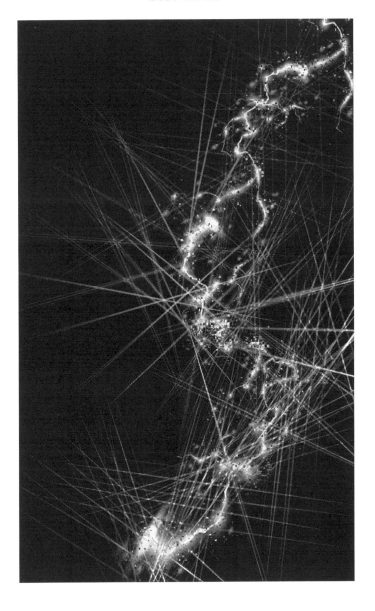

Braxton, quick as a fox, raised his wand in defence and conjured what looked like a type of shield.

"Pélti!"

The purple lightning reflected off the magical shield and dispersed into the air to be seen no more.

"YOU COULD HAVE KILLED ME!" he roared.

"I...I am sorry," I stammered.

"What a low blow using magic like that," said a snooty voice in the crowd.

I was in a panic. What had I done?

He circled like a tiger ready to pounce, I couldn't get any further back—I was already up against a wall.

"I'm going to teach you a lesson, Horny Boy, one you will never forget. Ádis pón—" began Braxton.

"Stop, He's not worth it, Brax," called a distinctly deep male voice.

Who said that? The tone in the voice hit differently...why?

The crowd of students parted and in walked a much taller older boy with fashionably styled raven-black hair with just a single curl forming a slight crescent moon on his forehead. He was film star-handsome and had skin the colour of caramelised honey. but the thing that stood out beyond his skin and muscular physique was his liquid-gold eyes that shimmered like burning, all-consuming fire.

My palms perspired as his gaze locked on mine. For the briefest of moments I could have sworn he looked at me as if he wanted to eat me. like a hungry wolf gazing at a rabbit ready to slaughter. I could've sworn that my antlers suddenly tingled, the sensation felt not unlike a toothache. I did not understand why.

Within seconds his gaze had shifted to one of clear dislike and contempt before lifting to something akin to boredom. Confused and more than a little shaken I wanted nothingmore than to get out of here and far away from both of them.

"But, Ace, this little punk—" Braxton began.

"Who cares. Why waste your time and besides, I can hear a professor coming."

Braxton looked annoyed before changing tack. "Fine, Whatever," he submitted, but as he turned back to me his eye screamed "you're dead meat."

Both boys quickly disappeared into the dispersing crowd. It seemed the idea of being caught by a professor was something to be afraid of...oh right the school rules. Yes...it's probably best that I too don't get caught on my first day.

After the altercation, I was left mentally spent. This was just my first day. What in the Jay Gatsby was my life about to turn into.

ATTICUS VALOR I

As Brax and I prowled through the throngs of students, I struggled to resist my vaewolf instincts. The sight and scent of the boy with eyes as violet as the dusk sky, skin as cold as winter, and hair as white as fallen snow, made my primal desires surge. The aroma of his spilled blood, a mixture of musky sweets and jasmine blooms, was an intoxicating call that I longed to answer. My vaewolf was restless, eager to claim its mate. The very thought of it was enough to make me dizzy, especially since it seemed that Cernunnos had chosen a male to be my mate. Such a union was taboo and unacceptable.

I picked up my pace, leading us towards the seclusion of the school's greenhouses. I needed a cigarette and a glass of aged blood to quell the insistent urge that had grown within me.

"What stupid pansy," muttered Brax from beside me. He clearly was still wound up from...whatever that was. A fair duel it was not. Anyone looking could tell the new boy hadn't a clue what he was doing.

If I was being honest with myself I'd have to say that Brax would have to be one of my least favourite people in my friend group at Amethyst. His family owned several blood banks, which was why my father had tasked me to befriend the spoiled brat at the start of the school year. He was only a first-year and befriending someone that young was unappealing. His personality reminded me of a spider. Annoying, but had its uses at keeping the flies away.

Once we were safely behind a greenhouse I pulled a fag from my packet and set it alight with a snap of my fingers. Closing my eyes, I took in a few deep breaths of the tobacco. This wasn't commercial tobacco. No, this one was chemical-free and blended specially for blood drinkers. The tobacco was left macerating in blood for thirty days and thirty nights before being dried and packed into the papers and boxed for consumers. They tasted pretty goofy when I first tried them but after a while I acquired the taste.

"Whose classes do you think he will be in?" asked Brax.

"Huh? The boy? Let it go," I said, cigarette in mouth. "He's clearly not worth the energy."

"He could've killed me," Brax said indignantly.

"By Cernunnos, so what. Why are we still on this topic?" I muttered.

"What a freak with those horns," laughed Brax, pulling

out his own pack of cigs and lighting one. Good, now finally he'd hopefully move on.

CHAPTER 6

THE FEAST OF WINTER SOLSTICE

LÉONIDAS I

T hirty minutes later I arrived at the entrance to Kheîma Tower. I was still shaking with a heady mix of anger, intimidation, and, even if I didn't want to admit it—fear. I had been publicly shamed and humiliated. Why did I have to go and pull my wand out? I was such an idiot. I didn't know how to control magic but when I did my stupid antlers would be the first to go.

The tower from the outside was made from what appeared to be the same amethyst as most of the other buildings, though once I entered it looked dramatically different. It was winter personified. The walls shimmered like ice reflecting the moon's light.

Plush chairs and lounges were covered in the palest blue velvet, with cushions that resembled little clouds of snow. There was even a tree covered in snow that grew from the floor. Elaborate wall carvings that looked to be carved from ice; a fire place big enough to fit a bed was carved into the wall to my right. Winter-themed art and tapestries hung from the walls.

In an armchair against one of the back walls sat a girl with luminously bright pumpkin-orange hair. She had a neatly cut front fringe just above her accented brows. In her hair was a blue ribbon, though the bow was hidden from sight. The ends of her hair were rolled into what I think was called a pageboy hairdo, but I could have been wrong.

The girl looked to be reading a faded green book but I was too far away to see the title exactly.

"Think not I love him, though I ask for him: 'Tis but a peevish boy; Yet he talks well; But what care I for words? Yet words do me well,'" she read aloud. No one else paid her any attention. This must've been a regular occurrence for her to speak aloud the text she read, otherwise surely others in this room would have turned to look. Yet no one batted so much as an eyelid.

Standing there alone staring felt wrong, so I decided to walk over to her. Besides, I still needed to find which room I was in. Neither Coco nor the Headmistress had told me where my bed was, only that my suitcase was there waiting for me.

"Hey," I said, trying for cheerful.

"Allo," she said, looking up from her book. Her face was all almond eyes and warm sunshine smiles. She spoke with a light French accent.

I stood there awkwardly. "What are you reading?" I gestured to the book in her hands.

"Oh this? Is William Shakespeare's *As You Like It*. Have you read it?"

"No, not yet. Is it any good?"

"It is marvellous, one of my absolute favourites."

108

"Is it like the marvellous *Wizard of Oz*? Because I really liked that one."

"Oh, no it's eh more adult. Have you read any Shakespeare?"

I averted my gaze as I felt my cheeks flush pink with embarrassment. "No... Is that bad?"

"Really? None? Where did you go to school?"

"I...er...was home-schooled," I said, shuffling my feet.

"You must be Léonidas." She beamed, closing her book with a *thwop*. "I'm Tamara Alair Masayá. I'm your new tutor to help bring you up to speed in classes."

"Really?" I said, shocked.

"Most certainly." She nodded. "You've been put in a majority of the same classes as myself."

"Is there much I need to catch up on? The headmistress said most Mondays would be spent catching up on classes. Also do we really only get one day off? Seems a bit excessive doesn't it?"

"Trés Excessive," she agreed. "But eh next year we will get more free periods so it hopefully it will get easier."

"Right..." I said, doubtfully. This school seemed like a lot of work for a teenager.

Ding ding ding

Spooked, I jumped a little. "What's that for?"

"It's the thirty minutes to dinner bell, you best get ready. The headmistress is very strict on correctly worn uniforms."

Tamara hopped off the chair and began to walk away.

"Wait!" I called, panicked.

She turned around worried. "What is it? Is everything okay?"

"I don't know where my room is," I admitted.

"Didn't Coco show you?" said Tamara, frowning.

"I haven't seen her since I went in to see the head-mistress."

"Hmm, very unlike her, maybe she had last minute prefect duties. Students are constantly breaking the rules and duelling. Well anyway, not to worry, I know where it is."

"You do?" I said, delighted.

Tamara led me over to a set of stairs.

"It's trés simple, just start walking up the stairs and think of an item you own that would be in your bags. Like a favourite shirt or pair of shoes. Once you do a door will appear and *poof* that is your room." She said this all very matter-of-fact with a smile stretching wide across her face as if this was all very normal. But normal it was not.

"Go up now and change. I'll wait for you down here and we can walk together!"

"Oh okay, sure thing," I agreed eagerly. Maybe no one would look at me if I was with Tamara.

I started to walk up the stairs when she called, "By the way, nice horns!" I lowered my head in shame even though I couldn't hear any malice in her voice, in fact quite the contrary. But I had just learnt that teenagers could be trés cruel and I had had enough of that for today.

ATTICUS VALOR I

The dinner bell rang and I was still in a putrid mood. Brax did not shut up about the piss-poor duel for what felt like an eternity. And the blood fags had done nothing to quench my cravings. Even after having a few glasses of blood it did only little to quench my vaewolf's thirst. If it was to keep acting up like this I'd have leave the school gates and shift for a few hours tonight. Agh.

Pulling open a drawer, I fetched the stupid waistcoat we had to wear for dinner. It was made from the same purple wool that our trousers were. I hated having to dress up. Give me a leather bomber jacket any day. At least it wasn't as bad as when I was home—always having to dress to impress. There were only so many times you could visit Windsor Castle before the novelty wore thin. Being a prince was overrated to the extreme. Privilege equalled duty which equalled people constantly watching and writing about you. The trade-off was abysmal.

News article after news article about everything from who I was supposedly dating, right down to which brand of blood I preferred that season. It was pathetic.

Grabbing the family ruby cuff links, I quickly replaced the basic amethyst ones I was already wearing. I straightened my tie and tidied my hair, making sure I still had one slight curl loose and free, my own private rebellion. I was ready for dinner. But was I ready for... Him? To see him? Smell him? I'd better have another fag before going. Stupid purple eyes that looked like flowers I wanted to run free in.

Down in the Metóporon common room I was greeted by red-haired Lindon Addams and blue-eyed Camella Teasworth who both were dressed ready for the winter solstice feast.

"You ready to head off, Ace? Addae, Brook, and Klaus have already left," said Lindon, his southern American accent prominent.

"Yeah, Lin, in a bit, just going to have a quick... breather," I said, patting my pocket.

"Another one? Do you know there was a study published in the British medical journal a few years ago that linked those things to lung cancer? It was conducted by Dr. Richard Doll and Dr. Austin Bradford Hill," sighed Camella.

Rolling my eyes, I replied, "Whatever you say, Cam."

Camellia's father was a celebrated surgeon, so she was always spouting off random facts like this. but being a vaewolf meant I was pretty impervious to most things. Pretty much only decapitation or black fire would make my death stick and neither was likely to happen at this school. So smoking was fine.

Leaving the autumn house tower, as much as I tried not to, all I could think about was that pale boy, his flushed face and the antlers atop his head. What a pity he wasn't a girl. He may have been as pretty as one but that did not mean squat to society. I would fight this bond and like all challenges I faced as a prince, I would win.

LÉONIDAS II

After I closed the door, everything stopped, a suspension of time. Noise was gone and like a flash so too did my energy depart. I was left only with my chronic emptiness, the giant chasm that was once my heart. It was like a radio being switched off and with the silence so did come a void like a toxic mist of doubt that fuelled my loneliness.

The words "*horny boy horny boy horny boy*" rang through my ears on repeat as flashes of the confrontation played though my mind's eye. I wouldn't give them the satisfaction of making me shed a single tear. They were not worth it. But that did not mean I didn't hurt.

My life for the last twenty-four hours had been so go go go that now standing alone I hadn't a clue what I was actually supposed to do.

So caught up inside my head, it took me few moments

to realise I was in the room that was to be my private space for the foreseeable future. The room was smaller than my bedroom on the farm but I supposed it was big enough for what I'd need it for.

There was a single bed, a dresser, and a chest of drawers with an antique oval mirror. To the side of the bed was a single window.

On the blue sheeted bed was my suitcase, wand box, and what appeared to be a neatly folded uniform with a square bit of parchment on top. Picking it up, I read—*Dear Mr. Nightshade, Welcome to Kheîma Tower. I hope this letter finds you well. I am writing to provide you with the necessary information regarding your uniform for dinner.*

Please be advised that cuff links are mandatory at all times, including both during feasts and celebrations, as well as during school hours. The only exception to this rule is the waistcoat, which is only required to be worn during dinner, feasts, and celebrations.

In your dresser, you will find five quantities of your uniform, consisting of five shirts, five trousers, five silk ties, and five pairs of blue socks. Additionally, you will find two sets of shoes, one for dress and one for school.

It is of utmost importance that at the end of each day, you place your dirty uniform in the designated dirty clothes basket, which will appear in your room at the end of each day.

Please let me know if you have any questions or concerns regarding this matter.

Kindest regards,

T. Kaptein

Assistant Head of Uniform Dress

Looking around the room, I did indeed find the two sets of shoes. One brown and the other purple. But which was which? The only thing on the note I couldn't find was the dirty clothes basket. Perhaps it would be placed in my room after dinner? Oh right, dinner! I needed to get ready. Quickly I started to strip away my clothes before starting to replace them with the uniform provided. Everything fit perfectly, better than anything I had ever owned.

Standing in front of the oval mirror, I tried to place the cuff links in the cuffs but I was having trouble. I only had ever seen a memory of my father doing so when I was very little. The sound of Mother's warm laughter as he would turn around smiling. Unfortunately, the memory was a faded one and resembled spoiled film with large burnt holes.

In the end I thought I did an okay job. The cuffs didn't sit super neat but at least they were closed. Practice makes perfect, right?

Wow.

I was really this high up? I was looking through the window and all I saw was the cotton wool of clouds.

"I'm glad I didn't have to walk up that far. It'd probably have taken me hours."

Before leaving the room I wondered if it was too early to already miss home? Was it also a bad reflection of my temperament?

Downstairs, I met back up with Tamara who was dressed the same, only now she was standing beside a familiar figure—Coco.

"Where have you been!" I blurted out, relieved to see her again.

Coco looked a little affronted. I couldn't blame her. She had only known me for a few hours but still, I felt I had formed a bond with her or hoped I had.

"Well darlin', after my rendezvous with Professor Arundell, I got roped into playin' prefect. You found the tower smooth as silk so just chillax, sugar."

Coco yanked on her hair causing my mouth to fall open as it sprung up into a short burgundy bob not unlike that of Louise Brooks in one of her silent films. There was still a slight wave to her hair, which made it feel unique to Coco, kind of like 1920s at the front with a modern Hollywood at-the-back situation.

But in being so surprised I almost had completely forgotten about how she hadn't been there to meet me even though she said she would. Maybe that was her motive in that little bit of magic or maybe she just wanted a new do, I couldn't know for sure. Probably should've just asked her but I wasn't sure if that was an appropriate thing to ask a girl, after all Grandma had said to me once, "that a girl's got to have some mystery about her." This might have been what she meant by that.

Coco turned in a little twirl and a few wrinkles from her uniform faded away.

"Goodness," I said, magic was the coolest.

Five minutes later Coco and Tamara led me out of the tower, following a small crowd of other students all dressed in the same blue shirts and blouses as us. It was late enough that the embers of the sky had completely extinguished and the ever so watchful gaze of the moon had begun its rise of victory across the sky.

Our path was lit with a candlelight glow from large candles resting in sconces on the walls made from a wax that matched the moon's hue.

"Aren't having so many candles lit a fire hazard?" I asked no one in particular.

"Léon, sugar, these ain't just any ol' candles. They're spelled to light up the minute that moon rises and to not extinguish until the sun does. Practically speakin', they're just fancy lamps with style," responded Coco.

"Oh," I said simply.

"Don't candles just make you want to smile?" chimed in Tamara in a dreamy tone.

"If I'm being honest I don't think I've ever thought about it before," I admitted, but the truth was very few things caused me to genuinely smile and magic candles were not on that list so I told a white lie. After all, I didn't want others worrying about me. And no one wanted to know how I was really feeling.

As we continued to walk I could not help but notice a few people glancing at me before sharply looking away when caught. I felt my cheeks redden. Stupid antlers.

"Hey, Coco?"

"Yes, Léon?"

"Is there a spell to...you know..."

"I know what? Come on, spit it out, cupcake."

"Hide my...er antlers." I couldn't meet her eyes.

I could feel her gaze intensify on me, my cheeks reddened further.

"Why?" she said simply.

"Because people are staring."

"Honey, let 'em gawk all they want. If they ain't got nothin' better to do than gawk at you, well, darlin', that's just a reflection of their own shortcomings, ain't it?"

But was it though? Was it really a reflection of them? Or just a reflection of how freaky I looked. I was silent as we continued to walk.

"I like them," said Tamara brightly, breaking the tension, "I think they add character. I wonder if they will continue to grow as you do?"

Goodness I hoped not.

Walking out of the corridor, we stumbled upon a serene garden dotted with orange blossoms and wisteria. In the distance stood a breathtaking crystal tower, its raw crystal point shining brightly against the night sky. It was like a beacon, casting a soft blue glow that made it stand out from the other structures. It was the tallest building I had seen yet, towering above all the rest.

"Is that the dining hall?" I asked, staring in wonder at the tower.

"Oui, tres grand, don't you think?" Tamara replied, equally mesmerized.

"Tres grand indeed." I nodded in agreement.

As we approached, we were swallowed by a sea of people, all making their way to the crystal tower. Lines and queues stretched far into the night, but Coco guided us to a shorter line filled with first-year students like us. With a sense of excitement, we joined the queue and eagerly awaited our turn to enter the magnificent dining hall under the starry sky.

"There are so many people," I commented.

"Well yes, after all there is only one true magic school," said Coco. "I told you earlier that the student count was in the vicinity of four hundred thousand, give or take fifty big ones. Did you think it would be small?"

"Oh my..." I gaped. That's a lot of people. A sickening inner voice whispered, "That's a lot of people to stare at you." I gulped, retreating inwardly.

The lines were moving inside pretty fast, we went from around thirty yards away to the head of the line in only a few short moments. It seemed like they had a pretty efficient system going here.

"Coco, you were saying about the accident between the two second-year girls?" asked Tamara.

"Oh yes, Listen up, dolls. After my little tête-à-tête with Professor Arundell, which went off without a hitch, I got my extension, so you can stop sweatin' it. Anyway, I was sashaying my way back to meet up with Léon outside the headmistress's office, when I heard a ruckus coming from a nearby staircase. Being the responsible prefect that I am, I had to go and see what was causing all the fuss. And let me tell you, it was quite a show. Two little second-year fillies were getting a little too frisky, and one of them, bless her heart, took things too far and gave the other a love bite, but not just any old love bite, no sirree. She started drinking her blood. Well, the other gal didn't take too kindly to that, not one bit, and she pushed her away, and before you could say Jack Robinson, blood was spurting all over the place, and she wouldn't stop screeching until I got there. By that point, she'd lost a fair amount of the red stuff."

Did she just say two girls were getting frisky? I didn't know that was such a thing… Could two people of the same gender do that? Wasn't that illegal?

"So then I had to summon a teacher plus one of the school doctors. It was a whole debacle. When will people learn to talk to each other. I mean this all could have been avoided," Coco finished.

"Which second years?" enquired Tamara.

"They were two in the summer house. Who can remember all their names? It could have been a bunny and Lola or a fanny and cola—"

"Carly and Nola?" Tamara suggested.

Clicking her fingers, Coco replied, "Yes, that was them, it was Carly and Nola."

"Are they from a progressive country?" I asked.

"Who? Carly and Nola?" responded Coco.

"Yeah."

"Oh, absolutely not, Carly I think is from Texas in the Americas and Nola is from Russia—at least her accent suggests," chimed in Tamara.

"Really? What does a Russian accent sound like?" I queried.

"Hmm tough maybe something like..." Coco began some sort of accent. Having no memory of hearing one I couldn't tell whether it was a good impression or not. But by Tamara's laughter I guessed it was probably on the more comical side. I wondered if I had ever watched a film with a Russian actor before. I made a mental note to ask Grandma next time I saw her, she'd know.

Through a doorway carved in crystal and etched in gold we came to a room bathed in warm refracted light. The ceiling was high and consisted of geometric pyramid-like shapes. Though it wasn't anywhere near as high as it appeared on the outside, which told me that there must be several rooms above.

"Hey, Coco?"

"Yeah, sweetcakes?"

"Does every student eat here? It seems pretty impossible if there is as many students as you say that attend."

"Once through the next set of doors you'll see how it's possible, don't you be worrying." She patted my shoulder.

"Really?"

"Coco is correct," added in Tamara, "there is a magic enchantment."

"What does that do?" I failed to see how that was going to fit four hundred thousand plus people.

"It is a godly enchantment and was used to make sure the room would be as big as it ever needed to be without taking up any more land mass on the outside."

"Will I ever not be in constant surprise?"

"Probably not, no," said Tamara put her hand on my other shoulder.

Great.

A portly man with greying brown hair who must have been in his mid to late fifties sat atop a tall chair behind a wooden lectern. On top of it was a ginormous open book with pages the colour of watered-down tea.

"Next in line," he called in a rather pompous high-pitched voice.

We approached.

"Names, house, and year?" he asked but not once did he look up from the book in which his nose was all but glued.

"Tamara Alair Masayá, winter house, first year," responded Tamara, her voice was light and full of respect.

"Coco La Roux, winter house, prefect, third year," Coco said next.

Then there was silence as no one spoke. Suddenly all eyes were on me. Even the man glanced up for the first time.

"Psst. It's your turn," nudged Coco.

"Oh right, sorry. Um I'm Léonidas Agápe Nightshade, I'm in the errr winter house and I'm a first year," I tried to announce confidently.

Looking back down at his book he began searching pages, maybe he was searching for our names? "Masayá, head through the first door as usual," the man responded, having found Tamara's name in the leatherbound book.

"See you soon," she called merrily as she skipped towards the doorway on the far left.

Soon?

"La Roux, head on through door three," said the man once more.

Coco nodded but turned towards me. "You only sit with

people in your own year. So I'm sure Tamara will save you a spot." And with that she was off heading towards the third doorway on the left.

Suddenly I was alone again. Surrounded by strangers who watched me and muttered amongst themselves. The hairs on my neck lifted up like trees searching for sunlight. I had a bad feeling.

It took the man the longest time to find my name. In fact in the end he had to grab an entirely different book that was hidden beneath the lectern. This book wasn't large or made of leather. No, this book was made of something else that seemed far older than any type of fabric I had seen thus far.

"There you are, Prince Nightshade. In the future you must inform me of your royal status," he chided me.

"Oh," I responded, simply. "Does that make a difference?"

"Well, of course, boy! Royals only sit with royals!"

"Oh?" Now I knew I was in trouble.

"Certainly. You will enter through the door on the very far right."

I looked towards the doorway the man pointed at. It was different to all others. This one was covered in unmistakable opulence. It was also the only doorway that actually had a door in it.

Gulping I asked, "Do I have to? Can't I sit with Tamara? After all, I am a first year."

"Gods no. Royals are to not sit with commoners, even spellcaster commoners. This law is iron-tight. Now head off. You are holding up the line."

Oh gosh darn it.

ATTICUS VALOR II

Bored out of my brain I watched as the giant hall filled with the bland and vapid students. I'd rather eat dinner elsewhere alone but even I was forced to partake in these nightly spectacles. The ancient crystalline structure may have looked to some as a giant amethyst shard on the outside but inside it resembled a giant colosseum housing pretty much every spellcaster offspring who had come of age.

First years sat on the ground level and so did the teachers and professors. Second years on the first raised level and so forth. As a member of one of the few truly royal families I sat on the highest level. Father had told me once (before my first year) that it was a form of security in case of an attack; we would be shielded by all those bodies and have a chance to escape through hidden passages but I had my doubts that was the truth. Personally, I thought it was just a way of keeping the royals separate from the others. Something to just enforce the establishment and social control.

Another thing I *hated* was the royal protocol of announcing every single one of us who took a bloody seat. I was just glad there were only around a thousand of us and it wasn't also done for the non-royals, otherwise it wouldn't shut up all night.

People like Brax hated that he wasn't included as one of the royals since he was from one of the wealthiest families here. But as they say, rules are rules.

"Introducing third year Jessamine Vickers, daughter of the Duke and Duchess of Sussex. Followed by—" said the amplified voice of the master of ceremonies.

I tried my best to drown him out like I always did.

Having amplified senses sucked sometimes. This was one of those times. I took another sip of my O-positive blood-spiked wine. My cravings had only just begun to recede. One pack of blood fags, two ounces of blood, and a glass of spiked wine was what it took. The gods could be cruel.

My nose itched, bloody thing.

Ugh, The colosseum suddenly felt sluggishly warm. They really needed to invest and add a cooling system. All of our family castles had a system installed. Don't be left in the dust of progress, time to catch up *Amethyst.*

Sniffing the air I caught a trace of...was that night-blooming jasmine? No, it couldn't be... I groaned with irritation.

"Léonidas Agápe Nighshade, Prince and heir of the Belladonna Fae Court," announced the master of ceremonies.

I turned to face the entrance and sure enough the pale boy with snow-white hair was standing sheepishly in the doorway. My throat went bone-dry. Hurriedly I refilled my glass from the carafe. My eyes zoomed in on his neck as my vaewolf started to take control. He... I wanted the boy's blood on my tongue.

"Ace, man, are you all right?" inquired a concerned Elias, the prince and heir-apparent of Basutoland.

"Yeah," I choked out. "Just peachy."

"If you say so. You look like you're about to shift and chase a rabbit."

This is stupid. I'm a prince, gods fucking dammit, I should not be acting this way.

"Just hungry," I muttered, downing the blood-infused wine.

"Looks it," he replied.

Food needed to hurry up and arrive. It was safe to say

that after dinner I would be shifting and hunting most of the night. Pretty much anything to not feel this...this...ugh!

I watched as the pale boy who smelled of night-blooming jasmine, with hair the colour of snowflakes took a seat next to...

"Hey, Elias, who's that guy the new kid just sat next to?" I asked, trying to seem more bored than like I actually cared.

"Him on the left?" He pointed.

"Yeah, you're right on the money."

"That, if I'm not mistaken is Aamin, a first year."

"Aamin huh? How is he royal? Who are his parents?"

"Don't know their first names exactly but I'm pretty sure his parents are the spellcaster monarchs of Malaysia. I think their last name is Kebaikan. Why do you ask?" Elias said, raising a brow.

"No reason, I'm just hungry, that's all."

"Right..."

"Royals always want to make gossip when there is none," I said dryly.

Elias choked on a sip of his black tea.

LÉONIDAS III

"Thank you..." I smiled at the boy in the red shirt. As I took the seat next to him. I had learnt that every house wore a different coloured shirt, so the colour he wore meant that his house was the autumn one.

"Aamin," he replied jovially, holding out his hand for a handshake.

"Thank you, Aamin."

"New here, huh?"

"Very. How could you tell?" I asked.

"Well there is like only a thousand of us who have royal blood so you kind of stand out, plus the horns," he said, gesturing to the antlers. How could I forget...

"Oh," I responded. That was right. Also, what had the announcer person said? Prince and heir of the Belladonna Fae Court? Could I be called a prince if my family were dirt-poor? I wasn't left pondering for long, as Aamin broke into conversation about a horror film he had just seen.

"Wait, this school has a cinema?" I asked excitedly.

"Of course it does! It has six!"

"Six?" I gaped.

"Each house has one in their tower, then there is one for teachers and of course, film studies has one."

"There is a class devoted to watching film?" Why didn't I know about this and how could I get myself into that class?

"Not exactly, it's more about the technical side of film, but I hear it's a great class."

"Wow!" I responded. If I ever get to choose my classes in the future, that was going to be the top of my list.

"You'll have to wait for third year to take it," commented Aamin.

"That's if I last it here that long," I mumbled, evidently not quietly enough.

Aamin responded, "You'll make it to third year, why wouldn't you?"

"I don't know..."

"So, what classes are you in? If we have any of the same ones, you can sit by me," Aamin offered, a glimmer of kindness in his eyes.

"Really?" I asked, surprised by his generosity.

"Yeah," he replied with a nod.

Excitedly, I pulled out my schedule and to my delight, I

saw that we had a great number of the same classes. Aamin's act of kindness immediately washed away any anxiety I had about starting classes the next day.

The table we sat at was long, curved, and circled the room, with seats only on one side and a small rail on the other. Sitting next to Aamin, I had a breathtaking view of the other levels below us. Each level had a table just like ours, with the same curved design and one-sided seating. I tried to spot Coco or Tamara, but my eyes strained to make out their faces, causing only a mild headache.

Amber light began to fill the void between floors as four giant faces emerged through the smoky magics. It was quite a shock to see that I couldn't help but jump in surprise. I only hoped no one noticed. Transparency enriched and within a few seconds the faces began to lose their ghostly appearance. It was the unmistakable face of Headmistress Guaire times four, with each of her faces facing a difference direction. She began to speak.

"Welcome, students, teachers, and royals alike. Tonight we pay our respects to those who came before us, those who were persecuted, killed, and enslaved. Those who sought for a more holistic world, one where the earth and humankind worked together as one. On the night of winter solstice we acknowledge the pain of Persephone and Demeter as she was taken away and forced into a marriage of which she did not consent."

As Headmistress Guaire spoke a cold frost fell upon the room. My breath became a puff of vapour in front of me.

"We mark the rebirth of Cernunnos as his former becomes the magics that fuel the solstice sun. And on this day of the shortest sun we welcome those who are born during this time of celestial convergence. We wish you a new house Kheîma and the students who reside within."

"PRAISE CERNUNNOS, PRAISE PERSOPHONE, PRAISE DEMEMETER!" chorused the room alike. The sound was deafening.

"And with that we wish you a warm and welcome feast."

She disappeared back into amber smoke and within a few seconds the table erupted with food. Mountains of mashed potato and sweet pumpkin, bowls as big as washing basins filled to the brim with sauces of gravy and apple. Plates piled high with roast vegetables of carrot, beetroot, squash, and artichoke. Turning my head I saw whole pigs right from the spit and chicken carcasses with dripping, oily flesh. The smell hit me and I felt sick. Aamin must have seen something in my face because a second later he waved his wand and the meat dishes had moved a few more places down the table.

"Thank you," I said.

"Don't mention it," he responded with a wide smile as he helped himself to a plate of what looked like a type of Cornish pasty.

I didn't know where to begin. The food was so grand, so elaborate, so utterly endless. Having lived for so long with so little I was in a state of suspended reality.

"Go on, eat something," said Aamin as he filled his plate with even more delicacies.

Slowly, I reached for the mashed potato and when no one stopped me I placed a spoonful on my silver plate. Next, I grabbed a pair of tongs and selected some char-grilled carrots and a slice of baked eggplant. When I put the tongs down and selected a knife and fork from the selection, Aamin added, "Is that all? Are you on a diet or something?"

I felt my cheeks redden. "Er...no."

"Then why so little?"

"It's all I need. I'm sure others will want some."

"No, look," Aamin said as he gestured to the dishes I'd selected food from. The plates refilled themselves before my eyes.

"How in the...?" I was more than amazed. And while I thought about it, my heart stung at the idea of my grandparents sitting down for dinner with none of this food and going to bed hungry. My eyes began to sting but Aamin brought me out of it.

"Hey, Léonidas, why is the prince of the vaewolves looking like he's about to jump the table to eat you?"

"Huh?" I said confused. But as I looked in the direction Aamin gestured, my eyes were met with the much taller older boy with golden eyes, honey-bronze skin, and raven-black hair. My mouth went dry for he indeed looked as if he wanted to eat me. I gulped in air as an irrational fear filled me. His eyes seemed to glow like lit candles... I could see this even from what had to be eight or nine yards away.

It took me a few moments to realise what Aamin had said.

"Prince of the vaewolves?" I asked, not quite remembering what Coco had told me earlier about them. Looking away from the—hungry?—gaze I looked back at Aamin who explained.

"Vaewolves are essentially vampire wolf shifters," said Aamin.

Now that he had mentioned it I could recall Coco saying something similar but I didn't think I truly understood what that really meant.

"By the look on your face I can tell you don't understand what that means. Didn't your family ever tell you of the world?" stated Aamin, slightly in shock. He must've thought my family was lazy or incompetent. But the truth was I could read and write and knew the basics of mathematics. I could also plant seeds and forage for mushrooms.

"Well not exactly. My parents are…dead." I said before adding, "but my grandma did read me stories of the folk legends and histories. So I know what a vampire is. It's a dead person, right? Who drinks blood like Dracula." Aamin looked sympathetically at me. I could tell he was about to ask me about my parents or something like that so I continued. "And a wolf shifter is someone who puts on wolf fur and turns into a wolf, right, like in the Nordic folktales?"

I could see the moment Aamin chose to abandon his last train of thought and instead join onto this one to correct me. "No and no. Vampires aren't dead, they are immortal and drink blood but their hearts beat just like ours do. Vampires are just people who evolved differently somewhere down the line of evolution. And wolf shifters are the same. They evolved from prehistoric wolves rather than prehistoric apes or whatever they say we homo sapiens evolved from."

"Wait, we evolved from apes? That's a bit wow isn't it?"

"You didn't know that?" asked Aamin. "Where did you go to school before this?"

Just like before I could feel my face redden. "I errr was home-schooled by my grandma."

"Are you sure you're a royal?" he joked.

I didn't meet his eyes for I didn't truly believe I was really royalty. Royals had money and we…and we did not.

I looked back across at the older boy with golden eyes and honey-bronze skin but he was nowhere to be seen. He had left and I…and I felt…and I don't know what I felt but it was something akin to…maybe sadness or grief, but in a different way then I normally felt. How…odd.

CHAPTER 7
A MIDNIGHT MEETING

ATTICUS VALOR I

I rushed out of there like a bat on fire. I could feel my vaewolf clawing at my teetering control. It wanted to claim its...mate.

"Fuck the gods," I growled. Fuck Cernunnos, fuck the decorum, fuck everything. I tore out of the hall and onto the lawn using pure instinct. I raged at the mere idea that this pale, sun-starved boy could have any effect on me. It was ridiculous. A divine insult. Men couldn't be with men, everyone knew that. *It's fucking illegal that's what it is.*

Only some comfort was afforded to me, at least all the students and faculty were out of my way. I tore down hallways and corridors and only just started to break a sweat as I made it to the school boundary gates.

Chest heaving, I withdrew my wand and drew the symbol I knew would let me out. Fissures began to crack, fracture, and solidify as a gateway appeared through the amethyst. It hadn't even finished forming before I rushed through it.

Heading for the caves located west of the school, I wasted no time. While I sprinted I began to rid my body of these mortal bonds. My tie was the first to go followed by the vest, shirt, and finally my trousers. The moon hung bright in the night sky, bathing the land in its forever watchful gaze as I tore through the valley in only my underwear, socks, and shoes.

As I passed through the outer forest lands, the vast expanse of the sea came into view, and with it, the looming caves that ran deep beneath the sea floor, just a few hundred meters away. In that moment, I stopped in my tracks, quickly freeing myself of my shoes before transforming into my vaewolf form. The sensation of shifting was akin to submerging myself in a tub of water that was just slightly too hot, and as my body underwent the transformation, my skin was soon covered in a thick coat of midnight-black fur. The process only lasted a few seconds, as my bones snapped into place and I finally felt a sense of freedom. Shedding my human form was like removing a restrictive garment, allowing me to take a deep breath and feel truly alive.

With a hunger gnawing at my gut, I began to sniff the air for my prey. I craved the sensation of sinking my teeth into flesh, and draining every last drop of blood from my kill. Luckily, I was far enough away from the school that his scent no longer lingered in the air. I focused my senses, taking deep breaths as I searched for an animal with ample blood to sate my thirst. Circe's Island was teeming with wildlife, and the scents of rabbits and foxes were the first to reach my nose. But I was not after such an easy catch, so I continued to search. And then I found it—the faint scent of a bear, some distance away. My ears twitched as I listened to the sounds of the land, taking in every rustle of leaves, crash of waves, and pitter-patter of paws on the earth. As the breeze shifted, the scent of the bear grew stronger, and I knew exactly where to go. In a flash, I darted across the land, heading for the mountainous region where the bear was likely to be found. I knew that bears were not an easy kill—they were massive, powerful, and deadly at close range. To take down such a formidable foe I would need both stealth and agility.

PRENEURS DE MAGI I

London was a cesspool of depravity and corruption, where back alleys held rooms of sin and wickedness for all manner of beasts. Shifters, sirens, succubus, and incubus openly prowled the streets, their true natures hidden in plain sight. The stench of smog and ash hung heavy in the air—a foul miasma that clung to every inch of the city. The kind that could never be eradicated no matter how many coats of fresh paint one applied. A vampire is what he sought, one that could tell if the blood Jacquard indeed held in that glass jar was from a fae boy. He needed to know for if he wasted magic on summoning the boy and he turned out to be some innocent school boy with no magic...well, it was best for all that that wasn't the case for in his anger he'd do more than just drain and kill the child.

Vampires were not bound to the shadows like the old tales would have one believe. No, in fact that was exactly what they wanted norms to think. For the easiest way to deny being a bloodsucker was to walk beneath the sun's rays, was it not? It was quite possible that vampires set up those tales for that very same reason.

Jacquard wore the disguise of a pudgy banker with black lensed spectacles to hide his sinister eyes, and a suit of delicate pinstripe to fit in with the norms walking by at night.

The posse of criminals turned onto a main road when a brunette woman in her forties appeared from out of the shadows. She wore a poorly maintained carnival uniform with a tacky gold Lurex turban and stunk of cheap cologne and cigarettes. She waved her arms wildly in the air. "Cryptic Kandi will read your fortune," she chanted, her accent thick with the characteristically ill Australian pronunciation.

"No thank you—" Jacquard began.

Kandi placed a hand on his suited chest. "Acts of generosity give good fortunes."

"I'm really not interested," he said, pushing past her.

Kandi called from behind him, "If you're loose with your pockets the gods will be kind to you."

Ignoring her, they continued on their way. But that didn't stop Kandi, no, for she chased after them.

"Kandi Kandi Kandi sees something big for you in your future, just a couple of Goldies and I will tell all."

"No, not interested," snarled a member of the group.

"But everyone *loves* Cryptic Kandi," she called after them.

"Just give her the money to shut her up," groused Jacquard.

A moment later Kandi was slipping back down the street with a few extra gold coins now in her purse. Before she vanished out of earshot she told the group, "Beware of the power of friendship, it's often overlooked." And with that, she disappeared.

Finally she was gone.

Club De Sang was a vampire-owned bar that patrons in the know attended to be fed on. For the vampire's bite was an addictive drug, not even close to that of feeding on magical essences but desirable nonetheless, and for norms who only had drugs of the poppy it was unlike anything else.

Painted matte black walls accompanied a sign made from painted white oak signalling the entrance to such a private club.

Knock...Knock...Knock

A slit in the door opened and jade-green eyes appeared.

"Password," crooned a south Londoner.

Jacquard pressed two gloved fingers to his neck and tapped twice.

Shhhwoop. The slit was shut.

Click.

Click.

Click.

The door swung inward as red light filtered onto the street from the open entrance.

"Come on in, gentlemen. Downstairs is what you seek," said the south Londoner as she disappeared into the club.

Jacquard led three of his cronies all disguised into the club and with a click the door was shut behind them.

A jazz band played standards as a soft, delicate voice sung a song of how a man gone and done her wrong. "He was a bad, bad man, a bad man who gone done me dirty, stole all my money and left me when I turned thirty for a younger filly."

Vampires sat on seats of black plush velvet with norm feeders draped over them in various stages of undress. Not all vampires though chose to feed off a human. Some detested the skin-to-skin contact so in the centre of the room was a great, gluttonous gold fountain that poured a river of blood. Jacquard knew of the hidden floor beneath that housed the spelled norms who partied on drugs while repeatedly cutting open their vein to fill the tanks that fed the fountain. The magic on them stopped all thought and pain, they were what was considered amongst the vampires as zombies.

Any number of these vampires could probably have done the task that Jacquard sought but he wanted irrefutable proof of the kind that only Chinese vampires could give because their lineage was well-known for their unique breeding of sensory gifts. For they were descended from greatness.

"Fan out and bring me what I seek," he commanded in barely a whisper.

And with his command his followers dispersed into the crowd.

What he sought would be found. All he had to do was bide his time and wait.

Maybe he'd have an absinthe on ice to quench his thirst.

ATTICUS VALOR II

Blood clung in thick, wet clumps to my midnight-black fur as I dragged the heavy bear carcass into the open. The beast's flesh would be tough, but it was a shame to let it go to waste. I had managed to drain every last drop of the brown bear's blood, without sustaining any injury, and my thirst was finally quenched for now. The trick to hunting such a large creature was to attack from on high, to swoop down and deliver a deadly bite that would leave the prey helpless.

As I looked to the sky, the moon shone down on me

with an eerie light, casting deep shadows across the forest floor. Its song of sleepy renewal hinted that it was time to return to the school before the morning light came. Letting out a weary sigh, I started my descent down the rugged mountain slope, weaving my way through the thick bushes of Buddleia and Oleander that grew protectively around me. Even in these lands, where the watchful gods ruled supreme, I could find shelter from their piercing gaze.

Being larger than the average wolf, my agility was far swifter, and my power far deadlier than almost any other. As I leaped over fallen trees and bounded across the under-growth, the trees cast flickering shadows on the forest floor, creating ghostly visions of monsters long forgotten. Every step I took was careful, calculated, and powerful, for I knew that in these woods, the slightest misstep could mean my demise.

As I neared the school, its vibrant aura of pulsing purples and refracted moonlight shone like a beacon in the distance. With each step closer, I felt the familiar sensation of a swift, icy transformation as I shifted back to my human form. My skin prickled as fur receded and bones reformed, a howl in the night marking the end of my time as a powerful vaewolf.

I gathered my discarded clothes, feeling like a warrior fresh from battle, my skin stained with the blood of my kill. With each item collected, I dressed myself, leaving my chest bare and stained, a trophy of my triumph.

Heavy is the mind that ponders the games of gods for only the gods can see the cards remaining to be dealt. The thing I truly only knew for certain was that the pale fae prince was going to be an issue.

LÉONIDAS I

The weight of a thousand thoughts burned through my exhausted mind, each one more piercing than the last. I couldn't escape the feeling of being devoured by the golden eyes that followed me, or the guilt of enjoying a full meal while my grandparents struggled to survive on watery broth. The impending doom of classes starting tomorrow weighed heavily on me, and the fear of failure loomed like a dark cloud over my head. I couldn't help but wonder if everything was a cruel joke, and if I would return home empty-handed, a failure.

But the voices of the malicious strangers haunted me, chanting their cruel words "Horny Boy! Horny Boy! Horny Boy!" as I fell further into despair. The memory of losing my friend Henry, his blood staining my hands, only added to the suffocating feeling that closed in on me. I threw off the sheets, desperate for space, for air, for anything to help me escape.

As I headed for the window, I tried to open it, but the rusted bolts refused to budge. I thought about using my wand, but the memory of my untrained fight replayed in my mind, warning me of the dangers. I needed to escape, but I was trapped, suffocating in my own thoughts.

Waking down the steps, I found myself in the empty common room. Dying ambers from the fire place lit the room with a soft glow. Being in the room without people for the first time, I could really appreciate the beauty and craftsmanship of the seemingly magical space. Even though I had seen little of the world I knew without a doubt there was nothing like it anywhere else.

My need for air wasn't satiated, so against all better judgment I found myself leaving the common room. I was filled with such anticipation and need that when I pushed through the doors and the wind kissed my skin, I let out a soft whisper of a moan. I could finally breathe again.

Looking up into the starry sky I was transfixed by the constellations I had never seen before. I loved to gaze into their greatness and see them watching me. Sometimes in my darkest moments I would pretend they were my parents watching from on high, protecting me. It was a foolish sentiment but I knew I wasn't perfect.

Slowly as I continued to gaze I found the constellation Orion. Orion was killed by Artemis for boasting he could kill any creature. I searched for the other constellations I knew but came up blank. It wasn't until my neck ached that I looked down and to my dismay found that my feet had wandered as I searched the stars. How long had I been walking? This ability to be able to disconnect hadn't gotten me this lost in a long time. The only difference, of course, was that I knew every square inch of the forests back home and this school was a maze even King Minos would be proud of. Why hadn't I grabbed the map? I hit the side of my head in anger. I'm such a fool.

Examining the walls around me for any sign of where exactly I had wondered off to, I was gifted with...absolutely no help. I took little solace knowing at least I hadn't made matters worse by entering any of the many buildings surrounding me. One would assume all I need to do was turn around and walk backwards and hope that I walked in a somewhat straight line.

PRENEURS DE MAGI II

He was on his third absinthe before his faithful brought to him what he sought. In a back room for which he paid a high price for discretion he sat with his pudgy pinstriped ankles crossed. A vampire by the name of Wú Huì Fēn was led in to meet Jacquard. She wore a blouse with a pattern of briar roses with high pants with the fashionable empire waist.

"You wanted to see me?" she purred, trying her best at seduction though Jacquard had long since given up those desires of the flesh for the greater cravings of power.

"Yes. Take a seat," he said, gesturing to one of the other lounge chairs opposite.

"Money?" she responded, watchfully.

Jacquard pulled from his breast pocket a wad of bound fifty-pound notes.

"How may I be of service?" she asked, taking a seat, all at once dropping the temptress act. She was all business.

Taking a sip before placing the empty tumbler on the table, he wanted her to wait because in delaying his response he established the rules of this little meeting.

"I have some dried blood I need identified," declared Jacquard.

Wú Huì Fēn scoffed. "I'm no bloodhound, sir."

Jacquard pulled out another bundle of cash and threw it at her before ordering her to, "Sniff."

Anyone with eyes could see the fury igniting in her cold brown eyes. But she held her tongue. The amount of money was just too high to dismiss his request even if she thought of him as some disgusting fat pig not worthy of her time.

With a hiss she lowered her fangs. Most vampires only had elongated canines, but Chinese vampires also had elongated lateral incisors. This gave them a far superior bite that yielded twice as much blood as regular vampires.

Using a falsely gracious voice she asked, "What may I do for you, sir?"

143

"Tell me what creature this blood is from," he ordered as he placed the jar with blood-soaked dirt on the table between them.

"It's dirt," she stated, irritated.

"Oh, don't worry, there is blood in there, leech. Now hurry up and tell me what I have asked of you!" growled Jacquard.

Wú Huì Fēn was up in flash, baring her teeth, she would kill him for his disrespect but quick as lightning the pudgy banker disguise was gone. His face wrinkled warped into his true monstrous visage.

In complete horror she took a step back but was halted by his faithful servants.

"The Preneurs De Magi!" she gasped.

"I see you've heard of us." Jacquard smiled as he took off his concealing glasses and his poisonous blood-red eyes and ghost-white pupils stared her down. Wú Huì Fēn began to shake in fear. All magic kind knew of this band of monsters who killed and stole without remorse.

"Please don't kill me," she begged.

"But you bared your teeth at me," mused Jacquard. "Tell you what, you do exactly as I have asked of you and I may let you live to see another sunrise."

"Yes, yes whatever you say, I'll do it for free just let me live."

"Then tell me who this blood belongs to," he ordered, nodding at the jar on the table.

Wú Huì Fēn was pushed forward by the two lackeys behind her. Falling forward, she only just managed to not hit her head on the table. Breathlessly, she reached for the jar of dirt under the watchful eye of Jacquard. Twisting the lid, she inhaled the scent.

Notes of damp earth and scorching heat were the first

aromas to hit her nose but there was something more. Subtle notes of metallic jasmine and bitter iron musk. There was indeed blood here. But whose blood she couldn't be sure, not without...

"Yes," called Jacquard. "Eat it." he ordered. Could he read her mind? She worried that this was so but she really detested the idea of chewing dirt so after a warning look from the man she did as she was told. The grainy taste of earth choked her mouth as she began to chew. After a few minutes the dirt began to dissolve and the dried blood distilled on her palate.

It could not be, she thought. *It wasn't possible*.

But of course, in the end there was no denying whose blood it was.

"Fae!" she hissed in utter shock.

A smile as large as an automobile tire and more menacing than being run over stretched across the victorious face of Jacquard Morioatus. It was the boy he sought. Finally.

Swiftly, he re-established his disguise and swooped out of the room, but not before ordering them to, "Pull out her teeth."

"No!" Wú Huì Fēn screamed but it was too late. As he left, her screams were drowned out by the privacy enchantments that kept this club exclusive. After all, norms would often scream, only it was nominally in ecstasy.

LÉONIDAS II

I was hopelessly lost, wandering aimlessly through the winding streets of the castle in the dead of night. It was a labyrinth of purple crystal structures, which all looked exactly the same. Frustrated and exhausted, I couldn't help but curse the person who had designed this confusing and monotonous place. I was on the brink of being late to my classes and failing if I didn't find my way soon.

My desperation grew with each passing minute, my forehead and underarms covered in sweat. I had been wandering for at least an hour with no sign of anyone to ask for directions. The emptiness was eerie, not even a bird flew by, let alone a teacher or prefect.

Suddenly, in the distance, I spotted a shadowy figure moving across a courtyard. Was it a person, or just a trick of the light? My heart raced with anticipation, hoping that finally, someone would be able to help me. Without a second thought, I ran towards the figure, shouting "Hey! Hey, mister!" as I closed the distance.

As I drew closer, I could see that the figure was indeed a person. But when I recognized who it was, my elation turned to dread. It was Atticus Valor, Prince of the Vaewolves, and he did not look happy to see me. I skidded to a stop just in time to avoid colliding with him.

Atticus glared at me with his golden eyes, his voice low and menacing as he growled, "What are you doing here?"

I was taken aback by his hostility, wondering what I had possibly done wrong. After all, he wasn't a teacher, and I didn't think leaving the tower was a serious offence. Maybe he was a prefect, but even then, his reaction seemed extreme. I gulped, hoping I wasn't in serious trouble.

"I'm lost," I stated.

"You're lost?" He raised a brow, clearly not believing me. "Why are you out of bed?"

"I couldn't sleep."

"So?"

"I didn't bring my map and can't find my way back... wait, why are you shirtless...and why are you covered in...is that blood?" I gasped as I noticed his chiselled chest stained red with blood. It was unmistakable even in this dim light.

A chill ran up my spine making my neck hairs stand up. The sight and smell...I wanted to throw up. I might actually be sick.

"None of your business," he stated as he shoved past me, walking away.

"Did you kill someone?" I called after him.

He snorted out a laugh. "And what if I have?"

Ice water poured over my soul. "Really?" My voice was high-pitched with panic. Did I yell? What was the protocol?

At seeing my expression he changed tune, sighing. "Don't worry your cotton socks. It's just bear blood."

Dread and the tiniest bit of anger filled me. How could he say that so calmly. That poor innocent bear.

"THATS WORSE!"

"How is it worse? You know, I don't care. You're just a silly little first year." He chuckled callously as he resumed walking away.

"No! Please don't go, I'm lost."

"Agh," he sighed, stopping once more. He cursed a very obscene word before adding in a tone that sounded like he was chewing glass, "Fine, follow me."

So I did.

I watched as the much taller older boy walked in and out of the shadows created by the moon's reflection on the amethyst structures that surrounded us. I tried to catch up and match his stride but he always was just a few yards away no matter how hard I tried. So instead I tried to make small talk, after all that was the polite thing to do...

"So where are you from?" I asked. trying for a cheery tone.

"A place," he responded uncaringly.

What an irritating answer, but I didn't let that deter me, so I tried a different avenue.

"Do this often? Hunting I mean."

"Maybe."

What was his problem? Again I tried. "You're a prince huh, what is it like? Do you live in a castle or—"

"Can we not?" he interrupted.

A burst of anger filled me, it was so sudden that I couldn't stop myself and let it out. "Hey, what's the big deal. I'm trying to be nice!"

"Being nice is overrated," he commented.

"Well being rude isn't polite!"

Snorting, he replied, "Yes, that's the point snowflake."

"Agh!"

Atticus laughed a little at my irritation. "Definitely a snowflake."

"How am a snowflake?" I puffed.

"You're pale, white, and melt at the first shift in the weather."

"No I don't!"

"Exactly."

Crossing my arms, I huffed out a breath of indignation. Who was this guy to say such things? After all I couldn't help being so pale. It wasn't my fault I couldn't tan.

"We're here," he stated neatly.

I looked up in surprise at the tall familiar glistening tower. Being so in my head I hadn't realised that we had approached it. I could breathe again.

"Thank—" I began, but as I glanced back down and turned around, I couldn't see Atticus. He had disappeared.

What an...what an arsehole he was. But at least he didn't leave me stranded. Boy, did he have a fit body even if it was covered in murder. A sudden tightness in my briefs that made me feel uncomfortable. Adjusting ...down there I told myself it was just a reaction to walking and nothing more. Heading inside, I sadly knew I wouldn't be getting much sleep.

CHAPTER 8

WELL THAT DIDN'T WORK

LÉONIDAS I

After the events of last night, I was left feeling utterly confused, frustrated, and lonely. Why did he have to be such a jerk? And why did I care so much? The endless loop of questions ran through my mind, and as a result I probably only slept for a few short hours before I was abruptly awoken by the raucous crowing of a rooster, which turned out to be emanating from my class schedule. "Wake up! Wake up!" it announced between its obnoxious Cock-a-doodle-do's. Magic was an incredible, yet annoying new force in my life.

After dragging myself out of bed I quickly got dressed for the day. Downstairs I was greeted by sunshine Tamara and cool, calm, collected Coco. Today she sported yet another new hairstyle this one featuring Dorothy-style back braids with her signature dark cherry ombré. It was only my second day knowing her but in that time I had seen three new hairstyles. A pattern was becoming apparent, she liked new and fresh.

"Mornin', sugar! What do you have first?" asked Coco, sipping on a steaming cup of what smelled like coffee.

"Ummmm," I said, looking at my schedule. "A double Divination and Runic Studies with Professor Mary-Weather followed by a double Magic and Non Magic Animal Studies with Professor Sutpo."

"Hmm, I advise you to really be punctual for Mary-Weather. She is a known as a bit of a ballbuster. She takes Divination very seriously," Coco informed me.

"Right, will try my best," I said.

"Do not worry," said Tamara, smiling. "We are in the same class for Divination." Oh goodness, that was a relief, I'd have both Tamara and Aamin to sit with in class. I wouldn't be alone for my first time.

Eighteen minutes later we stood outside a large classroom. All around the arched doorway was filigree styled symbols of the moon phases. I knew them, thanks to Grandma. New Moon, Waxing Crescent, First Quarter, Waxing Gibbous, Full Moon, Waning Gibbous, Third Quarter, Waning Crescent, and finally New Moon once more to start the cycle all over again.

Tamara and I had arrived a few minutes early just to make sure there wasn't a chance I'd be late for my first day. On the way we called into the student centre and picked up a few miscellaneous things I'd need for the day such as exercise books, pens, pencils, and a purple satchel bag to store them all in. I felt really embarrassed that I didn't have these things already but Tamara assured me that most people on their first day didn't, not since the war. Many families nearly seven years later were still recovering from the financial, mental, and spiritual impact.

Only a handful of students had beat us there so we were in good stead for our pick of seats. I was pretty nervous after all of yesterday's experiences to meet new people, but as of yet no one had called me—

"Ay! It's Horny Boy!" laughed a familiar voice. One I had very much hoped to avoid at all costs. Turning around I came face-to-face with yesterday's bully, Brax.

"What did you call him?" said Tamara sharply, whipping around with all traces of her characteristic smile gone.

"Don't get your panties in a twist, toots, wasn't talkin' to you."

Tamara's already flushed cheeks turned the colour of a burnt rose.

"I'm glad. I wouldn't want to waste the same oxygen as you."

Brax turned to his gang of friends. "It's rag week," he quipped.

He was slammed hard into the wall by an invisible force. Dust fell from the tall ceiling coating Brax's mustard shirt in grey powder. I turned to look at Tamara, but it wasn't her who had cast the spell. Brax's gang separated and a kind, familiar face emerged with his wand drawn. It was Aamin. He walked in as though he hadn't a care in the world.

"Why you—" Brax began, but a much older female voice interrupted him before he could say or do anything further. "Welcome, class, to a new day. May the fates smile kindly down upon those who follow the school rules and *don't* wish for detention."

We all turned as one to face the short women with curly brown hair, skin the colour of burning embers, and piercing grey eyes.

"Good morning, Professor Mary-Weather," chorused the majority of the students as she led us into the classroom.

Professor Mary-Weather's classroom was all white marble. Each table was circular in shape with only three seats each. There were probably twenty tables in the room, plus the teacher's table, which was only a corner triangle at the very front of the classroom up against a freshly painted black chalkboard covering the wall.

Tamara, Aamin, and I took a table close to the front but not quite centre. We were careful to sit far enough away from Brax, who was shooting us murderous glances, but close enough to see the chalkboard.

Pulling out an exercise book and black fountain pen, I looked forward towards the teacher, ready for my first day.

"We have a new student with us today. Everybody wish Mr Nightshade a warm welcome!' About half the class wished me a "Welcome." Aamin and Tamara were by far the loudest in the group of well-wishers. Unsurprisingly, Brax wasn't one of them.

"For Mr Nightshade, could anyone tell him what this class is all about? What is Divination and Runic Studies?"

Hands shot into the air including Tamara's.

"Yes, Mr Sweeney, you have the floor," announced the teacher, pointing to a student with short red hair who sat a few tables behind us.

"Well, Miss Professor, Divination and Runic Studies is the art of prophesy and the examination of the facts as told to us by the magics that govern this world and the next," answered the student.

"Very good, Mr Sweeney, now who can tell me what we mean by runic?"

More hands shot into the air. This time Professor Mary-Weather pointed at a female student with long blonde hair waved in the popular fashion a few of the other girls in the class sported. "Miss Federicksen, can you tell Mr Night-shade what we mean by runic?"

Clearing her throat, the blonde-haired girl answered the question; her voice sounded possibly Nordic or at least what I imagined Nordic to sound like. "Runic refers to a system of symbolic letters from the Germanic peoples of Northern Europe that denote information not unlike that of which we use today to read and write. In divination we use them to channel the powers that be. In this instance we use the runic alphabet to establish a connection with the fates of the old Norse pantheon, the Nornir. Through that connection we either are casting magic, charms, or curses or we are using it to channel a small glimpse into their sight."

"Very good, both of you." The professor clapped. "The only thing left to add is that the future is always uncertain and so in layman's terms telling your fortune, reading your palms, casting your crystals, reading your tea leaves so on and so forth, only shows us what is the most likely outcome. To think it shows us a definitive answer is incorrect. Now, it is my understanding you will be tutored by Miss Masayá here. So today just try and keep up."

And with that the teacher sent me one last smile before turning to the chalkboard, wand drawn. A few waves and flicks later the board was completely filled with writing in a cursive style.

"Today's subject is a continuation on from Thursday's class on runes. The Elder Futhark is the oldest form of the runic alphabets. And is considered one of the earliest known writing systems used by the Germanic peoples of Northern Europe that has survived. This of course was the precursor to Thursday's class on the younger Futhark—"

Quickly I began trying to write notes as the teacher

155

spoke, unfortunately some of the words I hadn't a clue how to spell so I just did my best. Hopefully I could correct it later if needed.

"Pssst," whispered Aamin.

"What?" I replied low voice,

"She is just reading what's written on the board."

"Oh... Wait, can you—"

"Can I read your mind? No, I can just see your spelling errors," laughed Aamin softly.

"Darn."

Why is that everyone here seemed to be able to read my thoughts? It was getting rather irritating.

Hurriedly, I scribbled out the page, I'd tear it out later. Starting anew, I looked to the board this time instead of trying to write from the verbal cues the professor was giving.

Mary-Weather continued, "The Elder Futhark is an alphabet consisting of twenty-four letters or runes. Named Futhark after the first six runes' names: Fuhu, Uruz, Thurisaz, Ansuz, Raido, and Kaunas. When we talk about rune stones we can be referring to the sacred monuments from the Viking era or we could be talking about individual characters carved into wood or stone to be used for Divination."

Two hours later and I had a written what felt like a novel-length's worth of notes about Elder Futhark. I kind of got the concept when thinking about it, it was like our own alphabet but different. Though I was still rather confused about how exactly it could tell us the future. Maybe that insight to this would just have to come in time.

"Class, I want one and a half thousand words written

about the practical use of runes by Tuesday. Class dismissed," called Mary-Weather.

Through the entire class I felt Braxton's eyes continually burning into the back of my head. It was made even more apparent a few moments later as he barged right past me leaving the room. Under his breath he hissed, "Horny Boy, the p-p-pansy."

Next I had Magic and Non Magic Animal Studies with Professor Sutpo in the west fields, and just like before both Tamara and Aamin shared the same class. Sutpo's method of teaching turned out to be more look and learn, which I found I rather liked. In the class he introduced us to a baby mountain lion, which we learnt was called a cub. The majority of the class was spent on how to track mountain lions and the best ways to avoid them when out in the wild lands.

After a quick lunch, where we had this amazing flaky pastry dish called a spanakopita from one of the takeaway lunch spots, we headed off to Tinctures, Tonics, and Spelled Brews with Professor Evans in the Apothecary classrooms on the other side of the school.

With Aamin and Tamara to navigate this school with me I didn't feel so out of my element.

Like Mary-Weathers's classroom, Professor Evans's was large with an arched doorway with filigree styled symbols, though this one seemed to denote plants and vines, maybe even poppies, but the stylistic approach made it hard to be completely sure.

Inside the classroom was a series of metallic silver tables that looked the picture of sterile, which I guessed was probably really important in this subject. On one wall was a long bench covered with various glass equipment. Some were triangular, some was tubular, and others were circular. Basically on this table was every type of jar, container, flask, and bottle one could imagine.

On the opposite wall was a plethora of plants in pots and vases. What looked like the largest spice rack known to humankind and a bunch of fresh and dried flowers in large fish-tank sized bowls. It was a very interesting room indeed.

There were no seats in this room. It seemed as though we all must stand. The metallic silver tables were larger in height than the others I had seen so far, they came up to my bully button in height.

Professor Evans strode into the classroom dressed in an all-white outfit with a matching white apron that had a shine to it like cold custard. He stood tall, much taller than me, with brown hair and tanned pink skin with the smallest moustache above his lip—kind of like Clark Gable in the picture *Any Number Can Play* that came out a few years ago.

"Class, this afternoon we will be prepping some oil for the creation of a simple salve that will do in a pinch to heal injuries and to promote tissue regeneration."

My ears perked up, now this was something I could bring back home to help on the farm. I *loved* plants and herbs and so did Grandma and Grandpa.

"In groups of three please fetch the following from the supply benches."

Professor Evans turned to the board and began listing a series of herbs and utensils we would need.

The board read—

- *Dried Comfrey Leaf*
- *Dried Calendula Petals*
- *Dried Plantain Leaf*
- *Myrrh Resin*

- *Dried Rose Petals*
- *Dried Roman Chamomile Flowers*
- *Jug of Olive Oil*
- *Set of scales*
- *Stainless Steel Flask Stand*
- *1000 fluid ounce Heatproof Glass Flask*
- *One Five wick 14 hour long-burn candle*
- *A Set of Glass Measures.*
- *A Porcelain Dish*

The class chattered noisily, forming small groups of three. Thankfully, Tamara and Aamin joined me, making sure I wasn't left alone.

"Let me show you everything!" Tamara exclaimed, clapping her hands with excitement. Her energy was infectious, and I couldn't help but feel a thrill of anticipation.

Suddenly, our bench was transformed into a magical garden, brimming with glass jars filled with fragrant herbs and flowers. The jars had a futuristic quality to them, with their pyramid-like shapes and open spouts. I felt my heart skip a beat as I took it all in.

Next, we were instructed to take out our exercise books and transcribe the lesson. I eagerly complied, my senses tingling with excitement. The only thing that gave me pause was the fear of misspelling a word.

"Symphytum Officinale also called Comfrey or slippery-root is a slightly astringent herb that has been used for generations to aid in wound healing. Comfrey includes minerals that are important in the healing process and includes a substance that stimulates cell growth called Allantoin. Comfrey is for topical use only as some studies have found that it may affect the liver in an adverse way when taken orally. In the salve we are creating it is considered a key herb in the formulation.

"Calendula Officinalis also called Calendula or Common Marigold is a flowing plant in the Asteraceae daisy family. When used topically it may speed the process of tissue healing after burns, bruises and other injuries that present a 'wound.' Can be used both topically and orally when brewed as a tea but should not be used by anyone who is experiencing pregnancy or that's currently breast feeding—"

"Hey, sir!" called an obnoxious voice from the back of the room, One I was growing to dislike.

Stopping mid-speech, the professor turned to face the particularly rude student. "What can I do for you, Mr Salopard?" he asked.

"How big are the jugs we talkin' here?" responded Braxton, squeezing his nipples a few times for added effect.

The back of the room ignited in raucous laughter, with some students going as far to say things like "Good one, Brax" and "Brax, you're a funny guy." Even some of the feminine students joined in, though they had nasty pinched faces and cruel eyes. Not my kind of people.

Turning back around, I whispered into Tamara's ear, "Is Brax going to be in all my classes? Please say no."

Tamara chuckled softly, "No, but he is in all of them today."

I groaned. "Must he be?"

"He could be in all of them," she added.

I couldn't help but shudder.

The air in the classroom was thick with the sound of chatter and laughter as the students joked with each other, heedless of the lecture that was supposed to be underway. But the professor had finally had enough.

With a swift, decisive motion, he withdrew his spellcaster's wand and muttered a few words under his breath, his voice lost amidst the cacophony of noise. The wand flicked across his lips, and as it made contact, the room was suddenly suffused with a strange and eerie quiet.

At first, I thought I had gone deaf. I could hear nothing but a faint murmur of voices from outside the classroom, as if we had been transported into a soundproof chamber. But as I looked around and realized that the silence was not universal. The students' mouths were still moving, but no sound emerged, as if their voices had been stolen away by the power of the professor's spell.

The stillness in the room was palpable, like a physical weight pressing down on us all. I could hear the thud of my own heartbeat in my chest, and I held my breath in anticipation of what would come next. For a moment, it felt as though we were frozen in time, suspended in this strange and silent limbo.

"Good. Now that is better. If you wish to ask a question please raise your hand. Thank you." And with that Professor Evans went back to his dictation. Braxton looked furious but seemly had regained the ability to speak as he was heard muttering under his breath.

We learned that plantain was a soothing herb with inflammatory properties. I thought it looked familiar, I was pretty sure that Grandma gave me one once when I was suffering from a five-week bout of bad bronchitis. Another thing we learnt that Myrrh was a dried tree sap that had powerful anti-bacterial and anti-fungal properties.

After we had taken down Professor Evans's dictation, he instructed us in the practical. Setting up the stand and inserting the glass was easy so in our group I got to do that. It was a small task but I found it exciting, I was contributing to the team. Maybe even a slight smile stretched across my face.

Aamin set up the scales and after thoroughly sanitising our hands we each took turns measuring out the various ingredients and placing them into the flask with the oil for infusion. Apart from the ingredient quality the next most imported aspect in the preparation was making sure hygiene and sterilisation of equipment was upheld to a medical level of care.

After instructions it was decided that Tamara would be the one to use the heating charm on the flask. I was yet to learn basic magic properly and Aamin didn't care either way so Tamara it was.

Pulling her wand out I noticed that it was different to mine. Tamara's wand was a sunny meadow yellow with etchings of a slightly more consecrated hue banding around. It was a little more elegant than mine but fit her sunny disposition perfectly.

Professor Evans went about drawing the wand motion for the charm on the chalkboard. It was a kind of a circle twirl ending in a flick. He called it the ignition movement and explained it was used for spells, charms, and hexes that called upon the power of fire.

Placing the small porcelain dish underneath the flask Tamara readied herself to cast the charm.

"It is important, like in all casting, that your intent matches the casting. You must want a small flame to appear in the porcelain dish for this charm to work." And with that he wrote the spelled words on the chalkboard.

"The first spelled word is Áptein. This word is to give us the ignition in the spell. It is followed by Thermós. Thermós is the heat, the hot temperature element so it is giving us the fire for this incantation. So when we are using it together we are igniting a hot heat. When you're ready, begin."

Students around the room began giving the spell a go. But so far no one was successful. Concentrating hard, Tamara let out a small sigh as she began her attempt.

Professor Evans could be herd calling around the room, "You must concentrate!"

Tamara twirled her wand and as she went for the ending flick she chanted, "Áptein Thermós." At first nothing happened, it seemingly didn't work but just as her face started to show an expression of defeat a soft orange light begin to flutter into existence before growing into a candle flame.

The flame required no fuel other than the initial usage of magic. Aamin and I clapped which caught the attention of the professor.

"Oh, good work, Miss Masayá! Look here, class. Miss Masayá has successfully completed the charm."

The class circled around watching, though there was one noticeable absence from the gathered circle. Brax and a few of his thuggish friends had stayed behind at their table. What a rude, sad excuse of a human he must be. I turned back to face a very pleased, very smiling Tamara.

"Do you see how around the outer edge of the flame is a soft glow of blue? This is an indicator of how hot the flame is. If Miss Masayá pushed too much magic into the charm it would have turned blue. For some instances this may be okay and even desired but in this particular instance we want a low heat that allows infusion of plant matter and oil."

By the end of the class every group had successfully set up the oil and plant matter for a slow infusion under the steady, spelled flames. Professor Evans had informed us that the oils would need twelve to fifteen hours of low heat for a rapid infusion so it would be Tuesday's class that we would get to create the healing salve. I for one could not wait.

My last class of the day was Transformative Charm Studies with Professor Connaway. Sadly, Tamara wasn't in this class. Instead, she had Ancient Literature, but thankfully it was only a few classrooms away from ours so the three of us got to walk together.

Birds of a foreign feather chirped in the afternoon sky as we walked arm in arm across the open air bridge to the charms complex.

"So what is Professor Connaway like?" I asked Aamin,

Tamara and Aamin shared a look. Why did they share a look?

"She's great but if you are five minutes late to her class even just once you'll go on Connaway watch."

"What's 'Connaway watch'?"

"Think of it as a naughty list."

"Okay..."

"It goes like this: you do something wrong you go on Connaway watch, repeat said grievance and you go on detention, repeat it again and the headmistress is informed and that's not good."

"That's fine, so what you're saying is I just need to follow her rules and I'll be fine?"

"Precisely," said Tamara.

"That's not so bad——" I began.

"Just make sure your uniform is *neat*."

"It's not now?"

"No."

"Okay, can you hold my bag and I'll fix it."

I didn't understand why they were making a big deal about it. Arrive on time, dress neatly. All things my grandma would expect of me.

As we approached Professor Connaway's classroom, I couldn't help but be struck by its elegance. The arched doorway, unlike the other classrooms' purple entrances, was a deep, rich crimson that lent the room an air of sophistication. The filigree adorning the doorway was exquisite, with its intricate lines creating a detailed pattern of diamond and square shapes. Each element was painted in a lustrous gold, catching the light in a dazzling display.

As we stepped inside, my eyes widened. The room was a masterpiece of design, with its tasteful decor and fine furnishings. The walls were adorned with artful pieces, each one seemingly hand-picked to add to the room's beauty. The air was filled with the scent of fresh flowers, adding a touch of natural elegance to the room's atmosphere.

Despite the sense of grandeur, it was clear that this was a room meant for serious learning, but the elegant touches made it feel inviting, as if the knowledge we would gain would be a true treasure.

I was going to ask Aamin a question when Professor Connaway arrived. My mouth fell open. She wore a long ballgown-style dress made from what looked like expensive silk velvet in a deep emerald green. Her hair was obsidian black and was tied into a system of complex crisscross ropes arranged around her head in an almost crown like fashion. Not a single hair was out of place. Grandma would be proud.

As she walked by a soft smell of peony and rose filled the air. Without uttering a word the class took their seats. Even Brax, who up until this point had rebelled, seemed to fall in line.

Following Aamin we took seats a few rows back from the teacher's desk. Brax again took the desk at the very back of the room. I was careful to make sure I was on the opposite side of the room, no need to make the target on my back any larger.

The classroom was silent, save for the sound of Professor Connaway's footsteps as she approached her desk with purpose. She exuded an air of authority, and the entire class seemed to hold their breath as she began to set up for the lesson.

As she did so I noticed a girl in the back row frantically attempting to fix her tangled nest of hair. It was too late, however, as I soon realised when a glimpse of silver eyes met mine through a reflection in a tiny mirror just on the wall behind the student. As I continued to look I found more of the same small mirrors placed all around the classroom. These mirrors were strategically placed, reflecting every corner of the room. It was like being watched by a thousand watchful eyes, the thought of being under constant surveillance caused me to sit up that little bit more.

The professor could see everything in the room with her back turned. She had placed herself in a position of absolute control.

"Good afternoon, class."

"Good afternoon, Professor Connaway," the room chorused.

"It appears we have a new student in our midst," she said as her intense gaze met mine.

No one bickered and no one spoke. The class was the picture of well-mannered discipline.

"Let's all welcome Mr Nightshade into Transformative Charm Studies grade 1," she said before adding, "now, of course, starting mid-year is quite undesirable but here we are. I expect great things from you, Mr Nightshade. I will not be going easy on you just because you're new."

My cheeks reddened as I wished desperately to fall under my desk and disappear into the abyss.

"Roll call. Trisha Allen—"

"Here," responded the same girl who moments earlier was so desperate to tame her bushy brown hair.

"Mitchell Amours?"

"Hello, Professor," responded a student a few seats behind Trisha, with just as brown hair only his was far curlier.

"Rebecca Azeri?"

"Here, Miss...Professor"

Professor Connaway went through the class list and not one student was absent. I got the impression that missing classes would not fly with this teacher, not one bit.

"In this afternoon's class we will be working on our transformation charms. In groups of two we will practice the transfiguration charm. It is one of the lesser forms of charm metamorphosis, so even our new student should be able to achieve a result by end of class."

This sounded like a warning as if she was about to say "or else." You could tell she expected *all* her students to do well, even the one who knew nothing—me.

And with that she went about writing up the logistics of the spell on the chalkboard.

"What kind of accent is that?" I asked Aamin.

"Southside Dublin, I think," he responded.

"Oh, Dublin, as in Ireland?"

"On the money," he confirmed.

Professor Connaway completed the intricate theory and raised her wand with conviction, bringing it down in a sharp, swiping motion. The air around us shuddered as the wand tip drew a luminous *1* in the air. In an instant, the atmosphere came alive with glittering stars drifting down like snowflakes, forming a veil that shrouded the room.

As the sparkling cascade began to dissipate, small mirrors emerged from the ether, each one no larger than a square cake tin, yet gleaming with a lustrous sheen that filled the room with wonder.

"Look into the mirror," she instructed. "Find a small aspect to change. Example eye colour. Repeat the charm and focus. You must will it to change with all your focused intent or else it will not work. With your partner they must guess what you have changed. Class, begin."

And with that I turned to face my glaringly tired reflection. What was I going to change when I wanted to change everything?

A low murmuring began amongst the students as they began their attempts at the transformation charm. It appeared that most people started with their hair colour. Aamin now sported hair a shade of blond that seemed almost impossible to achieve.

"Oh goodness," I said.

"It's cool huh?"

"Very."

Looking around the room I saw that Trisha, the student with broom-like hair now sported a badly bleached nightmare that stuck out like bundles of straw. She seemed *very* happy about it. Mitchel, who she was partnered with, hadn't changed his brown curls...wait, had he just grown breasts? I averted my eyes away quickly but not without seeing him fondle them in a way that made me feel *very* uncomfortable.

"Focus, Mr Nightshade," called the professor from her desk.

Damn, okay let's give it ago. I stared hard at my reflection. Let's just change my hair colour like everyone else. Ordinary brown hair would be nice. Okay, half the work is the decision now it was time for the charm. But just as I was about to the attempt the charm I noticed in the corner of my mirror Braxton. He was laughing and pointing at another student who'd seemingly miscast the charm as all of her hair was falling out in awful clumps, she of course was in tears.

In that moment I flashed back to his name-calling. "Horny Boy." A name he'd given me because of the antlers. I wanted them gone, maybe then I wouldn't be such a target. Checking the theory notes twice and then twice again I stared back at the mirror but this time I focused on my freakish antlers. The unwanted curse given to me b... Him.

"Metaschimatízein," I muttered, focusing on my horns disappearing.

Nothing happened.

I tried again.

"Metaschimatízein." Still nothing. Why could I not do this?

This time I put everything I had in me. I drew magic in from what felt like my very soul. These antlers were going.

"Metaschimatízein!" I shouted. Giving it everything. All students instantly faced me, their eyes like knifes on my back. I pictured what I'd look like sans antlers and...was that a face I saw in the mirror? A bearded man? Was he whispering "no"? What in the... Lightning cracked, striking the mirror and sending glass shards all over me in a burst of glass dust. Pain lanced, burning what felt like my veins. A second later I heard more mirrors combust.

One—*Smash!*

Two—*Smash!*

Three—*Smash* and so on.

Had it worked?

Frantically, I turned to Aamin. "Did it work?"

"Did what work? Summoning lightning?" He looked puzzled.

"No! Are my antlers still there? Did the charm work?"

"Léon, is that what you tried to do?" Why did he seem so confused?

Looking around the room, I saw not one mirror still standing. Braxton caught my gaze as laughter erupted from almost every student.

"Horny Boy doesn't want to be horny anymore, haha."

"SILENCE," commanded the professor before turning to face me, her face the picture of fury.

"Gods be... Mr Nightshade, what on earth have you done? You silly boy."

Two hours later I sat alone outside the winter tower on a bench, legs tightly wrapped in my arms, completely miserable as I flashed back to the furious face of Professor Connaway. Not only did my charm not work but I had also destroyed several hundred dollars' worth of antique mirrors from the professor's own personal antique collection. To say she was upset was an understatement. Her words still rang like a tower bell in my brain.

"Mr Nightshade, you cannot undo the work of the gods. To think you can is just plain stupidity. Never have I ever seen in all my years a student so completely foolish. The bill for your reckless damage will be sent to your guardians—"

We couldn't afford to pay for the damage I had done. My grandparents were going to be so disappointed in me.

They probably wouldn't be able to put food on the table because of what I had done. I wished I was never born. Stupid stupid stupid fool.

I was nothing but a burden.

PRENEURS DE MAGI I

Pungent grey smoke boiled in the iron cauldron as Jacquard Morioatus poured in another bag of dirt from a grave long since lost to time. Next he added the scream from a cat caught in a jar with the power to steal sound. Following the scream he added three feathers from a blind chicken thrice drowned in a lake with no end. Finally, he added to his cursed brew a few pinches of the dried blood from the god-touched fae-born prince he so desperately sought.

Staring the pot, he watched as the smoky liquid changed from a sickly grey to a brilliant belladonna-bright. The invocation brew was complete. Smiling, he quickly ladled up a vial of the concoction. He would use this potion in conjunction with a summoning chant.

Jacquard sauntered over to his bound circle carved into the cobblestone flooring of the freshly acquisitioned house. The former owners of which lay discarded like broken skeletons in the corner of the room.

"It's time," he called.

The doors to the room opened and in marched a very select handful of Jacquard's most talented followers. Amongst the band of villainous evil were the Mauvais Twins—called the pied pipers of Bayeux for their abduction and murder of twenty infants. Sheila and Barry Ottomen— the faceless phantoms of Sydney. And Ronald Gilbreaith, the prized assassin from Hitler's inner circle.

Hand-in-hand, they began the chant. They spoke in the old tongue that translated to

To summon one, our magic we wield,
Across time and space, our plea be sealed,
With the power of wildfire, fierce and bright,
We call upon you to join us in this rite.
In this circle, your freedom we'll ensnare,
A captive bird, caught in our magical affair,
May our spell bind you, with unbreakable might,
Forever trapped, within our sight.
So mote it be, let this trap be set,
Our will be done, without regret,
Bound in this circle, our wish will unfold,
To keep you captive, as we behold.

The hiss of ignition sounded before a flame sparked into existence, lighting the bound circle of blood in a ring of fire. Jacquard, smiling, threw the vial of belladonna-bright into the centre of the summoning circle.

Smash. The vial broke, unleashing a mutinous purple smoke. It bubbled and oozed as it rose into the air matching the sinister hiss and crackle of the spelled fire.

"It is working!" called Jacquard with glee.

His followers began a chant of energy magnification. "Magnificamus virtutem nostrum."

The smoke started to take form, a face through the mist and…and…and…

Puff. The spell broke.

"NOOOOOO!" screamed Jacquard as he ran into the centre, pushing his followers aside.

"This should have worked!" Hurriedly, he grabbed at the mist as it faded from view. He sought it like a man lost in the desert desperate for water.

Muttering broke out in the room.

173

"Why didn't it work?" Someone asked.

"Did he get the cursed brew wrong?" asked another.

Fury unlike anything this world has seen before crackled in Jacquard's blood-red eyes. As the smoke finally faded away two things were left in the circle that had not been there prior. A purple feather that glowed from within and a chunk of amethyst crystal.

He let out a mighty cry of anguish.

The boy was at the school that could not be found. Circes Island.

CHAPTER 9

Homework, Why Do You Suck So Very Much

LÉONIDAS I

It was a dreary Monday afternoon, weeks after my mishap in Transformative Charm Studies, and the pile of homework before me loomed like a monstrous beast, threatening to swallow me whole. The essays for magic were multiplying like rabbits, and the equations for maths taunted me with their complexity. I had English papers that seemed to stretch on for miles, and star-gazing reports that required an otherworldly level of focus. The practical and non-practical charms were piling up, and the research topics on history were as dry as the desert. To top it all off, there were quizzes about flowers, which seemed like a cruel joke to play on someone drowning in a sea of homework.

The sheer volume of what I had to complete would have sent me spiralling into the abyss of despair, if not for the presence of my two loyal companions, Coco and Tamara. They sat beside me, offering their unwavering support and guidance as I trudged through the endless sea of work.

Aamin, my other friend, would have been there too, but he was serving detention with Professor Langford. Apparently, he had sent a counter-jinx on Braxton, who had tried to set my hair on fire when I wasn't looking. That malicious jerk seemed to have a personal vendetta against me.

I let out a deep sigh and read the essay question aloud once more, "What are the many benefits from including fungi in potions, brews, and drafts?"

"It's an easy question, Léon," sighed Coco.

"Is it?" I responded rubbing my tired eyes.

"Here," said Tamara, handing me a thick brown book titled *Fun with Fungi* by Fenalious Gilbert.

"It like a thousand pages," I moaned.

"Well, then best you get readin'," snipped Coco.

Tamara and Coco were helping me, but they wouldn't do the work for me. It just sucked that I had several months' worth of homework to complete to catch up with the other students in my year. Opening the book, I looked up the chapter index and quickly searched it for any keywords that may narrow my search but after reading the index three times nothing stood out. Slowly, I lowered the text book to peer over at Coco and Tamara. My eyes said help me but those that met mine said not a chance.

Sighing, I flicked through to chapter one which was aptly titled "Introduction to fungi." *Fungi is used in all matter of life for the human population from brewing beer to making bread. Even people who detest mushrooms in their risottos would be hard to not find it in one's home in an unconventional sort of way.*

I tried my best to read as quick as possible but after a few failed attempts I was left with little else but to read every single stupid word.

Afternoon turned to dusk and dusk turned to nightfall.

"It's done!" I yelled, putting my pen down with a soft clink.

A sleeping Coco jumped into the air. "What what what's goin' on?" Seeing that I was just finally done with the essay, she added, "Did ya have to yell? I thought we were being invaded by the Christians."

"Okay, Léon, hand it over," yawned Tamara, motioning with her fingers.

Handing it over, I grabbed the next paper I had to write. At this rate I'd never get any sleep ever at all period. People can say what they want about home-schooling but at least you didn't have novels worth of writing to complete all the time. How I'd ever remember any of this come exam time was a complete mystery.

The following Tuesday morning I had Defensive and Offensive Spellcasting with Professor Sokolova. Her class-room was in the building by the school entrance. This was another class I had without Tamara as she had another teacher, Professor Mills, but luckily his classes were also in the same building so I got to walk over with both Tamara and Aamin.

Getting up early for the morning classes I found to be rather difficult and over the past few weeks I had formed a rather abusive relationship with coffee as a result. I blamed Coco for introducing me to the American monstrosity.

Professor Sokolova was a good teacher, like many of my professors she was straight to the point, but unlike some she also went easy on me and so far hadn't expected me to be at the same level as my peers.

So far I had learnt a few basic shield spells that used little magic but would hold up against several of the more violent spells known to spellcaster kind. One of the aspects of shield charms that I found fascinating was that while they were up they continued to siphon off magic from your essence and that it was better to lower a shield then to allow it to break apart because the shattering of a spell as such would feel like an elastic band that had been stretched to far returning to your body tenfold.

Theory was also a big part of the class work in Defensive and Offensive Spellcasting. Professor Sokolova was adamant that the theory had to be correct before you were allowed to practice anything with your wand.

"What do you suppose we will learn today?' I asked the two.

"We should be starting offensive practical soon, I hope it's that," responded Aamin.

"We could be learning the next level in shield spells," chimed in Tamara.

I agreed with Aamin, I wanted to learn some of the Offensive aspect to the class. Especially if Braxton was going to continue trying to curse me every single chance he could get. I mean the whole thing on my first day was an *accident*.

Saying goodbye to Tamara, we separated and entered our different classrooms.

I admired Professor Sokolova's no-nonsense approach to classroom aesthetics. Her room was refreshingly minimalist, lacking any ornate embellishments or ostentatious decorations. It was simply a vast and unadorned space, dominated by a towering blackboard that loomed over us.

Despite its simple appearance, the room was massive, roughly the same size as my home. It was grand in its understated simplicity, leaving no room for distraction from the matter at hand.

Today's lesson was undoubtedly a practical one, and we could all feel the electricity in the air as we entered the room. All the desks and chairs had been stacked up neatly and pushed to the side, making way for the intricately carved practice circle that lay at the centre of the room.

Circles were a fundamental component of spellcasting, a magical barrier that contained and controlled the flow of magic. I learned that the concept was first discovered by the ancient Sumerians of Mesopotamia, who called it "Zisur-rû." Professor Sokolova explained that in the context of our class, the circle was used to prevent magic from going haywire during practice. However, she also warned us that it could be used to trap somebody or something and contain them indefinitely. Of course, she was quick to point out that such actions were illegal and should only be used in a dire, life-threatening situation.

We stood around the circle with the other first years in the class and in walked the professor. Her blonde ballet bun was as tight as always and her fringe just stopped above her arched brows. Today she wore a lime green boiler suit with a tightly wrapped belt.

"Dobroye utro, class."

"Dobroye utro, Professor," we responded in unison.

"Dobroye utro" of course was the Russian word for good morning which I had learnt in my very first lesson with this teacher.

"All right, class, today we shall take our first foray into the world of offensive magic. We shall begin with simple push-and-pull spells, which could come in handy should you find yourself in a spot of trouble and need a quick escape. I trust you are all excited to learn."

A buzz of anticipation hummed through the room.

Some of the students had grown up with magic in their lives, while others were new to the ways of spellcasting.

"Now, pay attention, please. The spells themselves are 'Apotheín,' meaning 'to push away,' and 'Epispán,' which means 'pull to.' The wand movements for these spells are quite basic. To push away, extend your wand forward from your chest, and to pull the object towards you, move the wand back towards your chest. Let us now practice these spells without incantation."

Wands at the ready, we each practiced the movements. Pushing the wand away, then drawing it back towards ourselves. After a few repetitions, the professor seemed pleased with our progress.

Professor Sokolova walked to the corner of the room and brought out a large orange ball.

"One at a time in the circle you will take turns practicing the spells with this here ball used in the American game of basketball first played in 1891."

Basketball—what an odd name.

"We will do this alphabetically, that means, Miss Allen, you're first up."

The bushy haired student whose first name was Trisha or Patricia—I wasn't exactly sure, stepped forward into the circle. Doing the motion for push she yelled the spell in a shrill almost comically witchy voice. "Apotheín!"

Instantly the ball went flying, it was as if a gust of strong wind had collided with the orange sphere. But instead of the ball flying into the wall its progress was immediately stopped as it made contact with the invisible barrier of the circle.

"Oh, look I did it! Mitchell, look how good am I!" squealed Trisha. She was of course talking to the same Mitchell who'd grown breasts in that first Transformative

Charms Study class. I had learnt since that the two of them were an item. Mitchell with his poutiest of lips blew her a very inappropriate kiss with a lot of tongue.

"Ochen khorosho, Miss Allen, very good. Now try the spell to pull."

And so Trisha did to a very celebrated success. We proceeded to go through the class list from Trisha Allen to Conner Myers. After about thirty minutes it was finally my turn and I was *dreading* it.

"Okay, Mr Nightshade, it's your turn. Please enter the circle."

Sweat slicked my palms as I withdrew my wand. I looked at Aamin with desperation.

"You can do this," he mouthed. I hoped he was right.

Entering the circle I felt a soft wash of cold energy pass over me. The sound outside the barrier was muted ever so slightly.

"Okay, ball, you're going to have to move for me, okay?" I whispered to myself. The orange thing just stared at me. To be fair, I didn't expect it to respond...

Raising my crystalline wand to my chest I pushed it out but instantly forgot the words. What were they a Arothin? a Pothiyn? Damn it.

"Look here! Horny Boy can't even remember the words to a simple spell! What a loser," laughed Braxton who was joined by what felt like most of the class. My already rosy cheeks turned a nasty shade of sunburnt blisters.

"Vedite sebya tikho. Be quiet, class," called Professor Sokolova before turning her attention back to me and telling me the spelled words once more.

I attempted the spell again and this time I was able to make the ball move. Not as much as some of the other students had, but it definitely moved. Apparently, my intent wasn't strong enough so it was a mediocre spell casting.

Next time I'd make sure to rectify my mistake. Intent plus focus equals a strong spell.

ATTICUS VALOR I

Wiping the beading sweat from my brows I picked my speed back up and took another run at the rope climb. Kicking down hard I propelled myself into the air. This time I succeeded in grabbing the end of the knotted rope. Muscles burning, I quickly climbed my way to the metal ring and swung myself over the wall barrier.

"GO ACE!" screamed supportive onlookers, "YOU CAN DO IT!"

Landing on my feet, I instantly dropped to all fours as I took on the barbed wire crawl. Using frog-like motions I dragged myself across the mud. I could hear my opponent catching up. He was not going to beat me, but the fact that he was catching up displeased me immensely. I was the best for a reason.

Just a bit further and...yes done. I made it through the crawl. After springing to my feet, I bolted to the rope ladder. The challenge wasn't necessarily the ladder made of rope but more so that the rope was slack. Had it been taut it would've been easy to climb over but because it was loose one could easily get tangled up in it.

Curls damp and body sticky with muddy sweat, I threw myself at the first suspended ring. I only just caught it. Hanging for a moment, I readjusted my hand hold. Flexing my core muscles I forced my body to swing back and forth. The next ring was two metres away so I'd have to gain enough momentum to be able to reach it. This, of course, would be super easy if it wasn't for the magic blocker we all had to wear. A small silver arm band that muted all magics including any extra strength or speed one would have if they happened to be a shifter, a shifter like me.

Grunting, I made the final swing. My feet made contact with the flat edge but not enough. I'd have to swing again, losing precious time. But the second attempt yielded another fail. Anger burned in my veins, I was normally able to do this one particular obstacle quite easily. It must have been the fact that my nights had been spent hunting to try to quell to bloody mate pull. I'd had barely any sleep in weeks.

Third year spring equinox house student Bailey Nelson was catching up fast. I could hear that he had made his first swing. It was now or risk coming in second.

"Aghhh!" I grunted, pushing myself. My feet landed firmly on the edge. Letting go of the ring I counter balanced my weight so I could roll forward. I made it but so had Bailey.

"Ace, you're losing your touch," he laughed breathily.

"Not a chance," I laughed back.

We both took the dive into the lake at the same time. The water was ice-cold. It was spelled to be this way. Literal ice chunks occupied the water as an extra obstacle on the course. The chill went straight to my bones and made it hard to breathe. We both chose a breast stroke and went hell for leather.

Coming to a section of large pieces of ice, I swam under whilst Bailey decided to go over. It was far safer to choose the up and over option. With going under there wasn't a guarantee when I would get my next breath, but the continued in and out would use three times the amount of energy. And the key to any obstacle course was the regulation of energy, making sure I could sustain the pace I've set. Use to much energy to early and I wouldn't make it to end. Nor using enough energy and I would come in last.

Damn it! I came to the end of the lake but the surface had iced over. Swimming back would put me behind. Not an option.

Smash smash smash! I thrust my fist into the solid sheet of ice. I needed to hurry, my breath was running out. Again, I smashed my fist into the ice. I felt the ice start to cut into my flesh, I didn't care. Once the band was off I'd heal the wound anyway.

Smash smash KRAAAWK! Finally, my fist broke through. Drops of blood fell in the deep water like ink droplets, but I didn't care because I could finally breathe. One glorious mouthful of air before I pulled myself out of the chill water.

Bailey had gained a stupid yard advantage but I took off after him. The next obstacle was the element of fire.

A forest lay before us, it was spelled with flames of nightmarish white. The objective was to cross the forest of around one hundred yards first. But this, of course, would be too easy, instead in the forest were creatures of mischievous fire—Kobolds. Small goblin-like creatures that shifted into any number of wild animal forms. Without magic I was only left with fists and whatever I could find to aid me in the forest.

Hand aching, I followed Bailey into the forest fire. The air was warm, filled with thick smoke that burnt my lungs and stung my eyes, making it rather difficult to see straight as the fire danced in front of me. If I kept breathing in this sludge I'd pass out long before I made it to the end.

Pulling off my blood-red sport shirt, I ripped it into large strips using the sharp tips of my fangs, which thankfully were still usable with the magic-muting arm band.

One strip covered my nose and mouth to help filter out the smoke and debris whilst another strip was wrapped around my head in a turban style and the last two strips I wrapped around my fists to protect them from the fire.

"Hehehehe!" sung a Kobold darting in and out of the tree flames.

"Show yourself!"

"Hehehehe!" it continued to sing. Its creepy little voice was a cacophony of sound, no matter which way I turned my head I couldn't work out which direction the Kobold was.

Picking up my pace, I ran through the burning trees.

Something shifted behind me and soon after I heard the unmistakable thud of large paws. The Kobold had shifted into a lion. I picked up a large burning branch that had long since fallen to its death and brandished it like some burning Spartan spear.

It was getting increasingly harder to see though the ash that fell like rain. Through the flames I'd lost complete track of Bailey. Hopefully, he had fallen far behind me but I doubted it.

"Hehehehe!" sung another Kobold somewhere to my left. Fuck—there was two of them on me. A second later I head the unmistakable sound of one shifting. Large wings flapped into the air. The mischievous thing had transformed into a bald eagle. I now had both a lion chasing me and a stupid eagle. I pushed even more strength into my pace but a burning in my arm muted my speed. It appeared I had reached the maximum a normal mortal could exert. Grabbing another fallen branch, I wielded the two as batons. twirling the burning sticks around me like a fire dancer. One shot is all I had and the plan I had formulated was very risky.

Ducking behind a burning tree, I propelled one branch into the air after the bald eagle. It missed, fuck, but the other stick I threw into the lion's mouth as it roared. It worked—the Kobbold was forced to shift back into its small ugly form.

I took back off into a run, the wings of the eagle fresh on me. I wouldn't get another chance like that. I only hopped I was able to outrun it by dashing in and out of the trees.

The end of the forest was fast approaching. *Damn it!* I could finally see Bailey and he was still in front, the lucky son of a gun.

"SKQARKK!" The eagle was coming in for a dive. Fuck. I stopped, darted, and spun. The eagle missed me!

One...two...yes three. I broke through the burning tree line, fresh air filled my lungs as I discarded the soot soaked rags.

The second last challenge was the dreaded fifty yard free form rock climb. There wasn't a risk of dying as there were magics in place to slow one's fall but that was an instant lose situation and that was *never* an option. Not for me, not now, not ever.

With my chest exposed I took on the rock wall, I had only sixty seconds before the rocks would disappear and move themselves to a new spot on the wall, this meant zero rest and absolutely no recovery time. If I thought my muscles were burning before it was nothing compared to how they were feeling now.

I was good at the wall climb, I knew it, I'd done it hundreds of times so it was no surprise to anyone that after ten minutes I had caught right up to Bailey.

"You were taking your time," he greeted me with a laugh in his tired voice.

"Thought I'd let you get a head start, handicapped and all," I responded dryly.

"'Handicapped'?"

"You must be, what with wasting energy talking."

"Hahaha, Ace, I'm still going to beat you."

"You wish."

Nine minutes later, two chipped nails and pain lancing my entire right side, we had both made it over the rock wall. We descended quickly over the other side using the knotted rope. What was a little rope burn to add to the list.

The truth was I liked the school sport because I finally felt a challenge, the injuries reminded me that I was alive, so what if I hurt myself with cuts and burns. They'd heal on their own after a few hours without the magic blocker.

Back down on the ground we ran over to the final obstacle, the only one without the magic band needing to be worn, as the last obstacle was one of magic although as I was still a shifter I wasn't permitted to shift, otherwise it would give me a distinct advantage.

Two Nalusa Falaya stood beyond us in separate circles. Their long shadow-like bodies with pointed bones and soulless eyes were the picture of violence. The obstacle was simple in theory, the first to immobilise their creature won.

Bailey and I looked at each, one breath, two breath, SPRINT. We took off as fast as we could. I pulled out my ruby wand at the same time as I pulled off the magical muter and prepared for battle.

The chill crept under my skin as I crossed over the circle barrier. Instantly, the creature slithered toward me like a serpent on the warpath. Right before it was about to strike, I bellowed, "Apotheín!" sending the creature back to the invisible barrier wall.

It hissed before melting into the shadows. It crawled

187

like a puddle along the ground, coming straight for me. What did the shadow fear? I hadn't much time, but I knew one thing—sunlight.

"Eílisis!" I screamed, jabbing my wand into the air before pushing it down to the creature that was about consume my ankles with its shadowy grip. Brilliant rays of light beamed from my wand tip, burning the creature and sending it out of the shadow into the same plane.

We circled each other like cats of prey, neither charging first, both biding our time. In its soulless eyes, I could see the venom of its hatred towards me.

"SSSSSSS." It bolted forward, its thorny fingers outstretched. I dodged and sent a blast of energy back. It swirled and made to jump back into the shade.

"Not today!" I growled.

Performing a freezing charm, I sent it out like a beam of icy blue. A second later it made direct contact with the Nalusa Falaya, its flesh froze mid-transition.

A horn sounded. The course had been won. Puffing out an exhausted sigh I sat down, finally able to catch my breath and the thought of Léonidas was driven right out of my mind and I could breathe again.

I just needed to keep myself busy and continue to push myself to my limits.

PRENEURS DE MAGI I

Jacquard was furious, he had been trying for weeks to secure the boy but alas nothing so far had worked. He'd tried every summoning in the book, and all he was able to summon was chunks of useless amethyst. He'd tried to travel to the island but it was protected by the gods so all attempts had led him back to Italy. What was even more infuriating was that he had once attended the bloody school and even taught there once upon a time. His only hope was that the god-touched fae-born prince left the castle city's walls, otherwise he'd have to wait until the end of the school year to nab his prize.

He sipped his boiled broth. He'd waited a long time for the boy, what was a few more months at the end of the day, when he'd waited so many years. After all, he knew where his prey was. The fact he couldn't get there yes was infuriating but just a practicality. He would get the boy and all the powers the incomplete prophecy promised.

Jacquard turned his attention back to his prisoners. Two men, brothers in fact, who were in their early twenties lay suspended in the air silently screaming in contorted agony. A silencing spell mixed with his favourite curses and charms for pain. The magical essences tasted all the better when the heart beat so rapidly and the soul screamed with the purest fear.

He was truly in a mutinous mood. "How about we skin you both, maybe that would enhance the flavour of this blasted broth." He smiled. The eyes of his prisoners bulged as renewed panic filled them.

"Yes. I think we shall."

Jacquard could, of course, have done this with magic be instead he decided to do it with a barber's razor. His first cut was on the taller man's thigh, long, and deep, not quite deep enough to hit the femoral artery but enough to expose it to his greedy fingers. Running the blade up and down, he drew one connected line around the entire body. Blood poured like the tears that fell from the dying man's eyes. But, of course, Jacquard wasn't going to have him die before his essence was taken. A quick little charm to slow the man's death was performed. He felt all the pain, but now it was if it was happening all in slow motion.

With his bony fingers Jacquard rolled back the man's skin. He couldn't help himself, he gave the exposed muscles a little lick.

"You taste good, Peter, very good." The blood stained his almost invisible lips. "You know what, I think I want to hear your screams." A simple wave of his wand and both men's screams rang like police sirens though the walls of his little den.

CHAPTER 10
A PARTIAL PROPHECY

LÉONIDAS I

J anuary and even February passed in a blur. By the second week of March I had *finally* caught up with all my schoolwork. Coco, Tamara, and Aamin even held a small little victory party, complete with cake, to mark the occasion and the cake was rather delicious.

The days had been long and exhausting, but as I looked back on them I had been so busy, running from one activity to the next, that I didn't have time to think about the darkness that had consumed me for so long. The moments of happiness were fleeting, but they were enough to make me smile and give me hope that I would feel that way again. I could recall the warmth of the sun on my skin during a picnic in the park where we ate brownies that Aamin had made, the laughter of my friends during a game night of *Sorry!* the board game where it was a race to reach the home space, and the feeling of accomplishment when I finally finished a project I had been working on for weeks. These moments were small, but they filled me with joy and reminded me that there was still good in the world. Slowly but surely, the fog that had clouded my mind began to lift, and I felt a sense of lightness that I had not felt in a long time.

With March came a new equinox, that of spring. Unlike winter, the city castle did change to reflect the occasion. Flowers sprung up everywhere—wrapped around castle pillars, growing up towers, and practically every field was blessed with a large section of Gaia's finest. With all the floral scents in the air I couldn't help but reflect back on the story of Hades and Persephone, the story my grandma would tell me. If all was true then she was now free and with her mother once more thus the fruits and grains of the land were happy.

The class I was excelling in strange enough was Tinctures, Tonics, and Spelled Brews. There was just something about working with the land that reminded me of home. Speaking of home, I had received my first letter from my grandparents on the 28th of February. The letter was short but sweet. *We miss you, can't wait to see you again on the 26th of July and don't you worry yourself about the broken mirrors. We all make mistakes. Love Grandma and Grandpa.* My heart bled just thinking about them.

There was one class that had me stumped, completely lost in an abyss of confusion, this class was Alchemy Basics with Professor Ceylon. It was as if mathematics had collided with the intricacies of spell-brewing and the complexities of transformative charm studies. The fundamental idea of transmuting one substance to another seemed simple enough, like transforming coal into gold, but beyond that, the subject was an enigma. The professor, often inebriated, rarely arrived on time to class, and when they did, their lectures were nothing short of a rambling monologue with no room for questions. It didn't help that their breath exuded a scent that was entirely otherworldly. Perhaps, it was this foul odour that drove my attention away from the subject, or maybe it was simply my inability to grasp the concepts presented. Either way, my proficiency in the course was non-existent.

Slowly, over the few months, I'd gotten better in Transformative Charm Studies. I still couldn't change any aspect of myself, let alone my antlers but I had been having success when using the charms on other students. Professor Connaway's current theory was it had something to do with how I'd received the antlers. Coco had suggested maybe it had something to do with the fae blood but when I mentioned it to the professor she shot it down. Apparently fae were great shapeshifters.

The one constant in my life, despite the ever-flowing sands of time, was the unwavering, intense stare from the prince of the vaewolves. Our paths only crossed during dinner, and we had not uttered a single word to each other since that fateful night. His golden eyes seemed to bore into my very soul with increasing intensity. I couldn't quite decipher if it was his contempt for me that fuelled his gaze or if he truly harboured an insatiable hunger for my flesh. To my shame, a part of me almost wanted him to devour me whole. I was lost, confused, and unable to make sense of my own desires. To make matters worse, I was experiencing a most inappropriate swelling between my legs, especially when he was watching me or when I woke up drenched in sweat in the middle of the night.

I had considered seeking counsel from Coco, as she seemed to have a wealth of knowledge, but a gnawing feeling in my gut told me that I wasn't ready for whatever she might reveal. So, I tried my best to ignore these confusing emotions, and eventually, I found that with enough effort, I could push them aside and focus on other things.

The 11th of March brought about its own challenges. We had moved into practical lessons in Divination and Runic Studies. So far everything had gone okay, a simple tarot reading and few sessions of tea leaf reading but today was the day we did crystal ball scrying.

Our classroom was set up much like it normally was, three seats per circle table, only today there were three purple amethyst balls, each around the size of a medium melon. They stood on stands of a polished mahogany hue.

"Come in. Come in," called Professor Mary-Weather.

Tamara, Aamin, and I took our regular seats. Braxton, of course, shoved into my shoulder as he walked by. I grabbed the table to steady myself just in time.

"Watch where you're standing, Horny Boy, you never know when your betters are walking by."

"'Betters'? Pfft," called Aamin.

"You're just jealous that Léon is a prince and you're not," added Tamara.

Braxton's face turned sickly red.

"What's the use of being a prince if your whole family is poor... Prince of the homeless." His eyes lit up and a sinking feeling dropped in my stomach—not another nickname.

"Prince of the homeless!" laughed Jerry and Kale—nothing students who appeared to live only as Braxton's sycophants.

"Students, please take your seats," called the teacher.

We took our seats, temporarily ending the constant fight with Braxton. Why did he hate me so much? I just did not understand it.

Professor Mary-Weather took her place in front of the room.

"Today as you all know we are doing our first practical with crystal balls. One of the oldest known written sources of crystal ball divination was written in the first century CE by the famed Pliny the Elder. The practice was later demonised by the early Christian church but regardless became wide spread within the soothsayer community by the fifth century. The objective is to read the images that are depicted through the stone. Some will see and others will not. The gift of scrying is not for everyone. So fear not, you will not fail if the ball yields you nothing but you all must give it your best go—"

That was a real relief. I had been stressed that I wouldn't see anything. At least now the pressure was off.

Professor Mary-Weather continued, "As you undoubtably noticed, we will be using amethyst stone balls today. These are not any ordinary crystal balls, can anyone tell me why?"

Hands shot into the air, including both Tamara's and Aamin's.

But instead of picking a hand in the air the teacher decided to choose someone else.

"Mr Nightshade, can you tell the class why these stones are special?"

"Er...er...er," I stammered. Why would these be special? I could practically feel Tamara and Aamin try to send me the answer telepathically but as of yet I was not gifted in that way. I'd have to do the work. Okay so what did I know about amethyst? It was a healing stone and one of mental protection. It was the colour purple and fluctuated between a dark purple violet and a light mauve. The name is derived from Koine Greek which intern was divided from ancient Greek. it was believed that wearing the stone prevented intoxication so it was often caved into drinking vessels, the school was made from amethyst...could these stones be made from the same amethyst that the school is?

"It's made from the same amethyst the school is?" I answered, though it came out more as a question.

"Correct, Mr Nightshade," agreed Professor Mary-Weather.

I slumped in my chair in relief, glad I didn't make a fool of myself. Answering questions was not fun. Not fun at all.

Professor Mary-Weather went on to explain why and her words echoed in my ears as I felt a chill run down my spine. The crystal balls, crafted from the very stones that made up the school, had a unique power that amplified scrying beyond normal measures. Instead of reading the clouds swirling within the sphere, some of us would witness vivid visions. We were instructed to jot down every detail, no matter how insignificant it might seem. I peered at the crystal ball with disdain, as if it were a cruel tormentor who had inflicted pain upon an innocent creature. I didn't want to know what the future held, for I feared that it would be a bleak and lonely existence without my parents. Or did I?

The tumultuous emotions of teenagerhood whirled inside me, and I struggled to make sense of my own desires. I gazed into the purple abyss, but all I saw was nothingness. I hadn't really tried, though. I looked deeper, hoping for a glimpse of the future, but the stone remained clear as glass. Turning to Tamara to share my lack of success, I was shocked to find her eyes had clouded over, and she was unresponsive to my queries. Panic seized me, and both Aamin and I reached out to touch her simultaneously. In an instant, all sound and light faded away, and we were falling, tumbling through the thick darkness of the night.

THUMP!!!

Aamin and I landed hard on the ground, the wind knocked out of us.

"Where are we?" I asked aloud, my voice echoing as though we were in a long cave.

"We must be in Tamara's vison," said Aamin with unabashed awe.

Must we?

Looking around, I saw absolutely nothing for there was no light. Just a vast black expanse. Getting to my feet with the help of Aamin, I asked, "Can you see anything?"

"No, not a damn thing yet oddly I can still see you clear as day."

Aamin was right, it was as if light was on us yet only us… Strange.

"HELLO!" I yelled, the sound echoing. "HELLO!… HELLO…Hello…hello."

Note to self, don't yell.

"Did you have yell, Léon?"

"Sorry, but how was I to know?"

Aamin rolled his eyes before adding, "Do you suppose we are in Tamara's mind or in her vision?"

"I don't know, maybe? It sure is a lot of void," I commented, confused.

"Hello, Tamara, can you hear us?" called Aamin.

SWOOOSH

"AHHHHHHH!"

The ground once more was knocked from under our feet and we began to fall. Aamin and I linked arms. Not from fear…no, so we didn't get separated…yes that was it. We weren't afraid…

197

Drip. Drip. Drip.

Colour fell like ravenous rain, pooling low beneath us, bringing a scene to light.

POOOFFFFT!

Sound escaped us as we both fell hard once more.

"Tamara, do you mind? Quit with the dropping us, okay? Twice is enough," muttered Aamin.

I felt a sudden knot in my stomach as I prepared to speak. The room was all too familiar—I had dreamed of it every winter since my parents passed away. The moisture in my mouth evaporated as a spine-chilling frost ran down my back.

"Where do you suppose we are?" Aamin asked, his voice echoing in the eerie silence. "Some sort of old library?"

I turned to face him, feeling as if I were wading through molasses.

"Léon? Léon, are you okay?" he asked, his concern palpable.

I nodded weakly, but deep down I knew I wasn't okay. The open doorway was covered in a neat border of golden filigree with matching gold doors with the same filigree as the connecting border. This was the very same one my parents would run through.

Aamin's hand fell on my shoulder, and I felt his presence grounding me. "Friend, do you know this place?"

I nodded, unable to find my voice. The memories were flooding back, overwhelming me.

He put the pieces together before I could speak. "This is where your parents died."

I nodded again, my heart aching with the realization. I had always believed it was just a terrible nightmare, a figment of my imagination. But being here, it felt too real to be just a dream.

199

I felt a sudden warmth encompassing me, and then I realized it was Aamin wrapping his arms around me. I returned the embrace, feeling grateful for his comforting presence. "Thank you," I whispered, my voice cracking with emotion.

A second later I felt another set of arms wrap around us. It was Tamara. Her unmistakable scent of frangipani and lilac was a much welcome comfort.

"Don't watch," said Tamara. A second later the sound of magic filled the room. It was a torrent of sound, a war of the heart. Even though I knew what was about to happen I couldn't watch, I wouldn't watch. Maybe I was weak but I'd seen this scene a million times over in my restless sleep. Living it whilst I was awake was a cruel joke by the gods playing the heartstrings of victims who are already taken by loss's sinister kiss.

My eyes were raw as I surveyed the aftermath. The stench of death hung heavy in the air, but I dared not look at the back corner of the room where I knew…where I knew they lay dead. Tamara held my right hand tightly while Aamin gripped my left, his knuckles turning white. At some point, the scene had paused, frozen in time as if waiting for us to make the next move.

In front of us stood a nightmare of a man with eyes the colour of blood and pupils the colour of broken porcelain. He was tall, gaunt, and terrifying, with skin as pink and hairless as a new-born rat. In his hand, he held a burned page, the only clue we had to the mystery that had brought us here.

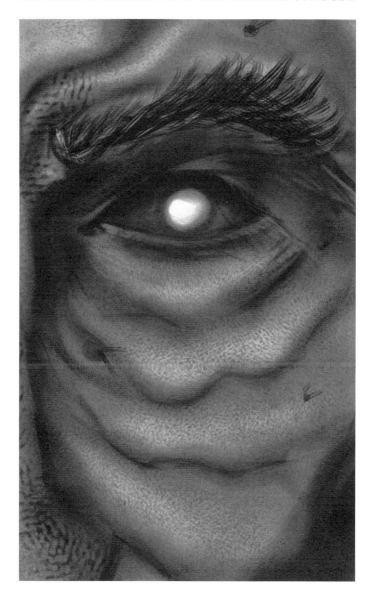

Deep in my gut, I knew this was what we had come here to see. This part of the nightmare, however, was new to me. I had always woken up before I could see this—before I could see my parents' bodies piled in the corner of the room, uncaringly, with their cold, dead eyes watching me.

But this time, I wasn't alone in this nightmare. Together as one, we walked forward towards the man with his sunken eyes and gangrenous nails that clutched the burnt page, as if it were the key to some unspeakable evil.

My heart pounded in my chest as we closed in on him, his horrid eye's locked onto us with a ferocity that made my blood run cold. Aamin reached out to take the page from the man's hands, but I couldn't take my eyes off his face. It was so lifelike, so vivid, as if he had stepped out of my dreams and into reality.

SNAP!

"Ahhh!"

We screamed, jumping in surprise as the monster's hand shot out.

The sound of bone cracking echoed through the room, sending shivers down our spines. Aamin's hand was taken in the grasp of the monster, and we had to act fast. Tamara rushed to his aid, but the man's grip was unyielding. I watched in horror as his lifeless eyes stared back at me. Was this even possible? Could he hear us?

"Help me, Léonidas!" Tamara shouted as she struggled to free Aamin.

With a sudden surge of anger, I let out a fierce cry, tears streaming down my face as I launched myself at the killer. His eyes remained fixed on me as his hand released Aamin's and shot out to grab me. I felt his fingers wrap tightly around my neck, crushing my windpipe, and lifting me into the air.

I gasped for oxygen, struggling to breathe, as my friends tried to free me. Tamara kicked at the man's shins while Aamin attempted to break his arm, but he was too strong. I felt my vision fading, my eyes heavy with exhaustion. And then, I saw it—the burnt page was falling to the ground.

We had come here for a reason, and I knew deep in my gut that we needed what was on that parchment. This was more than just a nightmare; it was a vision. We had to retrieve the information on that page, no matter what it took.

As I struggled to breathe, I watched as it finally landed on the floor. It was losing its hold in time, and we had to act fast for my gut told me that piece of paper was why we were here.

With my last breath I rasped, "The page, read the page."

Aamin looked confused but Tamara, she understood. Diving for it, she read it aloud.

"Lost, Ancient, forgotten and old, A great power will rise that was long foretold, When fae born prince becomes god-blessed—"

PUFF! The monster holding me vanished, I fell to the ground wheezing for breath. I was getting over falling on my arse but at least I could breathe again.

"The rest is missing... No, wait. There are a few lines at the very bottom. Glory, fame and fortune beyond measure, is what awaits this powerful successor."

"What do you suppose it means?" she asked.

"It's clearly referring to Léon, god-blessed fae prince, is there another one in this realm? No."

Tamara read it aloud once more. This time I got to my wobbly legs and with Aamin, read over her shoulder.

There were twenty-four lines marked on the page but as Tamara had said only five remained. It was just the top of the page and the bottom, the middle was currently beyond reading.

"Lost, Ancient, forgotten and old, A great power will rise that was long foretold, When fae born prince becomes god-blessed...Glory, fame and fortune beyond measure, is what awaits this powerful successor."

With a start of realisation the three of us said aloud, "Prophecy!"

Colour dripped like liquid paint as the scene around us changed. As the colours began to shift, swirls of gold, cream, and black mixed together, turning into a sickening display of reds, browns, and mustard yellows. The ground beneath us changed, transforming into a field of death, bodies strewn about in twisted, grotesque positions. The stench of decay filled our noses, as the screeches of crows echoed around us, drawn to the rotting flesh.

My heart felt heavy as I looked into the faded eyes of a man whose life had been taken too soon. Tamara was over-whelmed, she doubled over and vomited. Aamin was in shock, his face drained of all colour.

"This is the future, it must be," Tamara whispered, an expression of horror painted across her face. We were inside her vision, but never before had we been confronted with such a grim reality.

As we tried to make sense of the scene before us, thick smoke began to billow around, creating a hazy cloud that obscured our view. Suddenly, a voice spoke, sending chills down our spines. It was low and serpentine, full of malevo-lent intent.

"If on your journey you should fail, all you love will meet death's pale," the voice hissed. '"Prince of the fae, beware and heed, Evil's hunger grows with greed. Stand tall, seek the prophecy whole, Or risk losing not just your soul. Your journey starts, find the way, With friends close, through night and day. But beware the snakes in the grass, Ready to strike as you pass. For not all will have your back, Many have agendas, ready to attack."

"What do you mean!" I called after the voice but it was too late, the fog had vanished and a new scene was appeared before us. Tamara, Aamin, Coco, Atticus, and myself lay dead on the ground. A figure stood beyond us, naked and covered in blood. He laughed, a sound akin to rusty nails on a chalkboard.

"HA HA HA."

Whoosh

Bang

Pop

The feeling of someone grabbing me by the nape of my neck and pulling me through thick, sticky mud returned me back to reality.

Blinking, I soon realised I was once more in the classroom. Turning my head, I saw that all three of us were. A distraught professor stood watching us.

"What did you see?"

"Errr," I began.

Tamara, Aamin, and I shared a look. *What do we do? What do we say?*

PRENEURS DE MAGI I

On the late afternoon streets of Greenock he hunted. A foul mood had fallen over Jacquard. Whatever spark of grace or humanity he'd once owned had finally extinguished. It seemed as though the fact he was so close to having the boy yet was still so far was more maddening than if he were still searching for hope. Addiction was a funny rabbit in that way.

Holmscroft Street was busier the usual, the normally vacant back street was sadly filled with people exiting the red brick of St Patrick's Roman Catholic church. It appeared to have been a wedding celebration. Women wore colourful frocks and men dressed in Prince Charlie jackets and kilts of a familiar tartan.

Jacquard hated weddings, he personally wished the marrying couple all the unhappiness and marital misery. Once upon a time Jacquard had once held similar desires of the flesh, though in his pursuit of power he'd sold that emotional ability early on. In a way one could say that he was forever chaste.

He wore a simple beggar disguise, after all people were unkind and hated to be caught looking at the homeless, often this meant they were the most invisible in society. This train of thought was correct for not one person spared him a single glance.

A fiery drought itched Jacquards veins, he needed to feed. Subconsciously, he scratched his right cephalic, which was the main vein in his wrist.

Turning down Mount Pleasant Street, he caught a lucky break, not in the way he had thought but in the form of a newspaper tumbling in the wind. Jacquard didn't know why he did it but he reached out a filthy hand and snatched it right out of the air. The headline read "The last of the Nazi spies executed today by hanging."

A smile bubbled at his thin lips, *Now a spy, that was an idea*, he thought. Someone to lure the god-touched fae prince from the protection of the school that kept him safe.

Walking down the rest of the street, he had a renewed spring in his step. He knew precisely which family owed him a favour. There was a reason he hadn't been caught in all these years. In his early days he'd granted many favours with contracts of a blood oath nature. Pretty much all of the influential families owed him in some way and now the time to collect that of which they owed had finally come.

"Ohhh, from the place where they are hiding, slipping sliding they come gliding, short and tall see them all, shake like gelatine at the skeleton raaaag," he sung on his merry little way. Passers-by hurriedly tried to hide their children as he went by.

"An insane person," one said.

"Timmy, don't listen," said another, but they were safe this day for this news meant Jacquard had bigger fish to fry.

"At the skeleton raaaaaag."

CHAPTER 11

THE MILLION BOOK LIBRARY

LÉONIDAS I

W e sat opposite the headmistress. Her apple-green eyes watched us intently. Her lips pursed with what I could only assume was displeasure.

"Tell me again what the three of you saw in Miss Masayá's vision."

The three of us hadn't had a chance to decided what we were going to say but it seemed a partial truth was what we favoured.

"An empty void," said Aamin.

"And a lot of smoke," added Tamara.

"Yes and a red light," I finished.

"Did you see any shapes in the void? Nothing is too small, every detail matters in a divine vison," Headmistress Guaire pushed.

We shared another look as if trying to speak tele-pathically.

"I think I saw a snake in the foggy smoke," Aamin lied.

"A snake?" she asked sharply. "Hmm, that could mean mistrust. What else?"

"Maybe a raven or a crow?" I suggested, after all it wasn't a lie...exactly. There had been plenty of them feasting on dead bodies.

"Ravens often mean a need to seek a purpose. Why do I feel you three are telling me half-truths? Now the question is why? You must remember a problem shared in a problem halved." She echoed a sentiment my grandma would use all the time. It didn't work though, if anything the three of us zipped our mouths shut tighter.

Knock knock knock

"Come in," sighed the headmistress.

In walked a second-year student with a freshly split lip. He was accompanied by Professor Bodhi, his characteristic tasselled hat made for easy identification. I think he taught advanced Shakespearean Studies or something like that, I was pretty sure Coco was in one of his classes.

"Headmistress, I'm sorry to interrupt, but Mr Patrick here thought it prudent to start yet another round of fisticuffs with Mr Russell and Mr Duffy."

"Yeah they was askin' for it, they was," groused the student, crossing his arms.

Headmistress Guaire let out a short, sharp sigh.

"Very well, Masayá, Kebaikan, Nightshade, this conversation is *not* over. If you three think of anything else from the vison come find me at once, day or night. Is that understood?"

"Yes, Headmistress," we chorused.

"Mr Patrick, why do I have to see you almost every other week? The letters home are getting ridiculous."

. . .

210

Down the stairs, across a bridge, down more stairs, and across a courtyard, we finally felt free to speak.

"Do you think we made a smart decision? Lying to the headmistress and all?" asked Tamara, biting her lip.

"I don't know," I admitted.

"Personally, I think it was best, I mean what we saw was…" began Aamin.

"Crazy," Tamara and I said at once.

"Yeah, crazy," Aamin agreed.

"Should we tell Coco?" I asked.

"Tell me what?" said a voice behind us that made me jump right into the air.

"Coco, ummm how are you?" treed Aamin, aiming for cool, calm, and casual but failing hard.

Raising a brow she asked again, "Tell me what?"

"Do you always make it a habit to sneak up on people?" began Tamara.

"Tamara, you're not foolin' me, now cut the crap. Tell me what's got you three all spooked."

"How did you know we were here?"

She huffed a loud sigh. "Now you gotta be kiddin'. I saw you three practically flying down those darn stairs. You know I take legal studies in that building with Professor Arundell. Now come on, I'm a friend. I think I've proven that much. What's going on?"

As if the three of us were suddenly hit with the same verbal diarrhoea, words came pouring out. We told her how we fell into Tamara's vision, how the scenes seemed to drip away like liquid paint. We told her of the room where my parents had died and how I had always thought it was a nightmare but now it seemed that I was experiencing some sort of nightmarish memory, one that wasn't my own. We spoke of the burnt prophecy and its burnt missing lines.

Finally we spoke of the rotting bodies being feasted on by the crows and the fog like smoke that slivered its warning of what a journey ahead and what was to come if we failed.

"And you didn't think to tell all this to the headmistress?" she said in utter disbelief. "You realise lyin' to the headmistress is a punishable offence, right? Like it's expellable."

"But the voice said——" I began.

Coco cut me off. "Said what? Commit crimes?"

"No. But——"

"But what, sweetcakes? This is serious!"

Both panicked and pissed off, I raised my voice. "The voice said 'Your journey starts, find the way, With friends close, through night and day. But beware the snakes in the grass, Ready to strike as you pass. For not all will have your back, Many have agendas, ready to attack...' or something like that, there was a lot of rhyming going on."

Coco stopped and fell deep in thought. After a while she asked, "Tell me everything the voice said. Be as accurate as possible."

It was Aamin who spoke up next. "I remember it all." A shiver ran through him before he recited it all to Coco. After he finished talking, Coco fell into silent thought once more. It must have been five minutes or so before she spoke again.

"Okay, I'll give you that—maybe not telling the headmistress til we know more was a sound idea. But, Léon, and I can't stress this enough. *Never* raise your voice at me again unless you want to be turned into a toad. Got that, sugar?"

"Sorry, Coco," I said earnestly, though I couldn't meet her eyes.

"No need for an apology, just don't do it again," she said this before adding, "now you mentioned something about a partial prophecy?"

We nodded.

"Then it's probably best we head to the library, though something tells me that I won't be getting much sleep tonight."

Coco led us to the tallest tower in the whole of the Amethyst city castle complex. The tower was so tall that it was impossible to see its end from the ground. I had never been to this particular library before, though I had explored two smaller ones on the castle grounds. This one, however, had an air of mystique and wonder about it.

As we approached the door, Coco turned to me with a solemn expression. "I must warn you," she said, "first years are not permitted inside this library."

"Why not?" I asked, intrigued.

Coco's eyes twinkled with mischief. "Legend has it that this library contains a copy of almost every book, codex, and scroll ever written. But some of the texts are too mature for young eyes."

"How many books is that?" Aamin asked.

Coco grinned mischievously. "Oh, they call it the Million Book Library for a reason."

A million books—now that was a lot of reading.

Tamara's face scrunched in annoyance. "Why haven't we heard of it before?"

Coco's smile faded slightly. "Because as first years, none of your classes require books from this facility. You have access to four other libraries."

Tamara still seemed dissatisfied.

"Why are there so many libraries, anyway?" Aamin asked.

"Well there is the Normals Library which contains a large selection of books from the non-spellcaster world. Then there is the Spellcasters Library with an even larger selection of books and texts from our world. Followed by the Fae Library—"

"Wait, there's a Fae Library?" I cut in.

"Yeah, sugar, but there ain't that many books. I think maybe just eleven or twelve."

Wow, there was a Fae Library, maybe I could get some answers, answers to personal questions that no one seemed to know the answers to or at least were not inclined to tell me.

"The last library is the Royal Library, which I haven't personally ever seen because only royal blood is allowed in."

Aamin shrugged. "The inside looks like a cult den. I left pretty much as soon as I saw what was inside."

"Which was?" This time Coco asked the question.

"A pretentious display of wealth."

"Ah well no surprise there." Coco nodded.

The door to the Million Book Library resembled the school's entrance by which I meant that it had no door, just a place where a door should be. Like the most of the school, the exterior was made from amethyst, though like some of the older parts of the castle city, it had this almost glowing blue wisteria growth. If one was not looking for this building it would be quite easy to miss.

Pulling out her wand she drew what I could only assume was an entrance charm, much like the one for entering the school walls. Coco started down before lifting the tip in an arch before pulling it down and diagonally. With a breathy laugh, I realised she was drawing a star. To enter the Million Book Library all one had to do was draw a star with their wand.

ATTICUS VALOR I

In the infirmary, I sat waiting for a Doctor Upuaut to see me. I was absolutely furious. I couldn't believe what I'd done. What a complete embarrassment, losing control like that. Me, of all people! And everyone watching! The scandal it would be in the newspapers for damn sake. There I was working on my metalwork project, welding the frame of the motorcycle together when I vaewolfed out. I couldn't control it, my left hand just shifted of its own accord. Destroying the left glove and damaging the work bench I was using, which now had a gaping claw mark right across it.

Why was my vaewolf not listening to me? Normally I had almost complete control but ever since that boy appeared... I sighed bitterly. What more could I do? I hunted every single bloody night, I'd never had to do that to satisfy the beast, not even as a youngling. What's more as recently I'd begun to feel when he was near, as though my vaewolf would turn its head in the direction. The only benefit to this was it made avoiding him a lot easier, but that wasn't a solution. If I couldn't control him then I'd need to leave the school, it was that simple. I wouldn't put others at risk like that.

In walked Doctor Upuaut, a fiery redhead doctor with a uniform so starched you could practically eat off it. A small silver wolf-shaped lapel pin denoted his rank as a wolf shifter specialist.

"What can I do for you, Mr Valor?"

"I'm not entirely sure you can do anything."

He raised his brow as if saying, "Is that a challenge?"

"As I understand it, you partly shifted against your control during metalwork? Is this correct?"

"Yes." I reluctantly nodded, this was stupid.

"Why do you think that is?"

"I don't know otherwise I wouldn't be here would I," I partially lied. I knew deep in my bones that it was because I was denying my mate. But a male mate? Who'd ever heard of that. Gods were merciless in that way.

Doctor Upuaut proceeded to run a series of tests, knocking my knee with whatever that little hammer was called, checking my weight and height, drawing some blood for blood work and finally checking my pulse.

"All seems to be within normal parameters for your kind, your pulse is a little high but that could be chalked up to stress over the unwanted shift. I'm going to prescribe you a set of neutralising sedatives. This should help control your beast."

"How?" I asked suspiciously.

"The pill is called Animperium."

"Animperium?"

"It's a kind of shifter suppressant. Take one a day till you feel like you have regained control over your beast."

"I don't know, doc, if I feel comfortable taking pills."

"Why? There is nothing to worry about. We prescribe hundreds of medications for students. Trust us, we know what we are talking about."

Being drugged didn't sound like a safe alternative.

"Isn't there a spell you could use instead?"

"No, magic should not be misused like that."

Right....and medication should be? Whatever. I didn't care. Anything to stop this craving for...him.

217

Doctor Upuaut handed me a small white bottle with thirty blue pills inside.

"Come back in a month for a prescription refill."

Leaving the infirmary, pill bottle in hand, I headed to my house tower.

I was passing the restricted library when I caught his scent. My throat instantly evaporated all moisture and a carnal craving for his blood filled me, my vision darkened, the shift was upon me.

"Noooo," I grunted out, I wasn't going to be able to stop it...wait, I had the pills, quickly I took out a blue pill and swallowed it down, it tasted like dry yogurt that had turned for the worst. The pill was powdery without a normal waxy coating. It dissolved quick, I only hoped it was fast acting.

LÉONIDAS II

The library was unlike any other, much like all things within this castle city. It was a marvel to behold. Its atmosphere was unique, with a musty scent that lingered throughout, hinting at the age of the volumes that filled the towering shelves.

Amidst the room, there stood a set of polished wooden desks and chairs, which seemed to be intended for reading. The walls were adorned with an endless spiral of shelves, which one could traverse using a set of accompanying stairs. I marvelled at the sight, wondering if the tower had a conclusion, or if its ascent was eternal.

"Thankfully we're lucky, no one is here to check that you aren't permitted to be here, few classes prescribe reading material that would require students to come to this specific library," said Coco.

We made our way to the back corner and established a sort of encampment, hoping to remain undetected. Each of us procured a fresh notebook from a pile in the corner and looked to Coco, our appointed leader. We relied on her guidance, and it was only natural to defer to her for judgement.

"Ok let's start with the prophecy. What do we know?" Coco began.

Aamin raised his hand.

"Yes, Aamin?"

"The prophecy had twenty-three lines—"

"No it didn't, it had twenty-four," corrected Tamara.

"Ok, it had twenty-four but only the beginning and end survived. The middle of the prophecy was caput."

"Twenty-four lines." Coco Scribbled on the page. "Who remembers what the surviving lines were?"

We were silent as we thought back.

"Come on, someone must remember," Coco said, exasperated. "Think."

"Lost, Ancient, forgotten and old, A great power will rise that was long foretold, When fae born prince becomes god-blessed," I said, surprising myself. "And the last part went: Glory, fame and fortune beyond measure, Is what awaits this powerful successor."

Coco hurriedly wrote it down.

"Now what was it that voice said?"

This time it was Tamara who answered, "If on your journey you should fail, All you love will meet death's pale. Prince of the fae, beware and heed, Evil's hunger grows with greed. Stand tall, seek the prophecy whole, Or risk losing not just your soul. Your journey starts, find the way, With friends close, through night and day. But beware the snakes in the grass, Ready to strike as you pass. For not all will have your back, Many have agendas, ready to attack."

"So you remembered not much at all then," laughed Coco sarcastically.

"Pffft, the voice was scary," said Tamara in her defence.

On a separate page Coco jotted down the voice's warning.

"So we have the prophecy or what's left of it and the warning attached, I think now because it was a 'vision' the next practical thing is to write down and make a list of any and all visual, audible, and sensory symbols to cross-reference with some of the seer guides and prophetic ciphers."

Aamin raised his hand. "I'll do that, I like the symbol side of things."

Coco nodded. "Then that can be your task, don't miss anything, nothing is too small. Even a smell or change in smell could tell us something vital." Aamin agreed and set about collating a list.

"Tamara, maybe you can look through a list of libraries said to hold prophecies and see if we can narrow down where that room you mentioned was."

"On it," she responded, immediately getting to the task.

"What will I do?" I asked expectantly.

"You can—" began Coco.

"Ahhhh" A cry of pain broke the silence. Instantly Coco and I stood looking at each other, someone was in pain. Together we went to investigate. Aamin and Tamara were about to join us, but Coco waved them back to the task at hand. After all we weren't supposed to be in here.

Coco opened the door, it appeared that the locking enchantment only worked one way. People leaving wasn't the issue. it was people getting into places where they shouldn't be...like us.

Peering over the corner of the door like a slinking cat, Coco surveyed the outside scene.

"Ahhhh" cried the voice again. I didn't wait for Coco's assessment, something deep in my chest where my soul lived called me into action. I couldn't explain it yet here I was pulling the door that was only visible on this side of the wall all the way open, startling Coco. I only sent her a passing thought of apology. I *had* to move. My body was telling me I needed to check on this...person.

I ran out onto the lawn where I saw...where I saw... nothing. There was no one there. I looked at Coco in complete confusion. Had I imagined that? That pull?

ATTICUS VALOR II

I bolted out of there, the second I heard the unmistakable lock and caught a fresh whiff of his aroma, his scent, his blasted siren's song. Mid-shift or not I had to get out of there. I'd never let anyone see me like this. Let alone the one the gods had cursed me with.

The effects of blue pill thankfully had started to set in, I could feel a disconnection with my vaewolf like a muting of the bond. It was just enough for me to regain temporary control over myself. Thankfully just in the nick of time.

My hands shook as I pulled out a blood fag which I desperately lit and took in a large huff of its blood-infused goodness. I didn't care who'd see me breaking the school rules, I needed my craving fixed and that was that. The only real question I found myself asking was if it was too early to go out hunting. Not so much people seeing me, more if any of the bigger beasts would be out to play yet.

No, the moon had only just started its rise. Nothing worth hunting would be out yet. I'd have to wait until after dinner. During which I'd have to gorge myself on blood-infused wine to try to keep my cravings at bay.

Tonight it would have to be something big or maybe a few somethings. Either way, a bear on its own wouldn't cut it.

Fuck the gods.

CHAPTER 12

A POSSIBLE PLAN

LÉONIDAS I

Dinner that night was filled with charged energy, Aamin and I barely spoke a word the entire time. Both of us were still mentally back at the library where Tamara, Aamin, Coco, and I had spent over two hours trying to decipher what the vison, the prophecy, and well what everything in between meant. We had come to two consecutive conclusions; we must tell no one, and trust no one outside our group. We also agreed that time was of the essence. So much so that the four of us were going to return to the library after dinner if we could sneak away.

I was halfway through a pumpkin risotto topped with pine nuts when I felt his eyes on me once more. Atticus Valor was rather odd. If I were to look up he'd have already averted his eyes. But as I was eating I could feel his hungry eyes transfixed on my neck. Aamin had previously told me this so I was able to associate the sensation with the reality.

Strangely though, I didn't mind, I had grown to be comforted by it in a peculiar sort of way.

Dinner was also the only time we ever saw each other theses days. I knew he was an arsehole of epic proportions but there was this feeling in my chest that bloomed when I knew he was staring at me. I couldn't explain it, but for some weird reason I desperately wanted to.

When the final dinner bell rang Aamin and I hurried back to the library.

We had made it about a block away from the building when something strong yanked me by my neck.

"Ahh!What the—" I yelled as I was pulled backwards.

Aamin stopped and turned around.

"Where do you think you're going?" said the low honeyed voice of Atticus Valor.

"Let me go!" I grimaced, trying to wriggle free of his iron grip. Unfortunately, I soon learned that unless he wanted to let me go there was no freeing myself, he was that strong.

"Atticus, let him go, we are just going for a walk, what is it to you anyway?"

"If you're just going for a walk mind if I join the two of you? I mean if it's just a walk then you won't mind a chaperone."

Aamin and I shared a look. How the hell were we going to distance ourselves. Just when I thought we would have to go on some wild walk around the school, the unmistakable sound of Coco's Hollywood voice rang clear.

"Atticus, it's fine. I will chaperone the first years."

A flash of anger crossed his face before it vanished into something like nonchalance.

"Two is better than one—" he began.

"Yes, but as I'm a prefect I think I should be fine. After all, we're safe within these school walls."

"Fine, whatever, I don't care. Suit yourselves."

Atticus still hadn't let go of my collar. Did I want him to let me go? Wait why wouldn't I want him to?

CONFUSION!!!!!!!

But it was Coco who made the decision for me.

"Atticus, can you let go of Léonidas's shirt?"

As if he only just realised he was indeed holding me in the air, he dropped me immediately.

"Sorry," he mumbled tersely, a few seconds before he turned and walked away.

"What a weird guy," commented Aamin.

"Yeah," I agreed though I was puzzled by what I saw in Coco's eyes. But as quick as it appeared whatever it was had gone.

The three of us met up with Tamara outside the library before checking if the coast was clear. It appeared we hadn't been followed, though I still felt a familiar gaze watching me. But no matter how hard I looked I couldn't see him. I was probably just being paranoid.

Four hours later we had complied a pretty comprehensive list of imagery versus what it meant in regards to symbolic divination. A lot of the iconography from Tamara's vison told us a story of forced change, war, and tough decisions ahead—although we were not able to distil a particular time when this was all supposed to happen. It could be today or six years from now. I could tell the fact we had to keep this a secret from the headmistress was weighing heavy on Coco's mind, as a prefect this was literally her job to report. But due to the warnings in the vision she held her tongue and not just that she helped us regardless of the consequences that could come. This was what a true friend was and I couldn't believe I had found three of them. I was truly blessed.

I was currently looking through *A Seer's Guide to Partial Prophecies* by J. T Shearman.

'Through time many prophecies have been lost due to both the persecution and murder committed by the Roman Catholic Church on various polytheistic faiths that worshipped and cared simply for the land. It is unverified but is suspected that in the rumoured Vatican vault holds a scribed version of many of the prophecies that have been destroyed though the vault is said to be protected by the darkest of magics - Hate.

Some have found luck in retrieving more of the lost partial prophecy by invoking the three Moirai. Though this author strongly advises against such practices for the fates will ask you for a favour which you must pay. Moving on we have the Egyptian method of prophecy—'

Putting the book down, I called Coco over. "I think I've found something that may help us."

After bookmarking her place in whichever volume she was reading, she sauntered over. Wordlessly I handed the book over, after a quick read she handed it back.

"Possibly a solution, but I am worried about the favour they may ask. How do we not know the favour is what brings us all down in the end? But this has given me an idea..."

"It has?" I said, hopeful.

"Yes."

Coco took off up the staircase, three at a time. I sat there and watched as she spiralled up and up the stairs above us. I turned to Tamara; she was reading a thick leather volume with no title on the cover.

"What are you reading?" I asked her.

It took her a minute but she finally responded, her accent was thicker than usual probably due to how tired we all were.

"It is called *Théorie du Royaume des Fays: Une Étude Théorique*. It's an account on fae by a French historian Verdi Confeté from around the mid-15th century. His handwriting is so petite it's a rather slow read, I must say."

"A book on the fae?" I perked up. I was still to learn anything about my kind. Was this book a window into that?

"Don't get your hopes up, it's pretty vague on detail."

"Oh…" I said, slumping back in my chair.

She must have seen something on my face before she quickly added, "But, err there was this passage about how fae can summon creatures and magic from across the veil."

"Does it say how?"

"Err no, no it does not."

"Oh."

"Guys, I think I found something!" called Coco as she ran down the stairs, holding what appeared to be the largest book I'd ever seen. It was so large it covered her torso; the more I stared at it the more it kind of reminded me of that old spell book the queen used in *Snow White*—such a great film.

Aamin, Tamara, and I hopped to our feet as Coco approached in expectation of what she must have found.

With an audible puff Coco dropped the book onto the table. A thick layer of musty dust covered her uniform.

"Ehh. Yuck." She grimaced as she realised her grievous error.

Aamin laughed but quickly muffled it as Coco sent him scathing glare.

The book was titled *Pious Potions* by KJ Harding.

"The idea of talkin' to the fates reminded me of a conversation I had in Tinctures, Tonics, and Spelled Brews with Professor Evans last year. It was about the crossover between divination and potion studies."

"There is a crossover?" I asked, surprised.

"Yeah, sweetcakes, it's called reflection work, where we spell a potion to act as a divine mirror."

"Right, and through the reflection we will see what is to come," said Tamara as if she should have thought of this long ago. I was still confused and by the look on Aamin's face he was also.

"You got it, sugar," Coco confirmed as she opened the giant book. Dust puffed into the air, it didn't seem that this book got brought out all that often...

"Hey, err, Coco." I stammered to ask.

"Mmm?" she responded absently as she thumped through the pages.

"Is there any danger in this course of action? Because the book is very dusty..."

"Oh yeah, but don't worry."

"You say not to worry but..." I trailed off.

"Well, it just...the water acts as window, we can see into it but that also means that what we see can also see us."

"Has this type of magic ever gone wrong?" asked Aamin.

"Yeah, but, fellas, we are after a piece of paper that was destroyed, paper don't have eyes," she said dismissively. "If the magic goes awry all we need to do is disturb surface of the water to the end the link."

"So you've done this before?"

"No, but have done all the theory, which is like doin' it."

"Is it?"

367

Harken ye to these words, for they
bear a solemn weight

A reflection from the charities doth call
for an arcane brew.
Gather ye powdered moonstone, the
sightless eye of a cat, and thyme, and with
these add a secret that might fray the
bonds of kinship. Boil them in a broth of
still water till sourness takes hold, then
on parchment inscribe thy heart's desire
If in their grace the charities deem thee
worthy, the water shall reveal thy truest
longing .

"Well I don't see you comin' up with any solutions, Aamin," Coco said hotly.

"Fair enough," conceded Aamin.

With a sigh of triumph Coco had found the page. The three of us looked over her shoulder eagerly. The book was thankfully written in English, though after quick glance of the words it was in an older English dialect. Not Shakespearean but like thirty percent of the way there.

"Harken ye to these words, for they bear a solemn weight: a reflection from the charities doth call for an arcane brew. Gather ye powdered moonstone, the sightless eye of a cat, and thyme, and with these add a secret that might fray the bonds of kinship. Boil them in a broth of still water, till sourness takes hold, then on parchment inscribe thy heart's desire. If in their grace the charities deem thee worthy, the water shall reveal thy truest longing."

"A sightless eye of a cat? That's rather horrid." I shuddered.

"Where would we even get one?" added Aamin.

"Professor Dilmah's artefact closet!" said Tamara and Coco simultaneously before they both broke into laughter.

"Professor who? Wait...why is this funny? I don't think I've meet him yet. Can you two stop laughing. I'm so confused," I begged.

It took about twelve minutes but finally the two of them stopped laughing. I glanced at Aamin, he was equally as confused as I.

"What great minds be thinkin' alike," explained Coco still with a trace of humour.

"Professor Dilmah teaches the third-year class of Witches Brew," added Tamara.

"Witches Brew?" I asked.

"It is where fictional potion-making meets reality."

By the look on my face Tamara elaborated further. "It's where you use symbolism in potion-making to create a spelled brew that does more fantastical things than what we learn in Professor Evans's class. Think Snow White and the poisoned apple or like in *Macbeth*."

Okay, so that kind of made sense.

"Wait…I thought calling someone a witch was offensive?" I asked Coco.

"That's when it used in relation to a person, sugar, here it's used in a historical sense."

"Right…"

"Trust me, it's different."

"So creepy ingredients equal creepy results?" interrupted Aamin, getting us back on topic. Even so I was still so confused about the use of the word witch and when it was offensive and when it was not.

"You got it, sweetcakes," Coco confirmed.

"Don't suppose Dilmah will just give us the ingredients if we ask?" asked Aamin.

"No, probably not," agreed Tamara.

"Well then we will just have to come up with a plan," declared Coco, placing her hand on the table.

It seemed we were now in a meeting of strategy that felt not unlike some war preparation…was this not actually a war we were heading into? Strange thoughts, scary reality.

ATTICUS VALOR II

Waiting to spring, I watched as the white stag drank from the silvery fresh water stream that refracted the moons glow. Its thick and glorious vein beat with the pulse of its heart, a sight that made my mouth water. I was not only

231

thirsty, but also filled with a fierce anger that brewed within me.

Léonidas was the cause of my anger, and the feelings that arose from our last interaction. I needed not only to feed, but also to kill. However, since this was a stag, I had to be cautious, for the network of horns that he wore as a crown could easily spear me with a mere turn of his head. I would not die, of course, but the healing process would be a tiresome endeavour that would take a day or two.

The stags were considered off-limits by my kin, due to their connection with the horned god of the forest, the very god who had cursed me. However, as the gods did not walk amongst us anymore, I had no fear of being caught, and killing his symbol might even bring a sense of relief.

Inhaling deeply, I detected no trace of fear from the creature. Now was the perfect time to strike, before the wind direction changed and the game was up. I sprang into the air with my teeth extended. This kill would be a kill to remember.

My claws went to strike and...

Hawoooooooooofff

As I moved in for the kill, the creature turned to face me at the very last second. A burst of extreme white light blasted me back, and the surroundings cleared away like dripping paint. It was a stag no more—a bearded man appeared through the creature's form, his face one of fury.

"Atticus!" he called inside my head, his voice filled with barely controlled rage. His words rang like tower bells a moment before the rest of his form changed. The flesh bubbled and burst until before me, bathed in an all-consuming white aura, was a tall, naked, hairy man.

With a spike of fear I knew who this was.

"Cernunnos," I whispered, bowing my vaewolf head low. This was the god who had cursed me to lust after another male, and yet my duty demanded that I bow down to this figure. The injustice of it made my stomach ache.

"Atticus," he commanded, his voice echoing through the clearing. "You must stop fighting the mating pull."

"What mating pull?" I lied, for I dared not acknowledge the truth.

"Boy, you cannot lie to me," Cernunnos replied. "I see the thoughts in your head and hear the voices in your heart. Forget not who I am!"

"That's easy for you to say!" I yelled, finally breaking. I yelled inside my head as I was still in my vaewolf form. The fear and frustration building in me, like a kettle filled to the brim with boiling water, about to blow.

"Why are you resisting so? He is your fate, your destiny."

"Why a boy?"

"I do not understand your problem. Yes, the fae prince is indeed male. Why is this an issue?"

Did a god seriously ask me a question like this? He must know the torment he had inflicted on me.

"Men should not lie with another man as he does with a woman; it is an abomination," I responded, reciting the Catholic text used often in the norms' media.

"Says who?" the god queried, a look of disdained boredom spread across his godly features, the expression appeared ill-fitting for the divine being's face.

"Everyone!" I yelled bitterly. I hadn't realised, but at some point I had changed back to my human form. I lay naked on the ground beneath the feet of the towering god.

An insect, a servant, a slave to the god's will.

"Name the god who decrees this law and I shall summon them here to answer for such stupidity."

"I can't name the god for society just calls them God."

Laugher unlike anything this world erupted from the bearded god.

"Are you not a son of the Valor lineage?"

"Yes," I said curtly.

"Then, according to your rules I *am* your god and I do not say or decree such idiotic foolery. My ruling is this; you are to love your mate. For if you keep ignoring your destiny, for that is what he is, I will curse you a life of unimaginable horrid pain. Every step you take from this day forward will increasingly get more and more painful until each step you take is like walking on broken glass coated in fire ants. Do you understand me, Atticus Valor?"

"They will never understand!" I yelled.

"I care not for the opinions of man, humanity's 'rules' are not those of the gods. Ignore me again and you will regret it."

And with that the light flashed away leaving behind only shadow. What was I going to do? Turning my head skyward, I howled a song of pain and fury. My life was never my own, I was never given a choice and I would never be given one.

PRENEURS DE MAGI I

The room was grandiose, thrice the size of a typical abode. Seated around a colossal cast iron table were thirty-six of the Preneurs De Magi, their faces etched with a sense of avidity. At the head of the table sat Jacquard Morioatus, garbed in his true form, which was grotesque to the core. The folds of mole rat skin and wrinkles seemed to be ingrained upon his face. He appeared to be profoundly content for he had successfully hatched a new plan.

On the table, an enormous feast had been laid out, consisting of the most putrid human flesh one could imagine. It had been pickled and stewed, roasted and barbecued, smoked and boiled. However, this feast wasn't meant for them to devour, but rather to serve as an offering to the Kêres, which had infested their very souls. These Daemons were the reason why the Preneurs De Magi could pilfer and feed on a being's magical essence.

The followers of this nefarious cult had long since relinquished their own souls in exchange for that of these Daemons. In order to sustain their agreement with the Daemons, these creatures needed to be fed periodically; otherwise, there was a risk of them taking permanent control of their hosts. The Preneurs De Magi were careful to ensure that this never transpired, for living like a marionette would feel like some abominable, suffocating nightmare.

"We are gathered here today to say our thanks to the Kêres for granting us eternal life and power," Jacquard spoke with sly reverence.

"We give thanks!" chorused the room in a toast to their allies in darkness.

Glasses clinked.

"As they have so blessed us, we offer up to them this feast of decadent delights. May they bless us for many years to come!"

A round of cheers echoed once more around the creepy cult as they gave their audible appreciation to the Daemons who not just owned their souls but also inhabited them as well.

For this spellcasting ritual Jacquard chose to chant in

Latin as words written in this language were used often to persecute, demonise, control, and kill in modern society, so it held much in dark magics more so than in Ancient Greek or Afroasiatic languages.

Jacquard knew this incantation well but all these years later he still chose to lean into the theatricality of it by pulling out the old worn, tan book titled *Daemonium Malum Magicae*. It was the kind of book that one's brain automatically hears ghostly screams and thunder cracking away in the distance.

He flicked his way through to a page just beyond the middle of the book. The page in question held no title or set of instructions that one would assume to see for a such a ritual act. In a neat script centred on the page was the phrase *vos daemones vocamus, oblationem nostram sumite.*

Dragging a calloused hand across the page, he began the spell. Lifting his head skyward, they all began the chant, "vos daemones vocamus, oblationem nostram sumite,"

Eleven times the spell was repeated but it wasn't until the twelfth and final time that something magical happened. Slowly, skin took on a burning pink hue as skulls elongated and bones sprouted. The creaking and cracking, a sound scape of horror.

The only person in the room who remained seemingly unchanged was Jacquard though his pupils shone that little bit brighter.

CHAPTER 13

BREAK AND ENTER...
SCHOOL RULES? WHAT
SCHOOL RULES?

LÉONIDAS I

The next morning Aamin dragged me along to watch a sports match between the house teams. Sportwise at Amethyst, there was football, rugby, and a game that was like an extreme obstacle course that combined tactical knowledge, strength, endurance, and magical prowess or at least that's what Aamin told me. I kind of knew how football and rugby went so as I got to choose which one we were to see I went for the extreme tactical course.

"Who's playing today?" I asked.

"No clue which students, but it's Autumn and Summer's turn to face off."

"Cool."

The games took place in one of the school colosseums in the back west fields of the castle city near the merge point with the cliff. It was quite a long journey to walk so on our way we called into Shula's Shakes—a malt milkshake bar that only used the freshest of milk from cows living somewhere on the island.

We placed our order, which was a strawberry malt for Aamin and a vanilla malt for myself. While we waited, we perused through the selection of candies the bar sold, these seemed to look more artisanal than the other stores selling candy I had gone into whilst I had been at Amethyst. Luckily Aamin paid. I hadn't any money for such luxuries. My pride did sting but as he had reminded me time and time again, money for him was no issue. But to me it wasn't about the money, it never was.

Before long Shula handed us our shakes and we were back on our way.

Sitting in the colosseum we sipped our malt milkshakes through candy cane-striped straws while we waited for the games to begin.

The colosseum was much like the crystal structure we had our dinner in, only there were no tables, it was completely open aired and people could sit wherever they wanted regardless of their social class. I liked it a lot more.

Horns trumpeted as two large crystal orbs floated into the air. Before I could ask what exactly they were images flickered across them, almost like at the picture theatre, only in incredible detail, no Vaseline here.

From separate doorways the two competitors walked out. For the summer house it was third year Daniel Piston —his name flashed across the orbs thankfully because I hadn't met him yet. The other competitor was...Atticus Valor. I didn't even need to see his name to know it was him. That face, those eyes, that gaze...it was unmistakable. As if he could hear my thoughts he turned and even from so far away made direct eye contact with me. I gulped as I broke out in an irrational sweat. I must be coming down with something. I was about to say as much to Aamin but an announcer spoke, and everything went quiet.

"Good morning, ladies, gentlemen, and those who are somewhere in between or simply not at all. Welcome to today's Match Olympia—"

There was a boisterous cheer from the audience, so loud in fact that I thought I might need a pillow to muffle the sound or else risk damaging my hearing.

What was Atticus doing? I could still feel his stare, always hungry, always devouring. Shouldn't he be warming up like the other contestant?

COCO & TAMARA I

Professor Dilmah's classroom was located in the same castle complex as the other chemistry rooms. The rooms were built and spelled in such a way as to resist explosions, which in particular was needed for his Witches Brew class, where explosions were unfortunately common. Magic and chemistry didn't always mix.

At the end of last night's book search a plan was hatched to "collect" or steal the ingredients necessary for the divine mirror potion. The plan started with Coco staying until the end of class and once the last student had retreated away to the next class, she would start asking a few questions about homework and if there were any tips to improving her already impeccable grades. Whilst this was taking place Tamara on the other hand would be causing a distraction. A distraction of which she had been practicing since before the break of dawn. It was some pretty advanced transfiguration magic, way beyond that of which she should be at skill wise for her age. Coco was pretty melancholy about the fact she was going to miss it. But like Tamara she had a job and role to play.

It was rather tricky convincing Léon and Aamin to be absent from this particular event but with the hawk-like gaze that was watching him by the headmistress, faculty, and bigoted student body it was deemed by the group as too risky. It was bad enough that Tamara was involved after her very public premonition but this plan heavily required two participants and out of the group Coco and Tamara had the best grades, so if all went south there was a higher chance of not receiving an expulsion.

Professor Dilmah was a short Punjabi man with a greying black beard and thick bushy brows. He belonged to the Sikh faith so he wore his hair up in a purple dastar turban that matched the school's uniform colours.

"This is why it is imperative to sanitise your cauldron before working with poultry, if the chicken contains salmonella it will automatically turn your spelled brew to that of a curse. So instead of creating say, a potion of prosperity, you have created a curse of disease."

DING

The class bell rang, signalling the end of class, students began packing their bags.

"Class, I will not see you before Sunday so please prepare for me an essay on potion hygiene, include three sources and at least one example of it going sour."

Dilmah turned his attention onto a student in the first row. "And, Abdul, if you turn in another paper that has under a thousand words you will be on detention, is that understood?"

"Sir, that was one time—"

"One time to many, now you all best be off."

Coco readied herself with the series of fake questions as the final students began to depart.

Outside the class room hidden behind an amethyst archway crouched Tamara, her spellcasters wand firmly in her hand. She took in a deep breath and began to channel her magic.

Her wand pointed towards the sky, she drew a tendril of magic into the air, her concentration unwavering. The sweat on her brow began to seep through her perfect makeup as she continued to push the magic with her diamond will. Tamara could feel her body trembling with the effort, but she didn't give up. She was determined to make this work.

Summoning all her strength, Tamara willed the magic to change form. She closed her eyes and visualized the end result in her mind's eye. As she focused on her intent, she felt the magic respond to her command. It was as if the universe was bending to her will.

With a mix of her determination and a few spelled words, Tamara began to grab the sunlight and bring it all together. Slowly but surely, a butterfly made of glistening stardust started to take shape before her very eyes. The beauty of the butterfly was breathtaking, and Tamara couldn't help but marvel at her own creation.

Breathing out a sigh of relief, she congratulated herself on making it this far but as she well knew the hardest part of the spell was still to come. She pulled out a vial of earth from her pocket and poured it in a perfect ring around the sleeping butterfly. Not stopping there, Tamara reached for another vial, this time filled with bone-white salt.

Quickly but steadily, Tamara began to salt the earth,

each grain of salt creating a crystalline pattern on the ground. She continued until the ring of earth looked snow-covered, and then it was time to begin the final spell.

Tamara took a deep breath, steadying her nerves. She knew that this was the most critical part of the magic, and any mistake could ruin everything. But she had come too far to back down now.

With a flick of her wand and a whispered incantation, Tamara unleashed the final spell. The air around her shimmered with magic, and the butterfly began to stir. Slowly but surely, the butterfly transformed before her eyes, growing larger and more magnificent by the second.

Tamara smiled in triumph. The spell was complete.

"Miss La Roux, I don't think I can make it any more simple. Look through your class notes and summarise why we need good hygiene—"

"But, Professor, what if I wanna be more in-depth with my paper," Coco lied.

"Fine, then visit the main library and pick up this book," said Professor Dilmah exasperatedly as he quickly scribbled down on a piece of paper.

Handing it to Coco, she read, "Basic Cauldron Hygiene by Michele Toxicosa."

"Now, Miss La Roux, you must go. I have another lesson to prepare for and—" A loud rumbling began outside the classroom that cut off the teacher. Frowning, the professor made his way to the classroom door.

"What is going on—HOLY HELLS!" he yelled.

"Stay here, Miss La Roux. It seems a giant butterfly has been let into the school!" And with that he withdrew his wand and ran out into the corridor.

"About time," mumbled Coco as she ran to the corner of the room where the door to the Witches Brew artefact closet was. Checking behind she quickly opened the door, walked inside, and shut it behind her.

Inside a glass jar a small blue flame flicked into existence, bathing the room in soft almost candle like light. The room was maybe the size of a standard kitchen with shelves upon shelves of boxed and veiled ingredients.

"Where do I start," breathed Coco, looking around in confusion. Pulling out the list of ingredients she began exploring the closest box.

Powdered wolf wort and silver fang seemed to make up the majority of ingredients in this particular box which was not what she needed so Coco moved onto the next one. And in this one she was finally in luck and found the blind cat eyes, they sat in a series of glass tubes stacked in a neat row. Coco, being the smart spellcaster she was, grabbed one from the very back as to not alert the teacher to the theft until enough time had passed. Now all she needed was the dead water and powdered Moonstone. The other ingredients she had already sourced.

LÉONIDAS II

The gun fired and the race began. Even though I had never thought of sport in any form of positive enjoyment, my eyes were fixed on the sculpted form of Atticus Valor. The red shirt stretched across his broad chest, creating stress ripples on the fabric. My mouth became wafer-dry and my cheeks burned. Whatever I was coming down with was falling on me fast. Would I even be able to last the match? Though I knew the answer to that because there was practically nothing that could tear my gaze away from Atticus.

A wooden tower was the first obstacle, according to the floating orb. I could see small little mounds of prickly clay scattered across the tower in an array of technicolour. Atticus was the first person to hit the wall, grabbing the mounds he began to climb his way up. Daniel was only a hair's breadth behind and within a second was also climbing up the wall.

"Hey, Aamin."

"Yeah?" he responded.

"What are those bands for on their arms?"

"They're magic blockers, they render the wearer mortal, no magic, no shifting, no healing."

"Oh," I said simply, returning my full attention back on Atticus, though I had asked a question my eyes never truly left him. What was this feeling in the pit of my stomach? Almost like anxiety? Had I eaten something strange?

Atticus, with a burst of adrenaline made it to the top of the towering wall, his muscles flexing with every move. But instead of basking in his victory, he took the ultimate plunge and dived into the crystal-clear lake below.

Not to be outdone, Daniel was quick to follow. He didn't just dive though, he executed a series of flips and spins, his face a mask of pure joy. It was clear that he was having the time of his life.

As the competitors emerged from the water, a new challenge was announced. The next obstacle would involve each of them retrieving a key hidden amongst the rocks at the bottom of the lake. The key would unlock the door to the next stage of the competition. The speaker's words were met with a collective gasp from the crowd, who watched in anticipation as the floating orbs changed to display underwater views of the two competitors.

Lost in wonder, I found myself transfixed by the image of the underwater world. I had never seen such beauty. The colours of the coral were breathtaking, ranging from shimmering blues to verdant greens and oranges so bright they seemed to glow. It was a wonderland unlike any other, and I couldn't help but imagine what it would be like to swim amongst such a magnificent display.

For a moment, I forgot about Atticus and Daniel, so captivated was I by the underwater realm. But as the orbs shifted, my attention was once again drawn back to the competition, and I knew that if I ever got the chance to experience something like this, I would leap at the opportunity. Maybe, just maybe, if I got to do things like swim amongst such serenity, maybe I would think about joining the team.

"Daniel Piston has found his key!" called the announcer, shaking me back to the match at hand. What had happened to Atticus? Quickly I found him on the glowing orb, his red sports trousers had got caught on a piece of coral and Atticus was failing to pull it free. The orb zoomed in and only stopped when Atticus's crotch filled the space. We could all see what was caught, it was the laces that secured his fly trapped around a pale blue coral that spiked up like a crown.

My face flushed, as if I were caught in a searing heatwave. My heart pounded with such intensity, it felt as if it might burst out of my chest at any moment. A sickening churning sensation twisted my gut, and I feared I might vomit. And then, to my horror, a sticky dampness began to pool in my crotch, making me feel as if I was caught in a sticky spider's web.

"I might need to see a doctor," I gasped, my voice barely above a whisper.

Aamin's eyes widened in alarm as he looked at me, concern etched across his face. "What's wrong, Léon?

247

Should I get a teacher?" he asked, examining the sweat that drenched my body.

"I think I've eaten something bad. My stomach is all twisted up, my crotch is swollen, and my heart won't stop racing," I replied, my words coming out in a jumble.

Aamin tried to reassure me, speaking in a soothing voice. But then, his expression shifted, and he asked in a higher-pitched voice, "Um, have you ever had this feeling before? Maybe at night or in the morning, with…a sticky sheet?"

My eyes widened in shock. "Yes, several times," I said, my voice trembling with fear. "Oh no! What's happening to me? Am I going to die?"

The panic on Aamin's face disappeared suddenly, but before I could process the change, there was a loud rip. Atticus had broken free from his restraints, but his pants had not fared so well. His see-through white underwear exposed him for all to see.

And then, something erupted inside me, a feeling I couldn't describe. It wasn't entirely unpleasant, in fact, it felt almost wonderful, but it also terrified me to the core. Meanwhile, the image of Atticus's exposed member seared itself into my mind, an unforgettably large image.

"I think I've been cursed!" I yelled at Aamin, as his face turned pink with…embarrassment?

"I don't think you've been cursed…"

"What do you mean?" I said panicked as my skin burned hot like a flame from a candle.

"Has your grandpa ever given you the talk?" he said awkwardly.

"'The talk'? Darn it, I think I've wet myself." Could the world please swallow me whole? "Quick. What's a counter curse to fix this? It was probably Braxton. He's been threatening me for so long—"

"Léonidas, this is not a curse. So, I take it he didn't give you the talk."

With Aamin's words I began to wish I had been cursed, the flush that had filled me quickly disappeared as I felt all colour drain from my skin.

ATTICUS VALOR I

Pissed off, I swam back to the shore, I had lost the contest. Stupid trousers. When would we get a better uniform? One actually designed for the water tasks. Daniel had beaten me. I couldn't go on, too much time had passed to have a god's hope of catching him. Once on land, I pulled the band off my arm, forfeiting the game. A loud ring filled the colosseum and the announcement of my failure broadcast to all.

What an embarrassment. If my mind wasn't so unfocused I'd have never gotten myself caught in the first place. Stupid horned god, stupid ma... The muting effects of the band had vanished and I was assaulted by wave after wave of pheromones but not just any pheromones, but sex pheromones from my mate. The scent was so strong that I froze where I stood, dripping wet in my underwear as if I had looked upon the eyes of a Gorgon sister and joined her garden. I could only breathe in as I looked up to the seats I knew Léonidas was sitting in.

My nostrils flared in anger the second my gaze fell upon Léonidas crying. I couldn't stop it, my body shivered as I let out a blood-curdling howl. Léonidas's red-rimmed eyes found mine and in the second I lost the ability to hold myself back any longer. My body shifted. It was as if hot water was being poured over me as midnight black fur pushed its way through my skin. In just a matter of seconds my human body had completely disappeared and I stood tall in my animal form. I felt free, though that feeling was only temporary as I registered what had just happened to me...in public. I spared my mate...I mean Léonidas, one last glance, his mouth was left agape, and I quickly bolted out of the colosseum. I wondered which student would be first to sell the story to the tabloids, gods for all I knew it could even be a teacher. I was an embarrassment to my family name, and the shame of the day felt far from over.

I headed for Metóporon Tower. I would change, shower, and send a message to my family. They would need to be contacted to hopefully stop this story from hitting the papers. I could already feel the disappointment from my mother and father. My head lowered just that little bit more as I ran away.

AAMIN I

The moment the words had left Aamin's lips, Léonidas had stood and began to back away. It had seemed he did not know, which confused Aamin immensely.

"No, you're wrong." He shook his head.

"Léon, I don't think I am...you were looking at Atticus."

"Yes but—"

"It's natural." Aamin tried to sooth, though it did only the opposite.

"I'm not…"

"It's okay if you are."

Angry tears began to fall down Léonidas's face.

"I'M NOT!" he yelled, and people began to pear over at the two. Léonidas quickly shoved his fists in front of the dark stain that soaked his crutch so that no one could see. The swelling had completely vanished the second Aamin told him what he had just experienced and why.

In a whisper Aamin added, "Men have liked men since the beginning of time, it's natural, truly it is—you have nothing to be afraid of."

But Léonidas didn't want to listen.

DING

"Atticus Valor forfeits the challenge, Daniel Piston wins! Breaking Valor's winning streak," boomed the announcer. Léonidas instantly looked down, his face a mix of horror and sadness. Aamin followed his gaze, staring at Léon was none other than Atticus Valor. With a howl everything changed.

LÉONIDAS III

My eyes were held captive, unable to break away from his piercing gaze. It was as if I had been captured and owned by him. Aamin's words rang true in my mind, the realization hitting me like a ton of bricks. I was attracted to men, but it wasn't just any man—it was Atticus Valor, the prince of the vaewolves. Everything I had been feeling since I'd first met him pointed to this undeniable truth. I was foolish not to have seen it before.

A fresh tear claimed my chin as home. It ran down and landed softly on my shirt. That was when I saw something unexpected, something so unbelievably magical and terrifying that I couldn't even catch my breath. A ripple of magic danced across Atticus's skin, and in an instant, his tanned flesh was replaced by the darkest black fur. I was afraid, but at the same time, I couldn't bring myself to look away. The transformation was so quick I feared I would miss it if I blinked. In place of the man who had stood before me was a mighty wolf, staring back at me with those same, familiar golden eyes.

I was terrified, but I remained rooted to the spot. The horror of the situation was undeniable, but there was a strange, inexplicable beauty to it as well. It was a beauty I couldn't explain, but I knew it was there.

I blinked and the spell was broken, the mighty wolf had run away. I was hit with a wave of crippling loneliness that drained almost all my energy. In an instant I wanted to do nothing more than to just crawl into bed and cry myself to sleep. It had been a long time since I had felt the need to do this. So long in fact I thought this darkness, this suffocation, this pressure on my chest had left me. But I was wrong for these feeling of being not good enough, of being nothing more than a burden had just been hidden away by a temporary cloud of foolish happiness.

A soft hand was placed on my shoulder. I wanted to take comfort in it but my mind had restarted and all I could process was I was not just dirt-poor, not just parentless, not just some weird mixed species but I was also now a queer pansy—as the likes of Braxton would call it.

Maybe Atticus had the right idea to run away, just leave this all behind…though the hand on my shoulder told me a different story, I may run but my friends would never let me leave alone.

How was I going to deal with this?

People couldn't know.

"It's okay," soothed Aamin.

"Please keep this a secret," I begged.

"You don't even need to ask," he promised.

Maybe in time I would forget this…curse, or even find a cure.

ATTICUS VALOR II

With a loud *smash*! I felt the weight of frustration and anger bubble up inside of me. "FUCK!" I growled, pulling my fist back from the shattered remains of the antique mirror. Blood poured from the torn skin on my hand, staining the Arctic fox rug that covered my room's exposed floor. It was a memento from a family hunting trip to Russia before I had started attending Amethyst.

I knew I was acting like an idiot, but I couldn't help the racing thoughts and explosive temper that had taken over my mind. My vaewolf stalked back and forth in my head, demanding that I give in and claim my mate in front of everyone. I had been fighting this urge for months, but I couldn't take it any longer.

With a defeated cry, I turned my head skyward and yelled out to the god of the forest, Cernunnos. "YOU WIN," I shouted. "DO YOU HEAR ME? I GIVE UP…I give up."

I fell to the floor, cradling my bleeding fist as angry tears streamed down my face. It was all too much to bear, and I couldn't fight this battle within myself any longer.

THE SPY I

They sat back and watched the display as their target made a huge fool of themselves. No one would suspect them. After all, their grades were some of the best the school had ever seen and now they had the *perfect* way to steal the boy away. They had to do this because their family owed a steep debt to the Preneurs De Magi. Thankfully, society was cruel and the voice in the right ear at the right time would create the perfect uncontrolled chaos. Luckily, outside in the norm world being a boy who was attracted to other boys was considered illegal and punishable by death and forced imprisonment in most countries. A plan was hatched and before the week's end Léonidas would be captured and taken to the Preneurs De Magi. All it ever takes is one flick and the house of dominos would always fall.

Sipping on a Shula's shake they tried their best to compose themselves. After all, it was no fun giving up the game before it had even begun.

CHAPTER 14

THE SCENT OF JASMINE AND DESPAIR

LÉONIDAS I

The end of the school day couldn't have come soon enough. I felt so disordered and anxious after what had happened. I even lied to my friends about feeling unwell so that I could hide up in my room and miss dinner. I just couldn't handle the constant looks given to me by Aamin that told me in no uncertain terms that I should tell them the truth. But how could I tell them a truth I hadn't even come to terms with? What if Aamin was wrong and I was actually sick? Sick of mind...

Ughhh, why couldn't my brain just slow down?

Coco and Tamara had been successful in their mission and had retrieved the needed ingredients for the ritual, which it had been decided we would complete on the following Monday night. I was both anxious about it and mildly excited about the task at hand.

Something wriggled in my mind, and when I poked at it, I flashed back to my first day at Amethyst. I remembered the story Coco had told me about the two female second years and the make-out session that turned into a non-consenting blood-drinking situation. That was the very first time I had ever heard of two people of the same gender being intimate together.

In the months that followed, I had sometimes, though rarely, seen a few couples holding hands, who appeared to be of the same gender. While it had never bothered me, I had never thought I was one of them, as though that was an option. I had heard Braxton call these types of couples "*pansies*" or "*queers*" and that this type of behaviour was abnormal. Shaking my head, I knew I had never listened to Braxton before, so why should I start now?

But the weight of Braxton's words bore down on me like a ton of bricks. *Ughhh*. I rolled over and hugged my pillow tightly as a fresh wave of despair poured out of my eyes. I hadn't felt this lonely and lost in months. The giant sea of a rocky chasm I had grown accustomed to feeling in my soul where the death of my parents had left me empty had begun to fill with joy and, dare I say, happiness which was entirely because of the love and support Coco, Tamara, and Aamin had given me from my first day. But now, I could feel it all draining away. Like the basin plug being pulled, I began to feel empty. The feeling was unbearable, and I knew that I needed to find a way to make it stop.

I wished my grandma was here to talk to, to hug me, to comfort me...would she even want too once she found out that I was...that I was...angry tears fell like rocky boulders cascading down a mountain. Through the chaos in my mind I saw two golden eyes that looked at me hungrily whilst Aamin's words replayed in my head.

"Men have liked men since the beginning of time, it's natural, truly it is—you have nothing to be afraid of."

ATTICUS VALOR II

Fiddling with my cuff links once more, I looked around the queue for dinner, but Léonidas was nowhere to be seen. Where was he? Dinner was mandatory so he had to be here.

Fuck this. I was over waiting. I had made a decision and now I had to act on it. Shifting just my ears, they grew into points as my hearing magnified a hundred times over. I sorted through voices like one sorted through record vinyls.

"Wendy, just pass the duck, Michael is a dead hoofer even if he has great peepers," said one particularly obnoxious student blowing out a bubble of gum.

"Brother, can you believe that Ace lost against Dan? I for sure thought he had it in the bag," said another student farther down the line.

My ears burnt scarlet with annoyance. I'd lost once, it wouldn't happen again.

I went through fourteen other conversations that my hearing picked up with a majority either talking about how I shifted or how I'd lost the match. With so many people talking about it I was sure I'd wake up tomorrow to find it spread across every single radio station and gossip column. If anyone else had lost this wouldn't even warrant anything more than a stupid conversation but because I was prince amongst the most powerful in the world it was bloody headline news. Pathetic, truly it was.

I was about to give up my search when I finally found a familiar name being spoken. I listened intently.

"Aamin darlin', don't you go tryin' to pull the wool over my eyes," Coco drawled, a glint of emotion in her accent. "I can spot a fib from a mile away, and you're not getting away with it."

She leaned in closer, her burgundy locks cascading over

her shoulder. "Now, spill the beans, sugar. What's the real deal with Léon? You know I've got a sixth sense for these things."

Coco's lips curled down in a threat.

"Don't keep me waiting, honey. The suspense is killing me."

"I'm not lying," retorted Prince Aamin.

I could however tell he was in fact lying about Léonidas. I was so honed in on their voices I could hear the subtle inflection of a partial truth. For a human it was almost impossible to tell but for Vaewolves it was as easy as breathing. It was one of the many reasons our family and race had survived all these years, through all these wars.

"Then why didn't he see a nurse or a doctor? If he was sick would that be the smartest course of action?" she challenged.

"Maybe it's just a twenty-four hour bug," added, I think her name was Mara or maybe Lara, it wasn't important but she had come to the defence of Aamin which was probably important information to hold on to.

"You two are unbelievable you know, Tamara. He is clearly lying."

"Why would Aamin lie?"

"I don't know, why doesn't he tell us the reason?"

"I've already said, Léon is back in bed because he is...sick."

"See, there you go again with the pause and look. You can't even look me in the peepers."

I had heard enough, this conversation wasn't going anywhere and I had learnt what I had needed to. Léonidas was in Kheîma Tower. This was a relief. It meant he was alone and we'd be able to talk privately.

Slowly, I walked backwards until I was kissed by

shadow before turning and disappearing entirely from view.

LÉONIDAS II

The hot water enveloped me as I lowered myself into the scorching bath. The sweet scent of jasmine filled the room. The steam obscured my reflection in the mirrors, adding to the otherworldly feeling that had descended upon me. I tried to empty my mind and let myself become one with the water, but the worries and anxieties that had been plaguing me for hours now refused to subside.

As I sank lower and lower into the depths of the tub, I couldn't help but feel a sense of despair creeping in. Maybe if I stayed there long enough, the bath would wash away my troubles and grant me some peace. My skin was slick with sweat, a physical manifestation of the turmoil roiling within me.

But then, as if on cue, a different kind of chill began to spread through my body. It wasn't the chill of the cool air but rather a numbing coldness that emanated from my very soul. It was the kind of cold that made me wonder if I would ever truly be warm again.

As I struggled to keep my head above water, a dangerous thought slithered its way into my mind. What if I just gave in and let myself sink? Would the pain and fear finally stop? The temptation to surrender to the watery depths was almost overwhelming.

I knew Aamin said he would keep my secret but what if someone could just tell by looking at me? I was hardly the most masculine of men in looks and behaviour, I was no Atticus Valor. Until today I hadn't even seen sports nor even wanted to. Wasn't this a hallmark of being a masculine male? Normal? For if that is so then maybe I should have already known that I was... I could not even think the words. Why was this my reality?

If Braxton ever found out, I had no doubt he'd make sure everyone knew. I could already hear his ghostly insults in my head, reminding me of how abnormal and weak he thought I was. But what really frightened me was the idea that everyone would leave me just like my parents did. I had nothing of value except for the friendships I had built here. If they all disappeared, I'd truly have nothing left.

I was a burden and I would never be anything more.

In that moment, a response to my desire took over, and I let go, sinking to the bottom of the crystal tub. My body rolled over, blocking my access to air, my antlers made sure I was good and trapped. My final thoughts were of my funeral. If I kept my secret and died this way, at least I knew or hoped anyway that there would be three people standing there at the end while I was lowered into the ground. I just hoped they would forgive me for leaving them behind, for not being strong enough to face the truth and the consequences that came with it.

I wanted peace, didn't I deserve that?

ATTICUS VALOR III

As I ascended the steps and entered Kheîma Tower, the emptiness of the place was palpable, and it wasn't just because it was dinner time. It was as if the entire tower was holding its breath, waiting for something to happen. Despite being technically open to all students, each house tower had its own unspoken rules and etiquette. I wasn't accustomed to venturing into Kheîma, the winter house tower. To be honest, I didn't socialise much with other house students outside of Match Olympia.

But as soon as I entered the common room, I was struck by its ethereal beauty. The room seemed to be frozen in time, like a palace buried under layers of pristine snow. The pale blue armchairs and lounges were soft and comfortable, with cushions that mimicked the appearance of snowballs. Even the carvings on the walls looked as though they were made of glistening ice.

I knew that in every house tower, there was a living tree that reflected the season, providing magical energy to the walls. But in Kheîma, the tree appeared to be a towering Norway spruce, its branches coated in thick, winter snow. It was a stark contrast to the Japanese maple that resided in Metóporon, my house, whose leaves were the same red as our school shirts and ties.

As I made my way to the spiral staircase, I couldn't help but feel a sense of unease. The staircase had a mind of its own, transporting students to wherever they needed to go. But it only worked for those who resided within the tower walls, or if you were accompanied by someone who did. Unfortunately, I had neither. So I had to rely on my senses and my own two feet to track down the person I searched for.

I closed my eyes and focused on my hearing and sense of smell. It wasn't easy in a place as large as Kheîma Tower, but I was determined to find him. I took a deep breath and let my senses guide me, hoping to catch a hint of his scent, or the sound of his footsteps.

Where was he?

Sounds came to me like pictures in a black and white film. The steady dripping of a tap was punctuated by the *thud thud thud* of a frantic heartbeat. Léonidas wasn't in his room, but in one of the bathrooms. Something was wrong with his heart. It beat both rapidly and erratically, as though it was struggling to hold on. Panic set in as I tore up the staircase, taking five steps at a time. What was happening to him?

His heart was faltering. I could hear it in my bones as clearly as if my ears were pressed to his chest. *Thud. Thud. Thud.* I was taking too long. I had to move faster. I got on all fours, shifting my legs and arms, leaving only my main body and parts of my face human. Using my enhanced energy, I more than tripled my ascent, the sound of his faltering heartbeat pounding in my ears.

Thud. Thud. Th-th-th-d.

"FUCK!" I growled, truly scared now. His heart was failing, and I was still too far away. I pushed myself harder, my curls slick with sweat as I tore around the final corner and burst into the bathroom chambers. The room was a maze of non-gendered bathrooms, each door baby blue instead of Metóporon's signature red.

Th-th-th-d.

Th-th-th-d-th-d.

Thud.

Silence.

Thud.

My ears pricked. Léonidas was behind the second door to the right. His heart was barely beating. What was happening to him? I had a sick feeling in the pit of my stomach.

With one swift motion, I ripped the door off its hinges and stormed into the room. A thick cloud of jasmine-scented steam hit me in the face. In the centre of the room was a large tub made of polished amethyst.

"LÉONIDAS!" I bellowed, but there was no response. My eyes honed in on a limp body lying face down in the bathwater. My ears heard no heartbeat. Panicked, I bolted to the bath and hoisted the body from the tub not caring that water completely drenched me.

His body was small in my arms, and in this state the antlered youth looked so very young, too young to have a mate bond with someone three years his senior. I turned his body over so that I could see his porcelain beauty as I checked his pulse...there wasn't one. As I saw it, I had two options. I let him be dead and be free of this cursed mate bond or I feed him my blood to restore his heartbeat and be linked together forever more.

In the end, the choice was easy. As much as I hated the idea of being tied to someone forever, I would never be able to live with his death on my shoulders. My fangs extended and I tore my wrist open, exposing a bleeding vein. Blood began to fall like a slowly pumping river that pushed out blood with each beat of my heart. I lowered it to his puffy pink lips, my blood staining them scarlet as it made its way into his body.

My blood would not change him into a vaewolf—only my bite could do that but it would heal him. It was another reason why vaewolves were so rich and influential. Our blood could heal almost anyone at death's door. Even a heart that beat no more...well, only before rigor mortis set in.

In a matter of moments my wrist had knitted itself back together and the flow of blood stopped. I knew my blood had done its job when I heard the *thud thud thud* of his heart return.

His body was drawn to my touch as he subconsciously

nestled into my chest. I hadn't a clue what to do, I couldn't leave him like this.

"You stupid idiot," I mumbled as I kissed his forehead. To my complete astonishment he purred in my arms, nestling even deeper into my embrace.

"Why'd you do it?" I said hugging him tighter.

In his sleep he whispered, "I don't want to be left behind again." And if that didn't just flay my heart raw. I didn't know much about his family, but in the morning I'd be sending letters to retrieve everything there was to know about the small boy in my arms.

"I'll never leave you behind," I promised. My world was about to become a whole lot more complicated because of those five words. But it was a promise I was going to keep.

Léonidas lay in his bed, battered and broken, while downstairs I urgently contacted Tamara, Coco, and Prince Aamin. I needed their help to unravel the horrors that had befallen my m…mate.

Using a discreet spell, I summoned them to the winter common room, my message short and to the point: "Léonidas needs you. Come now, and tell no one."

In less than twenty minutes, the three of them had arrived, breathing heavily and looking stricken with fear. It was time to confront the truth head-on.

"Léonidas has suffered some serious traumas," I said, my voice shaking with emotion. "And he's done something terrible as a result."

Coco was the first to explode. "Stop talking in circles, Atticus!" she shouted. "What did he do? And why isn't he here right now?"

I ignored her anger, sensing the deeper undercurrent of terror and worry that lay beneath. "Our mutual f…friend is in crisis," I continued. "He needs his friends now more than ever. We must be there for him, physically and emotionally, in his darkest of hours."

"He tried to kill himself," rasped Aamin. "Didn't he?" Despair filled his scent whilst the clear guilt he felt was written across his face plain to see. Why did he appear so guilty? Did he have a hand in this? A growl began low in my chest. The biological instinct to protect my mate burned hot in my veins.

"WHAT! IS THIS TRUE?" bellowed Coco.

I gave a sharp nod, she whirled around to face Aamin, "Oh, honey, I had a feeling you were keeping something from us, and I was right on the money. But instead of coming clean, you kept lying and lying, and look where we ended up. Our friend almost slipped through our fingers. Let me tell you, Aamin, I'm furious, absolutely furious."

"D'accord Aamin, what are you hiding? Something clearly happened and I think now is the time to come clean." Tamara tried to reason with him.

He just shook his head. "I'm sorry," he mumbled before adding, "but I can't tell you."

"Cannot or will not?" interjected Coco, her eyes narrowing. I knew she was a prefect and in my year. We shared a few classes and I had never seen this side of her. It was plain to see that she was a fiercely loyal friend to have.

"I won't, Léon...Léonidas made me swear to keep it a secret and I will until he tells me otherwise," declared Aamin, puffing out his chest. A lesser man would have cowered at the death stare that was given him, even Tamara who I gathered was normally a jovial person appeared annoyed at this revelation or I should say lack of one.

What I wasn't expecting was the ice-cold glare that

Aamin turned upon me. "But what I will say is that Atticus here is at least partially responsible for Léonidas's actions."

Coco and Tamara whirled back around to face me like a couple of lionesses protecting their cub. Shocked at the outburst, I said nothing.

"You don't deny it?" hissed Coco.

"What did you do?" Tamara glowered.

I bristled at their tone. I'd done nothing wrong here and how dare they speak to me in such a disrespectful way. I was a prince and regardless of anything else respect must be shown for the crown. If there was anything that my family had taught me it was this.

I grew in the space, allowing my vaewolf to shine through my stature. It wasn't a shift but to them it would appear as if I were absorbing all the shadows.

"Watch how you speak to me!" I warned. "I did nothing. Nothing but save his life."

Tamara lowered her gaze, looking a little embarrassed but Coco and Aamin still met my gaze with distrust.

Sighing, I let go of my anger, this was going to get us nowhere fast. This event was something that would need to be kept secret. If word got out to the professors or worse the headmistress, Léonidas would surely be sent to an asylum for the magically insane. And no one ever returned after being admitted, no one.

After the initial hostilities, we eventually came together. It wasn't easy because it was clear that no one really trusted me but with the mutual link we put aside our differences.

Yes, I was an eighteen-year-old student but I was also a prince of the greatest empire, not just in the spellcaster world but also the entire magic world this side of the veil. I knew how to switch on when I needed to do my duty and that time was now.

We stayed in conversation about what we would need to put in place so that he got the support he needed to recover from this, until the students began to arrive back from dinner. I was exhausted. It was decided that I would stay in Léon's room until he awoke. Coco didn't like it but I gave her no choice in the matter. I'd found him, I'd saved him, and he was my mate even if I was the only person who knew it.

Léonidas Nightshade had just gained his biggest ally. I wondered though how he would react when he found out the real truth.

Before Tamara could lead me up the stairs to his room (saving me from having to walk a million steps) Aamin pulled me aside. He spoke in whispers as to not let the others hear.

"This was all your fault, don't think I haven't seen the way you look at him."

I froze, my tone turning to ice. "Then prince to prince why don't you enlighten me," I challenged.

"You're in love with him."

Laughter burst from my chest. "No, Prince Aamin, I can assure you I'm not 'in love' with him."

"Then you are in lust with him. I know what I've seen," he countered.

"Don't say things you could never understand," I warned.

"Oh I 'understand' all right—"

"Do you? Then say it." I growled low as I cornered him. "He's your mate."

Before I realised what I was doing I had picked Aamin

up by his neck and slammed him hard into the floor, buttons pinged everywhere as they were torn off his shirt.

My canines had descended as I snarled at him.

"So it is true," wheezed Aamin.

"You keep your mouth shut," I hissed.

"Only if you tell him."

Pulling my fist back before I smashed it into Aamin's face, my skin ripped as it transformed into claws.

"Pélti!"

"Fuck!"

My knuckles bleed as I withdrew my claws from the protective barrier, I turned around to face the caster, my temper in raged.

"If you're going to act like an animal then you can leave. Prince or no prince," called Coco from across the room, her wand raised.

It took a second for the fog of anger to dissipate from my brain but when it did I was horrified to see hundreds of eyes on me from the now filled common room. I had made a grave mistake.

Dammit.

Reluctantly, I held out a hand for Aamin, whose expression matched the anger I felt at being called out.

He took my hand and I helped pull him onto his feet. After which he hissed at me, "You tell him or I will."

"Fine," I gritted out.

Cernunnos had won. I wasn't going to fight it any longer.

Coco and Tamara stood in front of us.

"You two care to explain what that was?" said Tamara, her brows raised high into her fringe.

CHAPTER 15

A WISH SEEN, A DESIRE HERD

LÉONIDAS I

Standing on the peak of the mountain, I watched as the north wind brought a sea of congealing blood that consumed the landscape. My heart beat fast as houses in the valley below were destroyed. Farm crops of barley, and fields of cows and sheep were entirely slaughtered by the bloody typhoon. Empty mess and horror filled my soul. Should I join them? Just step off the edge?

"Noooooooo," whispered a voice. Where did it come from?

Curiosity won out and I turned around to see black poplar and willow trees bordering a cavernous cave where light seemed to die like the light on silk velvet.

How had I not seen this before?

I turned back to look over the edge at the sea of blood consuming all, only to find it had been replaced as if it was never there at all. But I knew what I'd seen...didn't I? A grove of trees similar to the ones by the cave entrance littered the small riverside. This wasn't a mountain after all.

"Come on, Léon, it's in here," called the distant voice once more. It was too faint to hear if it was a man's voice, a woman's voice, or something else entirely.

"Who are you?" I called as I turned back to face the blackness of the cave.

"Come on, Léon, it's in here," it repeated, ignoring my question.

The more I stared the more the blackness called to me, the shadows spewing out like the tentacles of a sea creature from legend or maybe even the souls of the dead.

I was so afraid yet I couldn't stop my shaking feet from meeting the darkness as something from within my very being pulled me into the cave. Quickly I was consumed by shadow as it licked across my body like a flame.

"Come on. Come on, Léon," the voice repeated as I was pulled deeper and deeper into the unknown.

"IT'S IN HERE!!!!"

I jumped, the voice was screamed into my ear. Something attacked me, was it bats? Their screeching abused my ear drums. I pulled my hands up to protect my face only to find them locked in chains.

"Help!" I screamed but no one listened or came to my aid. What had I done?

I fell to my knees as I tried to walk. They too were wrapped in iron chains. Crawling on the ground I tried to pull myself away, fingernails clawing at dirt as the acrid smell of decay petrified my senses and burnt my nostrils.

"AHHHHHHH!" I screamed as something pulled me by the chains, dragging me away. Where was my sight? I saw nothing.

"Do you want to die?" whispered another voice. Was

this the person pulling my chains? I could feel rocks and dirt bite into my exposed flesh.

"W...w...w...what?"

"YOU HEARD ME!" screamed the voice.

Did I?

"No," I said, surprising myself.

"Is that the truth?" The voice was back to whispering.

"Yes..." After a beat. "I think it is."

Instantly, the darkness washed away and I found myself lying on lush green grass as a ghostly blue figure stared down at me with kind eyes.

Tears burst from my eyes as I got to my feet free of chains, I knew who this was. It was my mother.

"Mummy," I sobbed, launching myself at her blue glow, The thing I wanted more than life was there in front of me but as I tried to hug her my arms fell through pale smoke.

"Darling, I am dead, we cannot touch." She tried to soothe me.

Not being able to touch her was like sitting to have a bowl of ice cream only to find out that it was mouldy cottage cheese.

"How is this possible?"

"Is this not what your heart most desired? After all, you tried to take your life for it."

Had I? Flashes of the bathtub flickered through my mind's eye like a hunting memory. I suppose I had.

"So I'm dead then?" I asked, heart beating rapidly as a fresh wave of ice-cold fear filled me.

"No, Thankfully your mate saved you," my mother soothed.

"My mate saved m—"

She silenced me as she pressed her ghostly finger to my lips. "Hush my child, all in good time."

This close, I could see her high cheek bones, my cheek-bones and the same doe-like eyes. She was here and yet she wasn't. A day ago I'd wanted nothing more than to see my mother and father and now that I could actually see her I wanted more, I wanted to have her arms wrapped around me. What a melancholy moment I had found myself in.

"Darling, don't cry, we have this moment."

"I miss you so much."

"I know you do, as I do you." Her voice was featherlight and airy with a richness that only age could give.

Blinking the tears from my eyes, I noticed something or rather someone was missing.

"Where's Father?" I asked.

A look of deep sadness flashed across her luminescent face.

"He...he is not here."

"Why not?"

"It is best we don't talk about that."

Again, I asked why not.

To which my mother responded, "We haven't the time. You have been brought here for a reason."

Face scrunched in deep confusion, I asked, "What do you mean?"

"I have a message for you," she responded.

My curiosity was piqued. "A message? Why? What is it?"

Before my mother could answer I felt a pull in my chest. Glancing down, I found a golden cord wrapped tight around my chest. How hadn't I seen it before? Or felt it? I panicked, my fingers instantly digging into the bonds. My attempts only served to make the cord grow even tighter around my chest.

"Mother, help! What do I do?" I whimpered in a panic.

The pulling was back, this time with a much greater force.

Frantically, I looked back up into her eyes. There...there was a smile in her eyes.

"Ahh yes, we are out of time, your mate is pulling you back."

"Pulling me back? My mate? You're making no sense...Mother?"

Cupping my face with hands I could not feel, she stared deep into my eyes.

"This is the message I must give you, darling. You have a greater purpose in this life. The fates have dealt you a destiny one must not hide from. Even the gods have stakes in you winning what is to come."

With a grunt I was pulled airborne.

"Mother!" I called after her as she receded far away in the distance.

"I love you, darling, and remember this, you are perfect. There is nothing wrong with you, nothing."

And with those final words shadows welcomed me like an old friend. Only the golden cord gave me any light.

"Mother!" I called into the void. There was nothing.

"Mother!" I repeated. Nothing.

"MOTHER!" I yelled, bolting up straight, my eyes desperately flying open. Where was she, it was too soon. I needed her.

I was slick with sweat...wait where was I? I was temporarily blinded by light. The cord had blinded me, I automatically patted my chest...my exposed chest...but there was nothing there, no golden cord. What was the light if not the cord?

Everything slowly dripped into focus, I was in my bedroom at school. The light was from the sun shining through the window. My hand lifted to block the light, the sun turning the edges of my white hand red. Was it all a dream? Did I want it to be? No, I told myself. I had seen my mother, I know I had...I hoped I had. But there was this feeling in my heart that told me it wasn't just some dream and if there was one thing I had learnt since being at Amethyst it was that anything was possible. So I'd hold onto that feeling until I was told otherwise.

A single tear echoed my loss as it travelled its solitary way down to my chin before disappearing into the unknown.

I jumped as voice spoke from behind me.

"Are you all right, snowflake?" asked none other than Atticus Valor, prince of the vaewolves. His low, sultry voice sent my cheeks flushing scarlet and a heart-stopping second later I became all too aware of how naked I was beneath my sheet which was the only thing covering my lower half. Why was I naked? I never slept naked...

"Er...um...what? Wait, why are you here...in my bedroom." I stammered, mortified. Why on earth was he here? And also how? This was not the autumn tower...was it? I quickly looked around and I was correct, I was in the right place and he wasn't. How does one ask someone to leave without being rude? I pondered.

He started to laugh, why was he laughing? I turned and meet his golden gaze. It was a trap for I was instantly dazed by their all-devouring all-consuming intensity. I was so enraptured that for the moment I forgot all about my encounter with my ghostly mother in the cave.

"Why are you here?" I repeated though it was barely more than a mumble, as his eyes were everything in this moment, like pools of afternoon gold I could swim in.

Atticus smiled, showing pearly white teeth. "Why I'm here to watch you, of course."

It took me a second to process what he had said. "Watch me? Why?"

"So many 'whys' snowflake."

"Why are you calling me snowflake?"

"See, again with the 'why'."

I felt a slight temper in me rise.

"Answer my question or get out of my room" I demanded.

"I am here to make sure *you* don't do anything so stupid *again*." His voice took on a steel-like intensity. I was trapped once more in his gaze as he stalked the distance over to me. My brain misfired as I tried to comprehend what he meant. Stupid? Again. Flashes of a bath and water filling my lungs played through my mind's eye like the flash of a malfunctioning torch.

That, combined with his intensity, locked my brain up and I was unable to do anything other than continuing to stare into his all-consuming gaze.

With a strong hand he gripped my chin, tilting it up with force so that our eyes stayed locked together. There was no safe haven for me, I was completely within his thrall. Why was it like this? Why was I?

Thud thud thud went my heart.

"You are mine," he growled.

"I am yours?"

"Yes. Eres mío." His gaze intensified further, how that was even possible was beyond me. We were close enough to kiss, just a bit further and... I was drowning in his pool of liquid sunlight, a field mouse in a spider's web, a lamb in a cage with a ravenous wolf.

Bang bang bang.

The loud knocking at the door broke the spell. I recoiled in horror. My back pressed hard against the smooth headboard as I frantically pulled the sheet up to cover my chest. What had I nearly done? To my horror. the swelling between my thighs had returned, stronger than it had ever been before. My member pointed straight into the air. I tried to hide it further by crossing my legs.

"You...you...you spelled me."

His face smirked. "Believe me, snowflake, I don't need to do that."

"Stop calling me snowflake!"

"No."

"Léon, you'll be late for first period if don't you get up now," called Coco's unmistakable voice. "Tamara and I will wait down in the common room to accompany you to class."

Accompany me?

"Why?" I called after her, but she must have already gone because no response was given.

A sinking feeling in my chest told me the answer, though.

"I didn't mean to..." I whispered.

"Didn't you?"

"I...I..."

"Let me make this clear, snowflake, you ever try to do that again I won't bring you back."

"You brought me back? How?"

Instead of answering he threw me a pair of purple slacks. "Get dressed, I'll meet you downstairs." His voice was back to the steel-like edge.

How had he brought me back? But the scarier thought was did everyone know?

. . .

Dressed with my books and bags packed, I made my way down the stairs. Palms dripping for I was so anxious I thought I would be physically sick any second. The common room was empty apart from the four faces of Tamara, Coco, Aamin, and Atticus. There was no happiness on Tamara's face, no humour in Coco's eyes, no smile on Aamin's lips, and Atticus...well, he looked the same— always staring, always brooding, always devouring.

Lifting my trembling hand I waved in meek hello. It was so awkward my voice even broke. "Hi."

"That's all you have to say? After you..." A tear ran its course down Tamara's soft face.

"I'm sorry—" I began but was swiftly cut off.

"Are you though? Are you realllllly, Léon? Because what you did...what you tried to do has hurt me, hurt all of us," clipped Coco, her emotions barely in check. I had never seen her so simultaneously angry and vulnerable at the same time.

"Did we not offer you enough support or..." said Tamara trailing off.

"You can tell us anything, you do know that, right?" Coco continued.

But it was Aamin who broke me, his face wet with tears as he threw the final arrow into my heart. "Are we not good enough friends?"

The four of us rushed together into a group hug, each a crying mess. I didn't know which of us started forward first, only that we did come together. All I could do was apologise profusely for what I had done. I never thought people would care so much about me to miss me when I was gone. In between hugs and tears I promised each of them that I'd never try to do it again. Yes, my heart was broken and I felt like a defective toy inside but I was not a cruel person, I knew that, and no matter what I'd never want to cause these people, my friends, this kind of pain ever again.

Their love shattered me into a thousand pieces, and in that moment, I swore an oath to do anything to make amends, for I knew that I would willingly bear the weight of the world for them.

CHAPTER 16
A SINISTER CHOICE

LÉONIDAS I

Defensive and Offensive Spellcasting with Professor Sokolova was our first class of the day. In some sort of weird unexplainable way, I felt like something precious being escorted to class by the three of them when really it was just Aamin and I in the same class. I could reason it was normal for Tamara to join us on the walk because she was in the class next door but Atticus and Coco were just simply too much.

Arriving at the classroom, Coco and Tamara said their goodbyes, it was pretty obvious they felt uncomfortable leaving me alone what with the darting glances back at me as they walked away. Before I could enter the classroom Atticus pulled me aside. Aamin stopped to join us but after a look from Atticus that turned Aamin's expression sour, he headed inside without me.

What was that all about? I'd have to ask Aamin later.

"You are to wait here until I fetch you to take you to your next class, is that understood?" Atticus spoke low, giving me what sounded in no uncertain terms like an order. Who did he think he was? My owner?

"What? Absolutely not," I bit back.

"Léonidas Nightshade, you are to await me here until I fetch you, understood? I'm ordering you."

"You're ordering me? And what pray tell, gives you that power?"

"I am your alpha and you *will* listen to me."

"My what? Atticus, you're talking nonsense. I'll speak to you later," I said, motioning towards the classroom door.

Suddenly, Atticus's hand shot out and latched onto my collar, pulling me back so quickly that my feet nearly flew out from under me.

"Where do you think you're going?" he demanded, his grip firm and unyielding.

I stared up at him, wide-eyed and startled. My heart raced as I tried to think of a way to escape his hold.

Atticus's expression softened slightly. "Promise me you'll wait for me," he said, his voice low and urgent.

I could feel the heat radiating off his body as he towered over me. His eyes were dark and intense, and I couldn't help but feel a sense of danger emanating from him.

"I...I can't," I stammered, trying to wriggle free from his grasp.

Atticus's grip tightened, and a chill ran down my spine. "Can't?" he repeated, a dangerous glint in his eyes.

Suddenly, the castle seemed to grow warmer, as if the air around us was becoming thick and heavy with tension. People began to stop and stare, but I hardly noticed. My eyes were fixed on Atticus, and I couldn't look away.

As Braxton appeared around the corner, my heart sank. He was always searching for new ways to torment me, and I knew he would use this against me if he had the chance.

With a resigned sigh, I gave in to Atticus's demands. "Okay, okay, I'll wait for you," I muttered.

Atticus's eyes bore into mine. "You are mine," he said, his voice low and commanding.

I swallowed hard, feeling a lump rise in my throat. "What do you mean?" I asked, my voice barely above a whisper.

"You belong to me. Say it," he demanded.

I hesitated, unsure of what to do. But Atticus's grip on my collar was unyielding, and I knew I had no choice but to comply.

"I belong to you," I murmured, feeling a sense of defeat wash over me.

For a moment, Atticus held me in his grasp, his eyes never leaving mine. But then, with a quick nod, he released me, and I stumbled backwards, feeling dizzy and disoriented. As I scurried away, my heart still racing with fear and confusion, I couldn't help but wonder what I had just gotten myself into.

It wasn't until I had sat down next to Aamin that my brain finally worked. What had I agreed to? I was his? In what way? Maybe that was not in my best mental interests to think about...after all I was already so emotionally exhausted and the idea of having to deal with yet another thing well...last time I couldn't trust my actions.

But no matter how hard I tried, those three words played over and over in my mind for the rest of the class.

You are mine.

Atticus kept his word, he was indeed waiting for me when class finished. I had to wonder how far he had to run to make it from his own class, yet there wasn't a hair out of place. The stupid prince was always the picture of masculine perfection. If I had to run here from somewhere my practically translucent skin would be flushed a patchy bright red.

After class Aamin and I parted ways as we had different second periods but we both had the same third so we would see each other again then.

"What's your next class?" asked Atticus.

"Cooking and home studies with—" I began.

"With Professor Albrecht. I know the class."

We walked in silence for a time. Students who normally called offensive remarks at me like horny boy stayed silent. It seemed Atticus had the same effect on others that Coco had though I guessed for an entirely different reason. Everyone wanted to be friends with the cool rebel prince of vaewolves, whereas everyone respected Coco, the prefect with the perfect grades. Either way, I just liked that when I was with either of them I was left alone.

After looking at his wristwatch Atticus pulled out a small bottle of blue pills, the label read *Animperium*.

"What are those for?" I asked curiously.

"Don't worry about it," he responded carelessly as he took one out and chucked it into his mouth. He grimaced.

"Tastes bad?"

"Yeah."

There was a flickering in his eyes that seemed to diminish the golden glow to something more subdued, not quite lifeless but not...him.

I wanted to ask him again what those pills were for but by his facial expression, I decided against it. We remained silent for the rest of the journey.

. . .

In the main castle complex, the cooking and home study classrooms resided, hidden deep underground. Like everything else in this place, it required several sets of stupidly long staircases to reach. These rooms served as both classrooms and kitchens, where the school prepared food for everyone here at Amethyst. And what we learned in cooking class would later appear as options for dinner. Cooking brought me a sense of comfort, a taste of home.

Like before Atticus left me at my classroom and made me promises to wait for him to escort me to my next class. I was really starting to hate this being babied nonsense. So I made a mistake…one I promised I would never made again. I couldn't handle this constant reminder, this weight in the air. I just wished everyone would forget about it and we could all move on, this awkwardness was killing me. I wanted to live in denial, could they not just give me that?

When I entered the classroom, I noticed someone had taken my usual spot in the back corner. It meant that I had to sit next to someone, which made me uneasy. Cooking was the only subject I didn't have either Tamara or Aamin with me, and I always preferred working alone. But today, I had to embrace change.

There was, of course, only two spare seats: one was on the right of Braxton, which was clearly not an option, and the other was across the room between two students I hadn't really spent much time with.

They both seemed nice enough, so left with little option I walked and stood in front of their table.

"Hey, Gabriella, hey, Harrison, would you two mind if I sat next to you? There isn't anywhere else to sit…"

Gabriella looked up at me through her long fluttery lashes. She had skin the colour of autumn and curly hair decorated with a kind of rope-like braid. She instantly smiled. "Of course you can, Léonidas. Isn't that right, Harry?"

"The more the merrier," he agreed. So I joined their table and waited for our teacher, Professor Albrecht, to start today's lesson.

Professor Albrecht was a man in his late 60s with a bald head and what I had learnt was a particularly strong German accent. He always wore the same white button-up coat that seemed like something an actor might wear when playing a doctor or scientist, and gloves, we never saw his hands for longer than a few seconds when he was changing them.

"Today, class, we will be preparing chicken for roasting. We will begin with the correct method of plucking the feathers. The second-year archery classes have provided today's freshly caught hens."

The idea made me feel sick. In my periphery I saw that Gabriella was also not thrilled about today's lesson.

Albrecht pulled out his spellcasters wand and with a small gesture dead animals appeared in front of us. I felt sick. Surely I wouldn't have to...disrespect a murdered animal. In fact I was so repulsed that I had to look away. Unfortunately, looking away meant catching Braxton's gaze. When he saw my obvious distress he proceeded to pick up the chicken and toy with its legs, laughing while he hummed the "Can-can." I pushed myself away, I needed to get out of the classroom. Everywhere that my eyes fell was a poor, innocent life that had been snuffed out. Life like mine, a life I'd wanted to end and now I was being presented with what that would be like if I had succeeded. Dualism of the two sent a haze over my vision.

This wasn't just so wrong and sick but also incredibly cruel. I got the concept of eating meat and normally had no problem with it…at least not in this intense way but actually seeing the lifeless eyes staring at me was just so, so wrong. If I wasn't already exclusively a vegetable-eater then this moment would have converted me, truly there wasn't a single doubt in my mind.

I'm going to be sick, I felt the bile rise in my stomach burning my throat.

After getting to my feet I started walking over to the door, unfortunately that was also closer to Braxton.

"Are you okay, Mr Nightshade?" called the professor, drawing all attention to me.

"Errr." I tried to focus on the professor's words and give him my attention but this feeling of dizziness only intensified the more I tried to focus and ignore that everywhere I looked cold dead eyes and lifeless bodies stared right back at me. I stumbled, catching myself at the last moment,. My brain took me back to the vision Aamin and I had shared with Tamara. All those dead bodies, and crows eating the lifeless dead. My body in a bath lifeless, my back and antlers the only things exposed. Dead. I was dead, everything was dead, everyone was dead.

The laughter of students brought me back out of my dire tunnel of sinking thoughts.

"Mr Nightshade? Are you listening? Are you okay?" called the professor once more.

"I just need…um…er I just some air, professor. May I please be excused?"

I didn't wait to see if he gave me permission to leave, I just continued my beeline for the door. But just when I could see the end in sight the cruel, callous voice of Braxton spoke to me.

"What's the matter, Horny Boy? Afraid of a little dead poultry?"

"Leave me alone, Braxton," I retorted, not stopping.

"You know you're not normal right? You're a freak, a F...F...FREAK...F...R...E...A...K."

"Stop," I begged as I passed him, but what he said next made me all out sprint for the door, a desperate dash.

"Guess what I heard? You're not just a horny boy but you're also a sodomite who's horny for taking it up the butt. Pillow-biter, such a freak. You are a horny horny horny boy. I wonder if your 'friends' will still be there when they find out how filthy you truly are?"

If I thought the world was spinning before it was *nothing* to how the world shattered now. I couldn't handle it. I was going to pass out be it from Braxton's words or the continuous stare of the dead watching me from every bench in the room.

A burst of cooler air—I made it outside the classroom. Shaking, I closed the door behind me.

How had he known?

Could he just tell?

Was it really so obvious?

Would I be left alone...if they knew the truth? My truth? A voice inside my heart told me they would stick with me through anything but an even smaller, tinier voice—one of doubt that came from the shadows of thought—told me a story of loneliness. How would I truly know?

I had already put them through so much in the last twenty-four hours...what if they just left because I was simply too much to handle, too much drama? Too much of a burden.

I had shed a lot of tears in my life and many in the last day but the one single tear that escaped my tired eyes now felt like the loneliest one I'd ever shed for it was filled with cruellest of thoughts—doubt.

I wasn't normal, like Braxton said. Anyone who looked at me could tell this by the antlers alone, the colour of my eyes—who had purple irises? No one, only freaks.

Once more I felt this giant emptiness threating to swallow me whole. As if I were on a raft out to sea fighting against endless tides, or standing in a barren gorge without a drop of life left in me. This emptiness I had grown to realise had always been a part of me. Even through the good times when I felt gay and merry, in the aftermath it seemed to always return like a curse.

Using the back of my sleeve, I wiped away the stale tear.

"Don't cry," said a voice in the shadow that caused me to jump in surprise.

"I'm not—" I began.

"You are and that is all right."

"Who are you?"

"Me?" said the feminine voice as they walked out into the light, "I'm Schuyler Warren. My family owns the Warren American Mining company and, dare I say it, I'm a friend."

Schuyler had rose-toned blonde hair curled close to her scalp. and wore the sunshine yellow shirt and tie of Théros, the summer house. She looked familiar, but not enough that I knew where I had seen her before. As she drew closer I could see she was holding a white pamphlet of some sort.

"A friend? Have we spoken before?" I queried.

"No, but I think we should change that, don't you?"

"Err—"

"Here, look at this," said Schuyler as she handed me the pamphlet.

"What for?"

"Trust me, it will fix all your worries."

"My worries?"

Looking down, I read *The sodomite cure, same gender attraction is wrong and Doctor Androsoff is here to fix you.*

My palms instantly dripped with sweat, I looked back up into Schuyler's green eyes. I didn't know what to say, so I just left my mouth open, dumbfounded.

Did everyone know?

As if she could hear my thoughts, Schuyler added, "Braxton's already gone around and told everyone, if people don't already know, they soon will."

"They will?" I said meekly, not even trying to deny it.

"Yes. But if you come with me now, I can take you to the doctor who lives just on the other side of the island. If we go now we can be back before dinner and you will no longer be a filthy sodomite."

"I...I...I—"

"Do you really want to be all alone? With no friends? Abandoned? Again?"

"They wouldn't leave me."

"Oh but they would. Everyone would."

"Noooooo I...I don' believe you," I stuttered, my resolve cracking.

"It is illegal, punishable by death in many countries, with imprisonment in most. Don't you want to be normal?"

Braxton's words ringing in my mind. "*You know you're not normal right? You're a freak, a F...F...FREAK.*"

"He may even be able to fix your gross disgusting horns of Lucifer," she continued. "You know they're a symbol of evil, right?"

"Lucifer?" I questioned, not liking the sound of the name.

"Yes, he is the devil, the king of sodomites, the man

with the horns. Master of trickery, deceiver of the right-eous, and the ruler over hell and eternal punishment."

That really sounded bad. I'd never herd of this monster before.

"Really?"

"Yeesssss, I promise."

"This person, this doctor will fix me as you say?"

"Fix you so good, Lucifer won't be able to touch you."

Thump thump thump thump beat my fearful heart. Maybe I should go, maybe it was what was best…I was confused, I was lonely and I was scared.

"Okay I'll go."

"Perrrrect."

I followed Schuyler up the stairs, my hands shook so bad I dropped the brochure, which fell back down the stairs.

As I left the safety of the main castle I could practically hear Atticus scorning me for disobeying his orders. And with that thought the emptiness just felt that little bit more vast and all-consuming. But I just kept repeating to myself, *I'm going to be normal, I'm going to be normal, I'm going to be normal. No one's going to leave me, not again,* never *again.*

GABRIELLA & HARRISON I

Sitting at their desks, Gabriella Jean-Bella and Harrison Knight stared in disgust at the dead chickens, their feathers strewn all over the classroom kitchen. The putrid smell of raw meat and blood filled the air, making them wish they were anywhere but there.

After a particularly loud shudder from Harrison, Gabriella broke the silence. "Someone should go check on

Léonidas, after all, he has been out there alone for a few minutes."

"And by someone you mean us? Right?" asked Harrison, looking relieved to have a reason to stop plucking chickens.

"Obviously," replied Gabriella with a roll of her eyes. "But first, let's not forget to say goodbye to our old carnivore selves. We'll be exclusively vegetarian after this fiasco."

Harrison nodded his agreement, adding, "I'm pretty sure these chickens were meant to be pets, not dinner. I swear this one is giving me a dirty look."

Gabriella giggled. "You're just imagining things, Harrison. These chickens are as dead as a doorknob. And probably as old, too."

Together, they had managed to pluck a total of one feather each, while most of their classmates had already completed the task.

As they raised their hands to ask the professor for permission to check on Léonidas, they couldn't help but feel a sense of relief.

"Can Harrison and I be excused to check on Léonidas?" Gabriella asked, trying not to gag from the smell of raw meat.

The professor raised an eyebrow, eyeing their practically un-plucked chickens. "Does that task require two of you?"

"Well, you know, we don't want Léonidas to get lost or something," said Harrison, trying his best to sound convincing.

The professor sighed. "Just make it quick. These chickens won't pluck themselves, you know with hundreds of thousands of people to feed you'll both be required to pluck a lot more than one each."

As if both on cue Harrison and Gabriella bolted for the door.

Outside the classroom the rest of the kitchens smelt like baking bread and clover, far better than the sterile smell of dead dead dead.

"Where is he?" asked Gabriella gazing around. The kitchen corridors were all empty.

"Maybe he went to the lavatory? Wait, what's this?" He bent down before picking up a white pamphlet with a large white cross across the front.

Gabriella and Harrison huddled over and read in unison. "The sodomite cure, same gender attraction is wrong and Doctor Androsoff is here to fix you"

In horror they both looked up, meeting each other's eyes.

"Oh no," gasped Gabriella.

"Who do we get?" added Harrison, "Surely a professor...right?"

"Nooo, I don't think that will help," dismissed Gabriella.

"Then who?"

After a moment of silence Gabriella suggested, "First I think he needs someone to stop him from going through with it, for that I think he will need his friends. Harry, isn't he close to a winter house prefect?"

"Yes, Coco, the one with the fabulous hair," answered Harrison.

"Where do you suppose she would be now?"

CHAPTER 17

OUTSIDE THE GATES

ATTICUS VALOR I

D uring our meeting last night, it was agreed that we would gather in the main library building, Atraios, during our second periods. Coco and I had a free period, and Aamin and Tamara decided to feign sickness to get out of their lessons. We discussed melancholia, a medical condition my father had once mentioned. It was a type of persistent sadness that had been known to drive people to end their lives. Although I had little knowledge on the subject, Prince Aamin was eager to explore the possibility of a magical cure for the condition, and thus, we were in the library. Unfortunately, we found practically nothing after around thirty minutes of searching.

Coco suggested a working theory involving electroshock therapy, but we were unsure whether fae or part-fae, like Léonidas, would have immunity or adverse effects from such treatment. The lack of reliable information on the fae made it difficult for us to draw any conclusions. As the saying goes, it was like looking for a needle in a haystack.

Tamara had floated the idea of asking a faculty member for access to the Fae library Frecia, though it was soon agreed that in doing so it would draw far too much unwanted attention since none of us took any subjects that would require its use.

Just after leaving Léonidas in the underground kitchens, I received the information packet I had requested. However, obtaining it quickly meant breaking the law and incurring significant costs. Nevertheless, being a prince had its advantages, and I couldn't resist my urge to uncover what traumatic experiences Léonidas had gone through to lead him down this path.

Of the seven pages, only about thirty percent were visible the rest completely redacted. What I received of course were only photocopies of the originals so there wasn't a chance to retrieve the lost information or at least not without laying my hands on the originals. Whilst I had already guessed a lot of the un-redacted information there was still one bit of information that made me raise my brows.

"Ah! J'ai mal!" cried Tamara, instantly snapping my attention to her.

"Sugar, what's wrong?" asked Coco getting up from the table and running over to her.

"My head...it hurts!"

We all gathered around Tamara. With eyes shut tight she gripped her head as if it were about to explode. I looked down at the book she was reading.

Beyond the Veil; a practitioners guide to theorising the possibilities of the Fae realm.

Frowning, I glanced back at her when her whole body shuttered, eyes flying open.

"Léonidas is in trouble!"

Outside Atraios we headed for the underground kitchens.

Coco was trying to gain as much information from Tamara as possible as it seemed she had had a vision.

"Okay, so you said you saw the same man again, the one from the first vision with skin warped like a mole rat? What else did you see?"

"Léon…oh the gods—"

"Keep going," pushed Coco.

"Léon, he was bent over, blood spilling from the mouth as the man…creature cut into his veins, pulling out the blue cords as if it were string from a yarn."

Aamin bent over and gagged, no vomit, but he did cough up a ball of spit.

I didn't stop, my…mate needed me.

"What about surroundings? Anything you could notice? Paintings? Time of day?" pushed Coco.

"Non… Wait oui, there was a…a…a large painting—I think behind the mole rat man, a kind of symbol like a diamond in front of a pyramid."

Coco and I both stopped looking at each other. It couldn't be…

"Was the symbol encapsulated in a sphere?" I asked sharply.

"I…I think it was, why? What does it mean?"

"Preneurs De Magi," Coco, Aamin, and I answered simultaneously.

We quickened our speed.

The Preneurs De Magi were a group of spellcaster terrorists who had evaded the authorities for many years. If they wanted Léon then something truly sinister was about to happen.

We weren't far from the main castle when we heard two people calling Coco's name. We had been lucky thus far with avoiding other students, due to it being class time and people were either in their towers, in classrooms, or studying in the libraries like we had been. I guess running into people was unavoidable.

Coco jogged over to them. The three quickly began a conversation. I tried to shift my ears so that I wasn't kept in the dark, but to my surprise I was unable too. It was as if my vaewolf was disconnected from me. My heart pounded in worry when I realised it was those pills. Fuck.

I had been taking them for a while without this kind of intense disconnection. Normally it was lightly muted but still present. Now it was as though my vaewolf was lost in the fog.

Before I could panic, I saw something white being handed to Coco. She took one look at it and raised her hands to her mouth. I couldn't wait any longer, I ran to join her.

"What is it? What's wrong? Is it about Léon?"

Silently she handed me the white pamphlet. The front was adorned with a white crucifix, under it said in a plain, easy to read script *The sodomite cure, same gender attraction is wrong and Doctor Androsoff is here to fix you*. My hands shook with rage. If something like this actually worked I'd have already tried it. This kind of conversion therapy did not work. I'd read all the research that backed this kind of false hope.

Coco whirled to face Aamin. "WAS THIS WHAT YOU WERE KEEPING FROM US, AAMIN?"

"What?" said Aamin, coming closer. He speared the front of the pamphlet a quick look, his face paling in what I could only assume was horror and maybe guilt.

Coco read his expression as confirmation. "Léon likes boys? Is that why he tried to commit suicide?"

"He made me promise to keep it a secret...I couldn't break his trust!" Aamin tried to explain.

But Coco was not having it. "Well, well, well, if it isn't the lot of us spending nearly an hour trying to figure out how to help him, when all he really needed was for his friends to give him some support and tell him that loving another fella is completely fine. Honey, I've said it once, and I'll say it again—Aamin, I'm just absolutely furious with you! Furious!"

They continued to argue back and forth but I tuned them out even when Tamara jumped into the conversation. Instead, I chose to read the content of the pamphlet. The second side was a map to a location on the island, but I knew this island better than most because after dark I hunted my prey and where this map led to was a swamp. No one lived there, it wasn't even near the other school.

"This is fake, no one lives there," I stated, fear fuelling my growing fury. It was a trap to lure him out of the school gates. "It's a trap!"

Not waiting for the others, I instantly began sprinting for the direction of the castle gates entrance. Once more, I tried to feel my beast but again this feeling of disconnection, of emptiness greeted my struggle. My knuckles closed into a tight fist.

"Fuck," I growled, pulling out the blue pill bottle and chucking it away as hard as I could. Because I couldn't handle having a male mate now meant I was going to lose him and it was all my fucking fault.

Class must have finished, because the hallways and corridors were filled with students and professors heading to their next classes I stopped for no one. People were staring but I didn't care, I just hoped I wasn't too late.

LÉONIDAS I

"Are you sure we won't get in trouble?" I asked Schuyler.

"Yes. Don't worry about it. Your life is about to be changed forever," she responded, pulling me along. I could see the gate now, just beyond another courtyard. Even though I went with her willingly I couldn't stop this persistent voice telling me something was wrong.

"Can you tell me more about the doctor? I've never been to one, at least not one I can remember seeing. Will this cost much? I haven't any money."

"It's all free." she said.

"Why?" I questioned.

She seemed to be getting more agitated as I kept asking questions. So to this question she simply snapped, "Because, for the betterment of society."

"Oh," I said meekly.

"We can't have freaks walking around."

"Am I a freak?"

"YES!"

With my free arm I hugged myself that little bit tighter.

ATTICUS VALOR II

I pushed myself to my newly suppressed mortal limit, I couldn't be late, I couldn't. Bursting into the last courtyard before the entrance, I sent blue and yellow birds into the sky.

"There he is!" I called, seeing Léon and some unknown girl at the large amethyst gates.

"LÉONIDAS!" I bellowed, but he didn't seem to hear me.

It was that second that everyone caught up with me, a feat only possible because my vaewolf was being subdued by pills I had no business taking in the first place. If my parents ever found out I was taking something like this behind their backs I'd probably be disowned.

"LÉON!" called Coco and Aamin.

"LÉONIDAS," called Tamara and the two new students.

The girl next to Léon must have heard us, for she turned her head to face us. I couldn't read her expression, but in a split second, she opened the gates and forced Léonidas through.

"FUCK!!" I yelled, breaking into a sprint and withdrawing my ruby and gold wand from my pocket.

I had an idea for a spell, something that might just work.

"Epispán," I chanted, pointing my wand at the gate and trying to pull it towards me. Of course, I couldn't move the entire structure, but as I'd hoped, the spell worked in reverse. I was flung towards the gate, propelled like a human catapult. I could hear the others doing the same behind me.

Who was this girl, and what connection did she have to the Preneurs De Magi? I didn't know, but I wasn't going to let her take my mate away from me. Not without a fight.

LÉONIDAS II

"Stop, you're hurting me. Let go of my arm," I begged, trying to break free of her iron grip.

"No, just a little bit further," she growled.

"Wait, I thought you said it was on the other side of the island?"

Something wasn't adding up, why was she so desperate to pull me away from school gates.

"Keep going. Don't you want to be normal, Léonidas?"

The words she had once said seemed to lose their power over me now that I was outside the gates. Schuyler had said my friends would leave me, but would they really? After all, Aamin knew the truth and he hadn't left me, in fact he knew and still sat next to me in class Atticus...well...he was the reason and he clearly knew what it meant more the I did by his words, "*You are mine.*"

I was being silly, my friends wouldn't leave me over this, I knew it in my heart, so then why did I let this person I'd maybe seen once before convince me of something different? Was it all because of Braxton's words? After all, it was just fuel to the fire he already burned against me so why should the fact that he knows affect me?

"Hurry up, move it."

"No."

"Move it, sodomite," she growled, yanking my arm hard enough it felt like it may have dislocated.

"Let go of me!" I demanded, digging my heels into the grass.

"FINE!" Schuyler shrieked, whipping around at the

same moment she drew out her spellcasters wand, it was made of what seemed like speckled granite.

"What are you doing?" I gaped, taking a few steps back, now holding my sore shoulder.

"If you won't come with me willingly then by force it is. YPÍK—"

"PÉLTI!" growled several voices.

Six beams of white iridescent light blocked Schuyler's spell. The force was so great that she was hurled backwards by several feet. It gave me enough time to fetch out my own wand. I didn't understand what was happening but I was filled with gratitude when I turned and saw who had come to my rescue. It was my friends, all of them even my two new ones, Gabriella and Harrison.

Standing there, they each looked like statues craved by Michaelangelo, mighty and unafraid.

"What's going on?" I asked, my voice cracking as emotion threatened to spill out and leave me dry.

Tamara was the first to speak. "Léon, it's a trap!"

"What?"

"She works for the people who killed your parents!" growled Atticus, the gold seemingly returning to his eyes. The world felt as though it shifted under me. She works for the person who killed my parents?

Stunned, I turned back to face Schuyler. Her face had turned a blotchy red as her eyes darted between us. She was like a wild lion looking for a place to pounce, but with the touch on my shoulder my friends had come to stand by my side. I was foolish to have ever thought they would leave me. This moment was all the proof I'd ever need that they truly loved me.

Coco broke the silence. "As a prefect I hearby place you

on detention. You can kiss your lunchtimes and day off goodbye."

"Hahahaha. You think I care about this school? You are wrong. ANANGÉLLO!" she shouted, waving her wand in the air so it spelled the name Jacquard. Purple light was summoned forth, spilling from the tip of her wand. A second later it crackled away leaving behind an intense smell of burnt wood.

Aamin waved his wand forth and Schuyler fell to the ground, laughing as she went. Vines from the earth rose up and bound her fists and ankles, her wand lay discarded a few feet away. Tamara pointed with her wand and chanted, "Epispán." Magically she pulled the wand towards her catching it, in her free hand.

"Hahaha! It's too late, they know your free to take now, bye bye, fae sodomite!"

"Silence!" shouted Gabriella, pointing her wand threateningly at Schuyler.

"What does she mean by too late?" I asked the group in between hugs. I was careful to avoid my sore shoulder.

Coco and Atticus shared a look. "We have to get you behind school wal—" Atticus began but he was rendered silent as a circle appeared underneath my feet, sound rushed in my ears, deafening me.

"Quick! Grab him!" yelled Coco.

Several sets of arms quickly wrapped their way around me in a python-like hug. A second later the ground fell from under me, plunging me into blinding white light.

CHAPTER 18

CIRCLE OF BLOOD

LÉONIDAS I

Not once did a single person let me go, through what felt like being dipped in ice-cold water, to the sensation of being blown through thick brush, we stayed in the embrace until the thud of ground once more hit our feet. Unsteady, we collapsed in a heap.

"What is this!" cried a malicious voice that chilled my bones, a voice I'd heard in dreams, in nightmares, and relived through an unwelcome vision.

I scrambled to my feet, the others following quickly. We stood in a circle of what looked like blood. Around us was chipped stone brick. The wet air smelled of decay and from the shadows a horrifying figure stepped out. Instantly Coco and Atticus stepped in front of me. Shielding me from the nightmarish monster, their wands raised.

"I am Crown Prince Atticus Valor, son of King Amadeus Valor and Queen Mariana Valor, and I demand you release us this instant!" ordered Atticus. I looked back to Tamara and Aamin who shielded me from behind. Aamin seemed to be assessing the symbols written in the blood circle whilst I could hear Tamara whisper something about doors or something to do with exits. She spoke only in French and sadly I had only picked up the bare basics since meeting her. Gabriella and Harrison were nowhere to be seen, I only hoped they hadn't been brought along.

"Let you go? Hahaha. No...no I don't think I will be doing that. After all you are all such tasty-looking morsels."

Coco raised her wand, a spell on her lips.

"Coco, no!" cried Aamin.

"KROÚEIN!" thundered Coco, lightning zapping forth from her wand directly at the man who looked like a monstrous mole rat with blood red eyes and white pupils.

The spell misfired, hitting an invisible barrier. The aftermath sent us all crashing back down to the ground like a house of cards.

We moaned collectively as the aftershocks zapped us.

"I was trying to tell you that we're in a caster's trap," grumbled Aamin.

"Well, sweetcakes, you should have spoken up earlier," replied Coco, helping me get to my feet.

Because of the misfire, I had momentarily forgotten about the monster of a man but his laugh snapped me back to reality. It sounded like cats being drowned in a river of acid.

"What do you want?" demanded Tamara, surprising me with a tone of voice so unlike her. The normally happy, sunshine voice had been replaced with one of utter contempt.

"Well, little girl, I had only planned on taking fae boy here but I've never been one to turn down a missed opportunity." His smile showed teeth blackened with disease.

I found my voice, finally. "If it's just me you want then let the others go."

"NO!" shouted my friends collectively.

"My dear, innocent fae prince, what makes you think you have a choice? How I see it I get you all."

"Then come and try me," growled Atticus, his wand and fist raised in a battle stance. It might have just been the lack of light but I could've sworn his golden eyes shone even brighter, more like himself.

Our captor laughed as more people began to emerge from the shadows like bats flying from a darkened cave.

"No, this is not for me," said Coco gesturing her hand at the newcomers.

Were my ears betraying me or was Atticus actually growling? It was like a low, guttural rumble. Stranger still, it was as though my blood responded to it, heating up, flushing my face. For a moment it was all I could hear...well, until he spoke that is. Atticus growled the words out, less princely and more...wilderness warrior. "Anyone who aids us in our return to school will be heavily rewarded."

The onlookers burst into a chorus of laughter.

"By all means," gestured their leader.

"Who are you?" I asked unable to keep the desire to finally put a name to the white middle-aged man from my nightmares.

"Me? Well...if you reeeeeaaaaaaaalllllly want to know, my name is Jacquard Morioatus, and these"—he gestured to his followers—"are my Preneurs De Magi. And the reason I have no qualms about telling you this is because none of you will live to see the end of this day."

Cold sweat dripped down the back of my neck at the confirmation of our impending death.

"How about you drop this barrier and fight us man to man," Atticus challenged. "Or are you too soft in your old age?"

I began to tune them out when I noticed in my periphery the reason why Aamin had become so silent. His wand wasn't standing tall like the rest of us, no, in fact he had let it fall down until it was pointing at the ground, but not the ground beneath our feet no, his wand was aimed at one of the symbols spelled in blood. Whenever someone spoke he fired another spell, using their voice as a distraction. The longer I observed the more I realised what his plan was. If Aamin could loosen one of the flooring stones, one that existed both in the circle and out, the circle's lines would be broken, deactivating the trap. My goodness Aamin was smart. We just needed to buy him more time.

I turned my attention back to Jacquard who was laughing at whatever Coco had just yelled.

"Why is it you want me?" I asked.

He stopped laughing but retained his blackened smile, "And *why* should I tell you?"

I just needed to keep him talking, even if I didn't get any answers. "Is it because of the prophecy?"

That zapped the smile from his wrinkled face.

"Ahhh, what you do you know of the prophecy?" he hissed as his eyes practically bored holes in my brain. There was no longer any humour or glee amongst the band of evil. All waited with foul, bated breath.

ATTICUS VALOR I

A weighted silence filled the air as Léonidas spoke. It was clear to me that this prophecy meant something to both parties. My anger spiked—Why was this the first I was hearing about this? I shot Coco a dirty look, she returned it with a challenging stare. If this prophecy was to do with Léonidas then it also concerned me, his mate, his alpha.

"If you're not going to tell me anything then I shall do the same," said Léon puffing out his chest trying to be brave even though I saw his legs shake.

"VRONTÍ!" Purple thunder flashed from Jacquard's wand, hitting the barrier. Pain lanced through me, we all were brought down to our knees. A howl escaped me. This shock was far worse than Coco's had been. For seconds afterward aftershocks travelled up and down, numbing my brain in a sea of pain. Like fire ants doing the cha-cha-cha over my flesh.

"FUCK YOU!" I growled, showing teeth. I could hear a small gasp from Tamara as a response to my choice of words.

"Tell me what you know NOW!" shouted the ugly mutt, ignoring me.

"You first," gritted out my mate.

Watching him like this, standing up against this person, showed me I was wrong. Léonidas wasn't as weak as I had originally thought. He was using a great deal of inner strength to face this man who'd murdered his parents...but then again maybe he was yet to work that out...

"I don't play word games with children, little pointy ears. If you don't tell me I'll kill one of your...friends."

"Don't listen to him!" called Tamara, "He's going to do that anyway."

"Yes, but if he doesn't tell me, I'll make him watch as I kill each and every one of you before me. He'll watch as I suck down your veins like spaghetti, he'll watch as you're all driven mad by pain and onl—" Jacquard was cut off

The trap barrier illuminated white for a spilt second before shattering like a broken glass. The barrier was down. Aamin had finally done it. Jacquard had made a grievous error leaving us our wands, now he was going to learn why the Valors were to be feared.

Wand pointed at Jacquard I sent a flash of red light, it was joined with two other spells from Coco and Tamara. Jacquard dodged the spells and sent one back of this own— a white and sallow shock wave that cracked when it hit an iridescent shield cast by Aamin.

It seemed that Jacquard must have given a signal for the others to join the fray because it went from one spell being sent at us to what felt like a hundred. The smell of burnt magic filled the room as our little group went on the defensive. In the corner of my eye I saw Coco, who was to my left, change her hair. It went from a curly number to instant military-grade shaved head and took on a khaki green. How she had the time in between sending spells back in retaliation I'd never know.

"Change of…hair, Coco?" I gritted out between shield spells.

"Well, of course. If there is no hair then there isn't anything to grab."

"Smart."

"I know."

LÉONIDAS II

Coco was to my right and Aamin was to my left, and in front of me stood a sea of nasty, deformed adults who looked as evil as one could ever imagine. I didn't know if it was just my fear of the situation making my brain tell me tricks but I could have sworn that behind their eyes I saw something else, something not human...

Coco and Aamin had me covered with shield spells so I took a different approach. Couldn't cast spells if they didn't have their wands...right?

"Epispán!" I chanted over and over again, using my wand to pull wands out of the aggressors' hands. For the most part it seemed to be working, I'd come a long way from my first lesson with that particular spell. Public embarrassment meant I'd made sure to nail it from that point onward. Thanks to Tamara staying up late correcting me on my approach. And now look at me, totally proficient at that particular spell. As I pulled them towards me they came in contact with the cursed spells the enemy sent our way. They hit the wands, either destroying them or at the very least sending them off dancing into the room somewhere unseen.

It wasn't necessarily the smartest plan but at least it was a plan and one I'd come up with on my own on the fly.

"I've had quite enough of this, AIREÍN!" snapped Jacquard.

Something large and green snaked out of his wand, there wasn't enough time to deflect. The shields Coco, Tamara, and Aamin had put up shattered into oblivion. The magical whiplash causing them to scream.

The spell hit me and felt like a fishing net sucking all the oxygen from my lungs. It wrapped itself around me in a stranglehold. I lost control over my body and no matter how hard I tried, I was motionless.

"Langdon, take their wands," he ordered.

"Fuck yo—" spat Atticus, but with a quick flash he was silenced. His face turned scarlet with anger.

"Leave him alone!" I yelled, but with a second flash and the sound of a whip I too was silenced.

"There will be no more talking unless I request it," he said, pointing his wand at Coco, then Tamara and finally Aamin, silencing them.

A short man appeared out of the crowd, his suit covered in all kinds of gross grime. A wash would not have gone amiss, that was for sure. Against my will he took my wand with his grubby little hands from my cold numb fingers. I tried so hard to move but not a finger would even respond. I was trapped in a prison of my mind, a new kind of torture.

"Now you." He pointed his wand at me. "Come here.

I floated towards him like a stiff board. Behind me I could hear the heavy breaths of my friends fighting hard against the spells that bound them tight and silenced them.

"It doesn't matter if you won't tell me, I only need your fresh blood to summon forth the missing prophecy."

He ran a finger down his bright wand, the appearance changing into that of a dagger.

"Shironia and Taran, bring forth the cauldron!" he commanded.

A few seconds later two haggard women almost as pale as I carried in a large grey pot. Next, he pulled out a scroll. It appeared to be empty with not a trace of wear apart from the two metal ends that looked to be somewhat weathered.

Jacquard walked the small distance towards me until we were nearly face to face. The dagger reflected the small light in the room, I had no doubt that it would be incredibly sharp. If I could have gulped I would have.

ATTICUS VALOR II

Struggling, I fought hard against the spell ensnaring me. I could do nothing but watch as the leader of the Preneurs De Magi took his transfigured wand and traced a line down Léonidas's cheekbone. A thread of scarlet fell, which he collected on the scroll of parchment.

The smell of my mate's blood sent a hunger through me that awoke something I'd thought buried, my vaewolf.

"Very good," the sick cad purred as he took the parchment over to the cauldron. He dropped the blood-covered scroll inside. A puff of moist violet smoke shimmered into the air, making the room smell temporarily of musk sweets and night-blooming jasmine—the scent of Léon. The distance between my vaewolf and me disappeared to nothing. I may have been trapped by magic but my wolf was not.

Jacquard spoke in the forgotten dialect of Ancient Samaria, I knew enough to understand the gist of the incantation. He called on Suen, the lord of wisdom, and beseeched that he returned what was lost. There was something about a sacrifice given is one received but that was where the extent of my knowledge fell. I was lucky that Mother made sure I spoke at least some of the old languages.

The spell seemingly finished when the violet smoke turned to ruby. And scent shifted to a bull-like odour.

"Weston, retrieve the parchment," commanded Jacquard.

A man with olive skin stepped forward, and without a

second thought, plunged his hands into the bubbling, boiling broth. Burning flesh simmered into the air as the devotee screamed in unbridled pain.

Snot dribbled down his tear-stained face as he removed his fingers from the cauldron. Skin dripped from bone like a ham hock stew. In his bony fingers was a scroll of a blue-stone hue.

"Give it to me now, Weston." Jacquard practicality salivated with greed.

But Weston's fingers were only bones and sinew. As a result they were bound tightly shut around the parchment.

Jacquard's face contorted in rage. "Give it NOW!"

"I...I...I can't," sobbed the man, trying desperately to move his fingers but there were no veins, muscles, or tendons left on his finger bones so he hadn't a dogs hope in following his orders.

His anger growing, Jacquard began to try to and pry the fingers open. He was distracted. A chance had finally presented itself.

A shiver rippled up my body as flesh became fur and human bones became animal. As soon as I'd finished shifting I was frozen no more. Pouncing, I extended my wolven canines to triple their size. I'd get only one chance at this so I aimed for his jugular. Teeth sunk into wrinkled flesh, a burst of rancid blue sickly blood coated my muzzle and burnt my throat.

"Ahhh, stupid mutt."

Wham

The former wand-now-dagger plunged into my shoulder. The cry of pain loosened my grip enough for Jacquard to pull himself free from my claws. He was a wrinkly, bloody mess and he had made the worst mistake a spellcaster could make—he let go of his wand.

LÉONIDAS III

NO! I tried to scream but my voice like my body was silent, ensnared by the monstrous magic. I could do nothing but watch as the crystalline dagger was plunged into Atticus's wolven shoulder. He let out a howl of pain, it was enough for Jacquard to break free. Blood spilled forth from an open neck wound. Only this man's blood wasn't red like any blood I had seen, no, this was a rancid blue colour that looked the picture of poison.

Atticus shifted back to his human body, he was completely naked. Large well-defined muscles glistened down his body, a small bush of black trailed down to his....large...yes.

Even though I was about to most likely die I could not stop the heat filling my cheeks. I was so consumed by this godlike sight that I had forgotten about the dagger buried in Atticus's shoulder. Until I saw him pull it out. Seeing his blood dripping down his solid form re-ignited my struggle. Atticus needed help. I needed to break free.

A hundred wands must have been pointed at Atticus. But in a flash he drove the crystal dagger into the stone of the wall, shattering it into thousands of pieces. Instantly, my body returned to me. I could move again. But it was Coco who sent the first spell. With her palm raised. "Psykhrostagē!" What seemed like a ball of snow and ice was sent forward. Towards the screaming Jacquard. I'd never seen another person use magic without a wand before. I had but I don't think that really counted in the scheme of things.

"GET THEM!!" screamed their leader, without wands I had not a clue what to do. My heart raced with a frantic beat that threatened to pound right out of my very chest, my breathing was shallow and I was filled with pure adrenaline.

Aamin tackled the man who held our wands. He slammed his fists into the short, portly man, the dirty ground only adding to the filth saturating his suit. Aamin had managed to get in three loud bone-breaking hits before being sent flying back by a beam of light.

"AAMIN!!" we all screamed.

He flew back, hitting the wall hard.

The crowd of sycophants closed in on us. We were going to be trapped again, without wands we might as well be sheep on the way to slaughter.

A glow appeared below my feet, a kind of ringed circle, what was happening?

Jacquard yelled his voice high with...was that desperation? "NO!! STOP THEM!" Spells of a rainbow hue came flying at us, I closed my eyes in fear. But just as I thought it was the end, I felt the ground beneath me shatter and I plummeted into the void once more.

CHAPTER 19

DOUBLE DOUBLE TOIL AND TROUBLE

LÉONIDAS I

Fiery light greeted me as me feet finally found floor once more. When all was grounded and my vison cleared, I found myself in a room of pure gold. Around the room stood six very annoyed, very angry professors and in the front leading them was Headmistress Guaire. Her midnight skin gleamed like royalty and boy did she seem thunderous. Beside me I felt the others, Coco, Aamin, Tamara, and Atticus. We had all made it out of there alive.

Thank the gods.

"Mr Nightshade, Prince Valor, Miss La Roux, Miss Masayá, and Prince Kebaikan, someone best explain why you were all off school grounds." When we all stayed silent, she added, "Well, I'm waiting."

In a torrent of jumbled words Tamara, Coco, and Aamin began trying to tell the story. Atticus and I stood back, not saying a word. The truth be told I didn't know what to say.

Around the room stood five other professors but only

one of them I knew... And that was Professor Connaway, my transformative charm studies teacher. She wore another gown of liquid velvet, her signature fabric choice. Her black hair was left long and curled into waves that fell below the middle of her back it was a style I had seen Coco wear on occasion.

The headmistress raised her hand and silence fell once more.

"Please, one at a time. As prefect, Coco, I want to hear from you first. Please let the faculty and I know how *you*, a *prefect* could have let this situation evolve to where it inevitably ended up."

It felt like we were on trial. Not one face showed us any sympathy.

Coco stepped forward, her expression one of solidarity. She had changed her hair back to her signature burgundy do but her outfit like all of ours was in a dire state.

It was looking at Coco that I finally made eye contact with Atticus, his shoulder had completely healed and only drying blood remained. But it was his golden eyes that stole my breath and transported me away. Away from pain, away from guilt, and most importantly away from sadness. A temporary calm.

"Mr Nightshade," repeated Headmistress Guaire.

Gosh darn it, I had zoned out.

"Huh?" I said stupidly.

Fenella Guaire looked mighty mad.

"Mr Nightshade, are we boring you?"

"No, Headmistress."

"Then why pray tell are you ignoring my questions?"

"Questions?" I winced.

"Yes, Mr Nightshade, my questions."

"Errr."

"He hit his head," lied Aamin.

"Yes, he might have a concussion." Tamara backed him up.

"Really? That is what you're going with? It was pretty clear to us all that he was not paying attention," spoke up a rather short professor maybe five-feet tall and with the face of a prune.

"Yes, that's because he is concussed," Aamin continued to lie.

Tears fell from my eyes, even in this my friends stood with me and lied to save my skin when it would have been far easier to just squeal on me. I was blessed and I needed to remember this even in the dark times, I wasn't alone anymore.

The rest of the interrogation went in turns and by the end we had told them almost everything. The headmistress seemed unfazed to learn that the leader of the Preneurs De Magi was after me. In fact, it looked like she had already known this was a possibility. The meeting ended with Coco being stripped of her title as prefect for not bringing the facility into the loop and finally we were each given an amethyst pendant that was made from a part of the castle. We were informed that it would prohibit anyone from summoning us as long as we never took it off, even in the shower. I was actually glad to wear it. I never wanted to see that man or his band of villainous adults ever again and if wearing it for the rest of my life meant that then I would wear it gladly.

"One more thing, starting immediately the five of you will start training," decreed the headmistress,

"What kind of training?" asked Atticus suspicious.

"Training to prepare for what is too inevitably come, now that we know a few of the missing pieces."

27TH OF JULY 1952

Months passed and without realising it the last school day had come. In the end the headmistress kept her word and Coco, Tamara, Aamin, Atticus, and I had spent every hour of our Mondays in private tutelage with the heads of the facility, training in case we were ever forced into an altercation with Jacquard and his Preneurs De Magi.

The types of magic we had been learning weren't the kind the school normally considered or even condoned teaching, but due to recent events, school rules and magical laws had to be bent if not broken entirely.

It wasn't just training we received but also endless detention and once the headmistress learnt of my...she called it melancholia, I was forced into counselling. Even though I was told to keep it from the teachers I thought maybe if I told them what I'd...done or at least tried to do maybe it would save the others from punishment. I was wrong.

Coco was unfortunately demoted from being a prefect and even though I knew this must have been really hard for her she never once let anyone see her feeling down. In fact, she tried to spin it as if she was glad to not have the responsibility anymore.

Another new development since the event that had come to pass was at dinner, I now sat beside Atticus, and Aamin of course sat on the other side. It seemed as though I was being courted by the prince of the vaewolves. No matter how ridiculous that may sound it was true. It was a slow courting and I was glad of its pace, I still didn't know if this was what I wanted but Atticus seemed to know for the both of us. Being mates—whatever that really meant. I had no doubt I'd learn its true meaning at some point soon.

Since Atticus had been hanging around me, to the point one could have called him my shadow, the bullying had not stopped per se, but had greatly lessened. The only person who really continued on the touch was Braxton who seemed more pissed at me than ever now that Atticus hung out with me over him.

I was on my way to English and Language Studies with Professor Nkrumah. Thankfully I'd finished my final class assignment. Our last unit of the year was on poetry and we had been tasked to create our own poem and recite it to the class. It was Professor Nkrumah's opinion that performance and poetry went hand-in-hand, and she taught us how tone of voice and melody could enrich text and give it a deeper meaning. We studied the art of Shakespeare and even the west African techniques of melody and beat.

At first I struggled to find the words to write, and making things rhyme wasn't easy but once I let the emotion take over, now that I knew what it was called, I was able to write it in a night. I chose to keep it to myself. The words I wrote made me vulnerable in a way I hadn't felt before.

So when it was my turn in class and Professor Nkrumah called my name in her kind yet direct way, "Léonidas Night-shade, it is your turn," I got to my feet and faced the class.

"What is your poem called?" asked the professor.

"It is called 'As you Say.'"

"Then when you're ready, begin."

My palms were sweating and I couldn't control the way my hands shook holding the parchment. There were so many faces looking at me, I...I was scared. But when my eyes finally fell on my friends Tamara, Aamin, and even my new friends Gabriella and Harrison, I somehow found the strength to begin.

"No, like you say—I'm not normal,

For I'm like a broken toy held together by duct tape and glue.

Some days on the outside I may seem fine even though on the inside I truly feel blue.

You see there is a void inside me that is eating me up inside.

Like a noose taut around my neck I'm all locked up in my mind.

I know it's stupid and it's really hard to describe,

But some days I feel like a raft at sea fighting against endless tide,

With vast oceans and storms that rage but all I can do is hold on for my life.

No I'm not normal like you say and maybe I'd be better off dead.

For maybe than I'll feel whole again lying in an eternal bed.

But even though this toy is worn out and used,

I have found my people and by some miracle,

They help see a day that lays beyond the sea,

For with their help I know I'll always be me."

A thunderous applause rang around the room, Even the teacher had a tear in her eye. I had faced demons this school year and I would probably in the next but maybe I was ready for it. At least with my friends by my side I felt as though I could take on anything this magical world could bring.

Professor Nkrumah walked over to me, putting her

hand on my shoulder. "Mr Nightshade, that was simply amazing," she said. "Your words were powerful and your performance was moving. I know this year you've had your troubles but take solace knowing you have truly captured the essence of poetry, well done."

ATTICUS VALOR I

With classes finished and bags packed I went to find Léonidas. In our new...I guess one could call it a group, I volunteered to escort Léon to the beach. Where we were all meeting before walking through the ripple home. Of course, everyone wanted to escort Léon but after his final class he had a support group, and since attending he had preferred to be alone for a little while after.

Not long after the events that took place with the Preneurs De Magi I found a group that meets up once a week filled with people who don't necessarily fit into society. It is a group of same gender-attracted people, people who had been born in the wrong bodies and people who just didn't fit into a box. The group called themselves "Circle of Friends."

I had attended one session/meeting and decided it was not for me. But after Léon attended one he was hooked and hadn't missed any since.

They met up in one of the language classrooms in the west side of the school. Normally it was in Professor Nkrumah's room as she offered it up many years ago for the course. She was a big proponent for change and led a lot of the school rallies over the years.

Making my way through the open door, I soon took a seat in the back of the room.

The circle was still in the process of going around the

circle speaking "their truth" and a student with black curly hair was standing. Their skin shimmered like sugar in water, denoting them part Merman shifter part spellcaster.

"Despite the challenges of being on land for practically a whole year I found that I was able to adapt and even thrive in this outer water environment. I think. Like a few of us have expressed, bullying has been hard but since finding a group of like-minded people it has definitely become more manageable. So as our group moderator Keely asked, this year I am thankful for meeting this group and also flowers, like this school grows incredible orchids and peonies that seem to never die."

"Thank you, Mark, you may take a seat. Next up we have first year student, Jade."

"Hey, everyone, as you know about three quarters into this school year I made somewhat of a huge discovery. Which was that I no longer identified with just the gender I was assigned at birth. And it wasn't just that, I've also found through the guidance of this group that societal labels are just not for me. I don't like them and I don't want them. So this year I am thankful that this group led me to the path that helped me find my truth."

Clapping echoed around the room.

Natasha Wilson, a fourth year, was the next to speak. "Like many of you know this year I lost my partner Loral who—" She stopped as she wiped tears from her large eyes. "Who took her life when her parents reacted badly to her bringing home me, another girl." A few students close to her placed their hands on her in a sign of comfort. Looking at Léon, I could see he had retreated within himself at her words.

"I am thankful for the love and support this group has given me when at times I felt too on the edge of giving up."

Three other students got up and told the room what they were thankful for before finally it was Léon's turn.

"Thank you, Rebecca, next up is our newest member, Léonidas. You have the floor. What are you most thankful for this year?"

Standing tall, Léonidas took a deep breath, this close I could hear the thudding of his heart, he was nervous.

"Thank you, Keely, for giving me the floor," he said before clearing his throat. "Err...r," he stuttered.

"Come on, snowflake, you got this!" I cheered, surprising myself. My cheer was carried on around the room, with other students like Mark, Rebecca, and Jade joining in.

His purple gaze found mine and he flushed a deeper, rosier hue which stood out on his winters milk complexion. But the support relaxed him. His heartbeat slowed. He was ready to speak.

"As most of you know I started this school year about halfway through. Having never attended school before it was a huge adjustment but thanks to the aid of others I pulled through and in the end of year examinations I'm proud to announce I got a yearly score of eighty-five out of a hundred, which is a passing grade! This kid from the forest farm passed his first ever school tests but it is all thanks to the fact I found my people. I've learnt that friendship is the hand that steadies us in the turbulent waters, the kindness and compassion that warms our hearts in our moments of ice, and the light that illuminates our journey forward towards joy and fulfilment. So this year that is what I am thankful for."

I got to my feet clapping. I knew saying this was a huge step for Léon. I was not the only one to clap, everyone did.

. . .

After, we walked together towards the school gate. Our bags had already been taken to the beach by magical means. It was just the two of us, most students had long since made their journey to the beach anxious to return home.

There was a charged energy between us and I for one wanted to do something about it, but Léon was fragile. Whilst I had come to terms with my mate being a male, he still had a long way to go. But I didn't want to leave him for the summer without him truly knowing he was mine.

We talked about stupid things, innocent things, things like favourite foods, favourite films, favourite actors and actresses. He asked me questions like how many houses did my family own and was it warm where I lived. We were so caught up in our own world that we had passed the school gates, the protective barrier, and were nearly at the beach. If I was going to make my move now was going to be the time.

LÉONIDAS II

Talking with Atticus was easy, there was this way he smiled that felt like the sun singing. I was actually sad at the thought that I wouldn't see him for several weeks. His hand brushed mine before capturing it with his much larger fingers.

My cheeks flushed, as my heart began to pound. What if someone saw us? Did he care if they did? Did I care if they did...?

"Come here," he commanded, pulling me into the safety of the evergreen trees and flowing vines that hung down like technicolour lightbulbs on corded ropes.

"What are you d—" I began, but was silenced by his lips smashing into mine.

He claimed my mouth, dominating me. I went to break away but his free hand shot up and gripped my chin hard, keeping me right where he wanted.

Through the kiss he growled, "You are mine."

The feeling of his lips against mine was unlike anything I had ever experienced. This was my first kiss and I was having it with a boy. Did they all feel like this? Like eternity and hope, fate and life, beginning and the end. I was careless in the kiss and my tongue slid against his sharp canines. The taste of copper filled the kiss. Atticus intensified our embrace, it was hungry and on another level entirely.

"You taste divine," he purred.

And with those words my heart sang.

I was his, I couldn't deny it. I didn't want to deny it.

Down at the beach the smell of salty citrus was a delightful welcome. We met up with Coco who had changed her hair into a coil of black curls, Tamara who was dressed in a simple pale blue shirt dress, and Aamin who looked like royalty, wearing a type of brimless cap that matched his loose silk shirt and pants that were a darker cobalt blue.

"I'm going to miss you," I said, my voice thick.

"You'll see us next year," Coco reminded me.

"Will I?"

"Of course you will," agreed Aamin, slapping me on my back.

"Promise to write?" I asked, voice sounding needy.

"You won't be able to stop us." Tamara smiled.

A second later we all converged into a tight hug. I held

on for dear life. How was I going to last so many weeks without them? Even Atticus after a moment joined in on the hug.

"Next school year we will do that potion and find the clues," promised Coco.

"Yes we will! And promise to find out everything on the fae to answer some of your many questions," added Tamara.

"And we promise to always be there for you no matter what," Aamin finished.

I'd finally found my people, my tribe, my missing family.

Each of us said our goodbyes and walked together into the water and bid the Amethyst School for Spellcasters goodbye for now.

See you next year.

EPILOGUE

LÉONIDAS I

Both my grandparents had come to pick me up. My Grandpa who was a man of few word, insisted on taking my one suitcase to put in the trunk of the old family motor vehicle. I knew he only insisted on doing this to hide the tears that I saw him hold back behind his happy eyes. He had missed me greatly and I him. Grandma was always put together and this occasion was no different. Her hair was immaculate and her dress pressed within an inch of its life. But something I didn't expect was the new single streak of grey she wore proudly in her hair.

"Hey, Grandma, what's with the grey in your hair?" I asked. "I thought you said you would never go grey."

"Hush you." She fake-swatted me. "I'm just trying something a little different." Then after a beat. "Does it look bad?"

"No, I like it, it adds character," I said, smiling.

"Character huh? Well this character needs to get us on the road before peak hour starts."

On the long drive home I couldn't help but reflect back on the year I had just ….survived is probably a good word for it. For this year I died not once but twice, met a god, grew horns, and was sent off to a school for magic in an unknown location, somehow made enemies, learnt how to cast spells and concoct spelled brews, learnt I wasn't entirely human. But the thing that seemed the most unbelievable was the fact that I, Léonidas Nightshade, had made friends who had showed that they would die for me. And because of this I somehow didn't feel so alone in the world anymore.

Taking my bag upstairs I noticed the house seemed extra clean, more than normal. And normally it was spotless but today it seemed almost brand-new. I wondered why?

On my bed I found a white envelope. Picking it up, it contained something that made it rather heavy. I placed my suitcase on the bed and tore it open.

Out fell a piece of paper and something long and silver. It was a key. Frowning, I picked up the folded letter and read the short message written in an elegant script. *Now that you have attended school it is time you returned home, Kind Regards M*

Did they mean my parents' house? Or somewhere else? And who was this M? Confused, I picked up the old key, feeling its weight and cold, rough texture. The metal was discoloured with small spots of rust that clung to the intricate floral design like a fly in a spider's web.

"Hey, Grandma?" I called. "I think you need to see this."

ATTICUS VALOR I

Juan, one of our family butlers, carried my bags up the stairs whilst I sought my parents. Our family owned several palaces and during summer we mostly resided in Borriana as our main residence here overlooked the ocean whilst having plenty of forest for pack shifting and hunting.

Only our family took residence in the place but in the nearby village lived the important people in our pack. Most of them travelled with us when we moved between palaces, so it became a necessity for the ruling vaewolves, (my family) to own most if not all the lands and associated houses closest to our residences. As not just a safety precaution but also a financial one.

Shifting my nose, I used my mother's scent like a roadmap to find her and Father. They smelled of home, comfort, and expensive wine. I breathed in again. They were out in the gardens, and with another breath I smelled the smokey scent of one of my father's lit cigars. I headed for the back entrance.

I needed to tell them about...Him.

Sunlight gleamed on the polished gold and silver decorating our home. Our doors, which could be sealed tight against an attack or an invasion, lay open and welcoming and through them bathed in sun were my parents. King Amadeus and Queen Mariana Valor.

Mother stood, paint brush in hand as she mapped out the rough blocking of a landscape painting, the smell of oil confirmed what paint medium she was using. Father sat on an outdoor patio chair as he read the current issue of *The Enchanted Echo*, the main newspaper for spellcaster kind.

Neither of them turned to look at me when I said it. Maybe that was why I found the strength to get all the words out or maybe I just wanted to get it over and done with.

"Madre, Padre—I...I have found my mate, the one destined by Cernunnos and he is not just half fae but also... a boy."

Mother's paint brush fell to the floor, leaving behind a green splatter.

There was no going back now.

PRENEURS DE MAGI I

Sitting on his throne of cursed skulls in the dark depths of the Fingal Sea cave was Jacquard. He was furious that not only had the child slipped through his fingers but now it would be impossible to snatch him. He had no doubt that the school would have given him a talisman or charmed item that could be worn that would prohibit summoning no matter if he was on school grounds or not.

In the months since the failed attack Jacquard had gone a little crazy, well crazier. He had slaughtered half of his legion of followers for their failure to keep the fae boy and his...friends from escaping. And he had also spent a few months on a soul-stealing bender.

Six towns had been completely wiped out. With not a living soul they had become nothing more than mass graves. This kind of accelerated abuse had warped his complexion even more. His body now gaunt and skeletal with a protruding spine and teeth that had grown into sharp stubby points. His blood-red eyes with white pupils now glowed in the dark like a malevolent spirit.

Transformative spells no longer worked to hide his visage. This magical change was permanent. The Algonquin and Ojibwe tribes had a name for a creature such as this, they called it a Wendigo. But Jacquard didn't care about his appearance, not one bit.

Pulling out the new copy of the lost prophecy, well what had survived after that stupid vaewolf attacked, he read the four new lines that completed the end of the prophecy. It wasn't everything but now Jacquard knew of what he must do. He read it for what must have been the six millionth time. *The only thing certain is the first to find the key of scarlet, Will be the one to get this war started, Who so ever wins this war ahead, Will be the one with the power to decide who shall wind up dead, Glory, fame and fortune beyond measure, is what awaits this powerful successor.*

A key of scarlet is what he now desired most in this world and may the gods have mercy on whoever stands in his way.

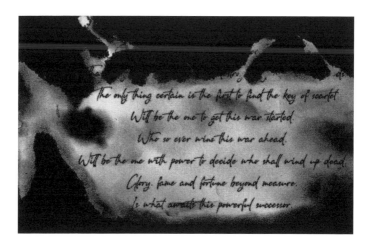

THE END...for now.

Afterword

Dear Readers,

First I want to thank you for taking the time to read my book but I think it is important to note that Léonidas Nightshade and the Amethyst School for Spellcasters explores themes of long-term depression and its associated factors, particularly within the LGBTQ+ community. Mental health is an important issue that affects many individuals around the world, and it is my hope that this book has shed light on this often-stigmatized topic.

If you or someone you know is struggling with depression or any other mental health issue, I want to remind you that you are not alone. I have been there, truly. I've been hospitalised and put on twenty-four-hour suicide watch. So I really want you to know that there are resources available to help. Here are some worldwide organizations that offer support and resources specifically for the LGBTQ+ community:

1. The Trevor Project: https://www.thetrevorproject.org/

2. GLBT National Help Center:
https://www.glnh.org/
3. PFLAG: https://pflag.org/
4. LGBT Foundation: https://lgbt.foundation/
5. Mental Health and Suicide Prevention Services for
LGBTQ+: https://www.nami.org/find-support/lgbtq

Suicide prevention is also a crucial aspect of mental health. If you or someone you know is experiencing thoughts of suicide, it is important to reach out for help immediately. The following resources provide 24/7 support for those in crisis:

1. National Suicide Prevention Lifeline (USA): 1-800-273-TALK (8255)
2. Samaritans (UK and Ireland): 116 123
3. Lifeline (Australia): 13 11 14

Remember, it is never too late to reach out for help. Your mental health is just as important as your physical health, and taking care of it should be a priority. The resources above are dedicated to serving the LGBTQ+ community and ensuring that every individual feels heard and supported.

Sincerely,
Dion Marc

ABOUT THE AUTHOR

Dion Marc is a bestselling Scottish Australian author who lives and breathes queer art. When he's not busy writing, painting, sewing, or dancing naked under the moon, he's practicing Hellenistic polytheism and spreading love with one hug at a time. But beware, if you offer him tea without a biscuit, you'll have committed a heinous crime!

Dion's work is as diverse as his interests - from Harry Potter to Moulin Rouge, Hamilton, Netflix series, feature films, and beyond! With over 12 years of experience in the industry, Dion's creative genius knows no bounds. You can join in on the fun and follow his adventures on Instagram @Author.dionmarc. Don't miss out on the ride!

Dion's Instagram can be found here instagram.com/author.dionmarc

Join Dion Marc's facebook group for all the latest news facebook.com/groups/953877695177248/

Printed in Great Britain
by Amazon